Calvin's Head

Calvin's Head

by

David Swatling

A Division of Bold Strokes Books

2014

CALVIN'S HEAD

ISBN 13: 978-1-62639-193-2

This Trade Paperback Original Is Published By
Bold Strokes Books, Inc.
P.O. Box 249
Valley Falls, NY 12185

First Edition: September 2014

Credits
Editors: Greg Herren and Stacia Seaman
Production Design: Stacia Seaman
Cover Design by Sheri (graphicartist2020@hotmail.com)

Acknowledgments

Writing may be a solitary pursuit, but getting a book out into the world is not—especially a first novel. I've been fortunate to have a great deal of support along the way.

I'm most grateful to publisher Len Barot and editor Greg Herren for taking a chance on an author arriving rather late to the literary table. Also, the rest of the incomparable team at Bold Strokes Books—from cover artist Sheri to copy editor Stacia Seaman, who patiently guided me into the home stretch.

An Amsterdam writers' group provided a safety net for the first chapters. That I threw them in a drawer for thirteen years doesn't diminish the encouragement from Martha, Pat, and Graham. The Brooklyn Book Festival inspired me to begin again, National Novel Writing Month (NaNoWriMo) kept my butt in the chair until I had a first draft, and ThrillerFest taught me how much more I still needed to learn.

Special thanks are reserved for my early readers: Mauricio Aguiar, Hiram Ed Taylor, Kate McCamy, and Arden Scott. Their keen enthusiasm and gentle criticism kept me moving forward. Jim Dempsey's sharp editorial eye was invaluable in later revisions. Also, I can't underestimate the importance of my personal writer retreats: Swee'Pea's House in the Catskills and the Inn at Whitefield.

Lastly, thanks to the talented authors I interviewed during my radio days. Too many to mention, but our chats were invaluable master classes. And though we didn't meet until the book was finished, John Morgan Wilson was a huge inspiration when first developing the story. The fact Bold Strokes Books had reissued his Benjamin Justice mystery series convinced me to submit *Calvin's Head*. Full circle.

For Calvin

St. Valentine

The slightest movement ignited flames of searing pain. Vicious welts crisscrossed his back and buttocks like a checkerboard designed by de Sade. He had slipped in and out of consciousness so often the concept of time had fled. He had no idea whether he had been imprisoned here for hours or days. Certainly not weeks, although in this state of near delirium nothing was certain.

In Case of Danger…he thought briefly. The rest of the warning eluded him.

Carl Orff's *Carmina Burana* blasted on an endless loop. *O Fortuna! vita detestabilis…* The Medieval Latin verses mocked him, as did the engraving on the wall behind him. *The Beheading of St. Valentine.* The picture was etched in his memory as if he had prepared the copper plate himself. He shuddered at the thought of hot wax, the drip of acid burning his body. Surely the martyrdom of his namesake so many centuries ago was not as cruel as what he experienced now.

Stocks encased his wrists and neck, bloody cuts and gashes scarred his knees and feet. Flickering candles provided the attic dungeon with dim hallucinatory light. Had a flame teased, singed, and burned his nipples, his genitals? He nearly passed out yet again.

Movement in a corner of the room caught his attention. His eyes widened as he watched the branding iron turn orange in the blue butane fire. He tried to scream but no sound issued from his parched throat. The glowing figure eight seemed to float through the air of its own volition and disappeared from view. He lost consciousness before it touched his skin.

Sometime later he remembered the story he had forgotten.

❖

Birdsong filled the air as he walked along a path between the forest and the open field of freshly plowed earth. He noticed a sign had been knocked over in the tall grass near the tree line. He couldn't read it from this angle, but assumed it was a No Trespassing *notice. He had no intention of venturing into the shadowy woods on such a beautiful day. The field was bathed in sunlight and the earth smelled of warmth and springtime. He was struck by an irresistible urge to lie naked in the upturned pasture, to soak serene energy from the sun into every pore.*

A quick look around confirmed he was alone and he stripped off his clothes. He lay on his back along one of the deep furrows dug by a farmer's plow. The dirt was surprisingly soft, supple. He adjusted his body slightly, shifted the soil around him, and closed his eyes, felt the earth's desire to envelop him.

He might have stayed that way forever if a deep grumbling had not disturbed him. He opened his eyes. A shifting mass of menacing dark clouds churned above him like an angry sea. The earth beneath him began to undulate and he sat up, alarmed. The birds had ceased their warbling. The only sound, more felt than heard, was an ominous rumble below him.

This was no earthquake, not even a tremor. Something loomed under the surface, ready to burst forth and devour him whole.

There was only one thing to do. He stood and planted his feet as firmly as the unstable ground would allow. He grabbed his head with both hands, ripped it from his neck, and threw it toward the trees. Earth and sky spun wildly as his head flew through the air like a rugby ball and landed with a thud near the uprooted signpost. From this vantage point he could read the words clearly.

IN CASE OF DANGER, HEAD OFF INTO THE WOODS.

❖

The acrid chemical scent from the small brown vial brought him back to semi-consciousness for the last time. The music was gone, the candles still flickered. He heard boot steps, heard metal strike the leather strop. Boot steps again. The last sound he heard was the soft whoosh of the heavy blade as it descended toward his neck.

PART ONE: THE PARK

"...how we have lived this night of June."

—Oscar Wilde, *The Garden of Eros*

CHAPTER ONE

I. CALVIN

calvin sniffing / furball hissing bravado warning
disappearing into bushes / stupid cat
calvin smart smarter smartest
mistercalvin calvinator calvin&hobbes
    - Yo, Calvin. Wait up.
calvin stopping / turning sitting waiting watching
dekker coming walking bad / graindrink smelling bittersad
calvin waiting tongue sweating
waiting dekker&willygone
    - Don't get so far ahead. Walk with me.
calvin&dekker&willygone walking together
calvin sniffing smelling danger / stopping looking
badman coming holding something / something
    smelling bad&bad
stopping waiting holding something / something
    smelling bad&bad
calvin growling holding ground
dekker calling stumbling falling talking
    - Shit.

II. DEKKER

The sudden impact as my butt hits the ground drives my teeth together, biting my lower lip, and my mouth fills with the coppery taste of blood. Fucking perfect! Drunk on my ass. Literally. I consider laughing but a belch intercedes. The bitter aftertaste of beer and tequila mixes with blood and makes me gag. I barely avoid the big barf-a-rama and spit a disgusting blob of tobacco-drenched mucus into the grass. I wipe my mouth with the grimy sleeve of my jacket and irritate my already swelling lip.

Happy fucking birthday to me! You're a case and a half, Dekker.

Which is probably how much beer I've consumed this night. Calvin stares at me with his head slightly cocked.

See what happens when you spend too many hours at the bar, me curled up in a dusty corner getting ashes flicked on my head? Or tail stepped on by your drunken friends?

- First of all, I don't have any friends.

I don't have to be drunk to talk to my dog, nor does being drunk hinder our communication. Calvin understands me in this condition, even if he makes no bones about expressing his disapproval with a soft steadfast growl.

- Guys I drink with are no more friends of mine than dogs you piss with are your friends.

Cal enjoys a good pissing contest, but his air of aloofness toward other canines doesn't make for many dog buddies. As for me, I had my star chart done by an astrologer who noted the absence of planets in my House of Friendship. She said that was not as bad as it sounded since my conjunct House blah blah blah combined with my natal cusp blah blah blah.

A bartender buddy who was into that shit put it more succinctly.

It means you're fucked, Tony quipped.

Fuck you, too, Tony, I said at the time. He was dead on, though. Dead now, too, Tony. Like Willy.

Don't go there, Dekker. Not tonight. Definitely not tonight of all nights.

- Second of all, where the hell are we supposed to hang out, huh? Or maybe you'd like it better if after your dinner I locked you up in Jax all night by your lonesome?

At the mention of the beat-up black Suzuki jeep we now call home, Calvin's ears lift the way people raise an eyebrow. He knows exactly what I'm talking about and reconsiders his position.

Maybe time for an attitude check.

- And last but by no means least, it's your fucking fault I tripped over my own fucking feet in the first place. What the hell were you growling at anyway?

Calvin trots to my side and licks my face, eyes bright with apology. He sits, whimpers softly, offers me a paw, turns his head into the darkness behind us. The uninitiated might mistake the minimalist growl that emanates from his throat for a purr of pleasure. I know better. I look back toward where he gazes but see nothing out of the ordinary. Probably just a cat on the prowl or maybe a duck he spooked at the edge of the water.

Cal paws the ground and continues his restrained grumbling, body poised in the direction of a barely discernible figure far off down one of the winding paths. I may not always understand why Calvin takes an instant dislike to certain people but I trust his instincts. Dogs know stuff we can't even begin to imagine. Once he started barking at a couple of middle-aged tourists who seemed perfectly normal. But a little voice in the back of my brain warned otherwise.

You never know. Maybe they're some psycho-killer duo on vacation in Amsterdam 'cause the good old folks from Quantico were gettin' a little too close for comfort. Or they could be aliens who've taken human form to facilitate abductions. So unless you wanna be the subject of their next anal probe, listen to Calvinator and make no eye contact whatsoever.

Vondelpark is a magnet for weirdoes. And here I sit on the wet grass in the dead of night having a heart-to-heart with a golden retriever like he's my goddamn shrink. The ludicrousness of this hits me like a ton of bricks crashing down on Road Runner's head and I start to giggle. Thirty-three years old, unemployed, homeless, drunk, and talking to a dog! Something inside does a little ballistic sidestep, which also strikes me as funny, and I reel over onto my back in a fit of hysterical laughter. Tears are rolling down my face as I try to stop but before I realize what's happening, I'm crying. Great heaving sobs of guilt, shame and, worst of all, self-pity. What an asshole I've become.

Excuse me, Doctor, but I seem to have turned into a giant asshole.

Bend over, Mr. Dekker, we're ready for your anal probe.

This is totally ridiculous but to my astonishment I'm laughing again. It's not at all funny and I can't help myself. Clutching my gut, I realize this must be what they call sidesplitting laughter because I feel like I'm breaking in two, which is not an amusing thought. It hurts it hurts it hurts and I'm sobbing again and the pain is unbearable.

I'm in mourning for my life, said one of the three sisters, and I'm laughing again at such sentimental bullshit and crying because I can't stop laughing and laughing because I can't stop crying and crying and laughing at the same time.

Laughing wild amidst severest woe, said the woman buried up to her neck in sand, and I've lost it now, am totally out of control, and I wish it would all stop, everything stop stop stop, just stop.

I lie in the grass physically exhausted, emotionally drained, staring up at the starry starry night. I search for the great hunter Orion, traversing the sky as he has for countless millennia, his dogstar Sirius trailing at his feet. I won't find him on this shortest night of the year. The daylight skies are his summer hunting grounds. But he's always there in my mind, one leg marked by Riga, seventh-brightest star in the sky, nine hundred light-years away; his opposite shoulder is Betelgeuse, a reddish supergiant large enough to swallow the earth's orbit around the sun. I've forgotten the names of the three stars that make up his belt. It doesn't matter.

What always intrigued me most was the Great Nebula of Orion. What appears as the middle star of his sword is actually an immense mass of swirling gas and dust, a thousand light-years from Earth. A nursery for stars in their infancy, its heat creates a cloud that glows steely cobalt blue in the center and soft ruddy magenta on the periphery. In several million years, young stars will materialize in the sky and Orion's sword will blaze with a new brilliance. Even as a child I knew I'd never live to see those stars.

I can't bring myself to look at Calvin but I feel his luminous presence beside me. If I died right here, right now, he would keep watch over me, through the night and forever, my faithful dogstar.

III. GADGET

Rosa Fairy, Tapis Volante, Finnstar, Snowballet, Hockey.

Just inside the rose garden where the first hexagonal beds of low bushes were hidden by tall hedges, Gadget paused to take several deep breaths and slow his heartbeat. Adrenaline pumped through his body as if he had taken a mega-hit of speed. This was not good, not good at all. That fucking dog! Of all nights to nearly tango with some snarling albino werewolf. If its drunken bum of an owner hadn't taken a tumble and distracted the stupid beast there could've been big trouble. He hated dogs, had even killed one once. The scrappy barky rat-coated rag of a thing had nipped at his heels one night not far from this very spot. He'd kicked its head so hard it flew through the night air like a spastic bat, disappearing into the shrubs. The memory of its owner calling *Alfie! Alfie!* over and over in increasing panic brought a smile to his face, relaxed him. Time to move on.

Paprika, Schneewitchen, Amsterdam, Corona, Marchenland, Lily Marlene.

Gadget stopped briefly to pay homage to his favorite, though in the darkness the tall blood-red blossoms appeared black. No big deal. He knew the rose garden by heart. Like a horticultural litany, he'd memorized the names of each variety from the small printed signs, catalogued their unique traits, methodical as any four-eyed botanist. Even in dead of winter he saw each of them in full bloom as he walked the brick pathways that separated the plots. He preferred this side of the garden with its hot profusion of reds, oranges, and pinks to the cooler whites and pale yellows that dominated the beds across the center lawn of lush green grass. On warm summer afternoons it was a popular spot for sunbathers and picnickers, young and old, locals and tourists. By night it attracted an altogether different crowd, not only in summer but all year round, and Gadget saw tonight was no exception.

Friesa, Pernille Poulseu, Orangeade, Anneke Doorenbos, Diabiotin.

Most of the roses had girly names but under cover of darkness it was the boys who came out to play here. Gadget had cruised the garden path for years. His technique of choice was to amble casually, avoid eye contact, pretend disinterest. This almost always kick-started the hunter instinct in someone seeking easy prey, someone who followed first with his eyes, then his head, then his body, without realizing that he was in fact the hunted, ensnared by a more clever fox.

A fox dressed as a chicken. Gadget snickered to himself. He wasn't so young anymore but in the moonlit park he could still pass for underage bait to those eager enough to believe in miracles. He was a catch, oh yes, make no mistake. Gadget was a lean mean machine, tall and dark, a drop-dead dazzler with chiseled features and a rough edge that spelled *Danger*, an irresistible combination to the lost boys who had become creatures of the night.

Else Poulseu, Alloria, ToJo, Blessings.

And whoa! Blessings, indeed. Parked on a bench, leather-clad legs spread wide and inviting, an older guy diddled himself with unrestrained abandon. His white T-shirt virtually glowed in the dark like a beacon, thick mustache to compensate for receding hairline, blissfully unaware he was being watched. This annoyed Gadget although he couldn't pinpoint why. The trick wasn't really his type, and he wasn't here for sex tonight anyway. He had pressing business contained in the black garbage bag gripped tightly in his right hand. Very pressing, he reminded himself, as his left hand absently wandered to his crotch like a baby's thumb was drawn to its mouth.

No!

Maybe?

Out of the question.

Just a quickie?

Absolutely not.

But what if—

Get a move on, punk, before you fuck up big-time.

Please?

Next time, Gadget! Next time.

Gadget shrugged and moved on.

Fragrant Delight, Tornado, Orange Wave, Olala, Fervid.

The names of the roses at the end of the garden beckoned him like the Siren songs of sexual promise that lured Odysseus and his horny crew. The bag or the bench? No contest. The bag could wait. The bench would not. Fuck his inner voice. He glanced around to see if anyone else was within cruising range. No other action in the immediate area. Anyone hidden from sight in the small grove of trees next to the garden would be otherwise engaged.

Gadget wanted to hurry but caution checked his inclination to rush, stupidly call attention to himself. He sauntered across the bike path and headed for the grassy strip known as the gay beach that bordered a shallow pond. By day, underwater spouts shot plumes of white spray into the air like multiple orgasms. They were quiescent now as he approached the water. Submerged wooden slats edged the pond. He took a few steps to where the dewy grass merged with shrubs and trees. Giving the knot a quick jerk to make sure it would hold, he set the bag carefully into the water, its weighty load pulling it down, while a pocket of air kept it barely afloat. He wedged the top of the bag between two siding slats and made sure it was secure with a firm tug. It didn't budge. The black bag would remain hidden in the black water until he returned.

In the meantime, a bit of fun was just what the doctor ordered. His body had built up a lot of tension in the last forty-eight hours and required release. There might even be a bit of cash to be made. Mr. Mustachio looked like tourist trade. Led by his hardening cock, Gadget headed back to the rose garden, his mind on one thing and one thing only, his near close encounter with a big white dog forgotten.

CHAPTER TWO

I. CALVIN

sun warming calvins nose / awareness waking eyes opening
damp cramp stuffy / sweet&stinky jax / calvin
    stretching long&hard
searching bluebear soft&worn / scenting
    willygone / missing more&more
missing bluebears longlost friends / missing
    gator hippo tigger hotdogman
humpbuddy all&more
sunshine shouting / dekker snoring sleeping moaning
sunshine barking / wakeup dekker
calvin licking furry faces / bluebear&dekker / tasting
    salty grainwater skin
wakeup dekker / sunshine shouting roaring
    barking / more&more&evermore

II. DEKKER

- Calvin.

His bark is so close to my head I can smell his mildly unpleasant dog breath. He apologizes by shoving his cold wet nose into my ear and licking the side of my face with his usual morning enthusiasm.

- Get off, you.

My head hurts, my body aches, I feel like I've been run over by a tractor. Great little birthday present I've given myself. A massive hangover. I can tell the sun is shining without rubbing the condensation from the jeep window. I don't want to be caught sleeping here by some local early riser who has a job to get to. Calvin's patience will be wearing thin anyway. He never barks me awake unless seriously in need of taking a leak.

I grab the steering wheel and pull myself upright in the driver's seat. Calvin jumps eagerly into the passenger side, wagging his bushy tail in my face. I pop open the door and the two of us tumble out in a tangle of legs and limbs. His leash, which hangs around my neck, catches the door handle and nearly chokes me.

- Jesus, Cal, you trying to kill me?

He shrugs, shakes himself off in overly dramatic fashion and trots to the edge of the parking space, lifts his leg and pisses like a racehorse, glancing back at me over his shoulder.

You see? I really did have to go.

I reach down to pick up my jacket, which has fallen out of the jeep with us. Underneath it the rubber hose lies on the pavement, curled like a venomous snake. I don't remember pulling it from under the seat last night. Truth be told, I remember fuck all from last night. I wasn't stupid drunk enough to attempt siphoning gas in the middle of the night, was I? Another possibility occurs to me, but that's too unsettling to think about.

Don't go there, Dekker.

I push the thought out of my head as I shove the hose back in its place and slam the door, hoping to lock my ever-lurking demons away for at least another day.

Despite the sun shining in a cloudless blue sky the morning air is brisk, so I slip into my jacket. It's a lightweight but bulky ski coat, wind resistant and surprisingly warm, black with a bright neon green pattern that looks like Jackson Pollock vomited on it. When Willy bought it at a flea market for next to nothing, I told him he'd never wear such a hideous monstrosity.

You're right. It's a perfect color match for you.

I knew better than to argue with his synaesthetic view of the world. But it turned out to be perfect to throw on for Calvin's early-morning walks, whatever the season, whatever the weather, and I could no more part with it now than anything I own. Not that I own that much.

It's still a free-parking zone at this end of the park, so Jax can stay put. I'll move him later because I don't want to attract undue attention. Jax being the only home Cal and I have, I can't risk the scruffy jeep might be mistaken as abandoned and towed off to God knows where. I'm probably just being paranoid. Homelessness will do that to you.

Calvin is waiting by the park entrance. He knows better than to go farther without me. Willy and I trained him well but it was easy. Even other dog owners comment on Calvin's extraordinary intelligence. *He's not like other dogs.* You don't often hear people handing out such compliments to dogs that aren't their own. But nobody needs to tell me.

- Okay.

That's all Calvin needs to hear as I walk toward him. He immediately shoots off down the path, sticking close to the green borders, sniffing for urinary messages left by canine comrades since his last ramble. This will occupy him more or less completely for most of the morning. In case his attention flags, I have a mud-stained tennis ball in one jacket pocket and a few dog treats in the other. For now, he's in a scent world all his own. I'm nearly invisible, subordinate to his unwavering mission.

I need a cigarette. I pull the nearly flattened pack from my shirt pocket. Three left. Shit. Maybe I should hold off until later. Fat chance. I shake one out, light it, take a deep drag. At first I feel light-headed, but then the welcome tingle arrives as the nicotine works its speedy way into my synapses. I'm still fuzzy from the alcohol I consumed last night but if forced to interact with anyone, I won't come across as a total moron.

Calvin bustles among the bushes and shrubs, busy as usual, snuffling dead leaves, stripping bark from fallen branches, jumping rotted logs, intermittently pausing to dig into soft soil and frequently, obsessively, leaving his mark to claim ownership of the spot.

Vondelpark is dog heaven, a narrow hundred-acre rectangle of woods, fields, dirt trails, bike paths, canals, and ponds. Dogs have free rein to run and play anywhere they want, except for a couple of children's playgrounds. Someone told me it was a condition imposed by whoever donated the land but Willy said that's just wishful thinking perpetrated by dog owners. I don't know. Picasso gave this gigantic fish statue to the park for its hundredth anniversary, with the proviso it can never be moved. It still stands in the middle of a big open field.

The first time Cal saw the statue, he barked his fool head off, as if he could scare it away. He has a conservative streak that doesn't allow for things to be where they don't belong: a refrigerator left on the street, a pigeon perched on a bench, even a bicycle lying on the sidewalk. He has berated a street performer with a marionette, a woman practicing tai chi on the grass, and a man swimming in a park pond to retrieve a football. That activity is fine for dogs, however. Vondelpark is their domain. Humans are tolerated out of necessity and within reasonable limits.

Calvin crouches among the bushes with the intense look of concentration that means he's finishing his most important business of the first morning walk. Given a choice, he prefers to do this in somewhat secluded locations as opposed to open grass, never on the sidewalk, and preferably not in the street. In a pinch, if he really has to go and I make it clear we're not walking all the way to the park, he'll submit to the indignity of a curbside undertaking. On the extremely rare occasion when he had no choice but to poop inside, his humiliation was so all consuming that any further punishment was rendered pointless. He stands, gives a couple of obligatory backward kicks, and is ready to move on.

I desperately need to take a leak myself and, seeing no one in the immediate vicinity, step behind a tall bush. The lack of bathroom facilities is the worst part of being homeless. Forget about brushing your teeth, taking a shower, or even washing your hands. The need to relieve yourself while walking the streets can be a bitch. Fortunately there's a café in the park where no one seems to care if you duck in to use the toilet without ordering a coffee. It's part of the reason we're hanging around here for the time being. Not that Calvin minds. This is just another big adventure for him, no different from a drive to the beach or anywhere else, for that matter.

My head is beginning to throb a little harder. I want to lie down. Calvin takes the path that cuts across Picasso field and leads to the gay beach area, by the pond next to the rose gardens. It's typical of him to anticipate my needs, even if it is our usual spot for a morning nap these days. Cal also knows I'll let him go for a swim afterward.

I slip off my jacket and spread it on the ground where the sun has already begun to dry the dew-damp grass. I pat the ground with my hand.

- Lay by me.

He needs no further encouragement and tucks his body alongside mine, his head resting in the crook of my neck. Side by side, we both heave a deep sigh.

High above our heads two bright green acrobatic parrots execute a noisy fly-by. A couple of strays that somehow were able to survive Dutch winters had prospered, grown in number, and adopted the park as their home. Willy had drawn my attention to the hearty pandemonium during a bike ride soon after I arrived in Amsterdam, a lifetime ago.

CHAPTER THREE

I. CALVIN

looking dekker sleeping snoring / calvin
    waiting wanting swimming
looking water blinking shining / sunshine
    warming tongue sweating
calvin drinking lapping water wanting more
checking dekker sleeping snoring / evermore&evermore
waiting dekker long&long / water calling needing swimming
jumping swimming swimming happy / paddling
    pushing pressing water
cold&cooling / circling cooling water
    splashing / yes&yes&yes&yes
something smelling darkness waiting / calvin sniffing
    something bad
smelling something swimming closer / something
    smelling good&bad
wake up dekker yes&yes / calvin swimming / football floating
wake up dekker / water football fun&fun
football inside garbage present / come on calvin present waiting
nosing pushing nothing moving / headbutt headbutt /
    no teethbiting no&no
calvin tiring swimming circling / sniffing snorting breathing hard
calvin jumping out&out / calvin landing dripping water
calvin shaking water flying / shaking flinging fast&fast

dekker sleeping calvin barking / dekker sleeping
evermore&evermore
calvin biting football present / pulling tugging out&out
sniffing smelling pacing pawing something smelling bad
come on dekker no more sleeping / calvin finding something bad
biting plastic garbage ripping opening present / calvin mad
present smelling bad&bad
garbage present shaking tearing ripping shaking /
calvin mad&mad
something flinging flying landing smacking dekkers head

II. Dekker

- What the fuck, Calvin?

Sometimes he finds it amusing to wake me by dropping a ball on my head. I prop myself up on my elbows, squinting from the bright morning sun. I assume it's still morning. I look for Calvin by the edge of the water where he always waits when he wants the ball thrown into the pond. I'm surprised he's not there and glance at my watch. Not even ten o'clock. He's usually begging for a swim by now.

He barks, and I turn to see him sitting a few yards away, near the area where the grass ends and shrubbery continues to border the pond. It's another of his favorite places to retrieve the ball, preferably if it gets stuck in a bush and he has to jump into the prickly branches for it. He barks again, impatient, twice this time.

- Okay. Okay. Hold your horses. Where'd the ball go?

I search the ground around me. No ball. Come to think of it, I don't remember taking the ball out of my pocket this morning. That's when a silvery glint in the grass catches my eye.

When you spend as much time in the park as Calvin and I do, you discover a lot of interesting bits of treasure and trash. Once Calvin found a billfold in the bushes of the rose garden stuffed with a wad of cash. I made a pretty big deal out of it, overdoing the praise and the treats, and for weeks he was sniffing out lost wallets and bringing them to me, tail wagging proudly. They were all empty, of course. When he dropped a particularly disgusting specimen in my lap one day, I taught him the word *Garbage*, something to be left alone, something not to be brought home. With a few choice examples, he got the idea. Tennis balls I don't want to fish out of dirty canals. *Garbage*. A big ratty stuffed animal left out on the street. *Garbage*. And, of course, anything in a black plastic bag. *Garbage*.

I reach over and brush the grass away from whatever is shining in the sunlight. Someone has lost their keys. I pick them up, dislodging a piece of black plastic stuck in the metal ring. Someone somewhere must be miserable. Before I can figure out what to do with them, I notice a reddish slime has smeared my fingers. I drop them and rub my hand on the grass to clean off whatever it is.

Calvin starts another round of barking, standing now, agitated and insistent.

- What?

I'm more concerned with the revolting keys than with Cal's antics. He dashes over to me, grabs my sleeve with his teeth, and starts to pull at my arm. It's this thing he does, sometimes annoying, but sometimes funny, so I've never tried to break him of the behavior. However, this time he's going at it in a kind of panic, as if trying to pull me away from some imminent danger, the edge of a cliff.

- Calvin, stop. What's the matter with you?

He doesn't stop, though. He's tugging hard enough I'm afraid he'll rip my shirt. I've never seen him like this before, and it's a little disconcerting. This is no game to him, but I have no idea what he wants me to do. I clumsily get to my feet and let him pull me. He almost immediately lets go of my arm, races away, stops just short of the bushes, turns around, and barks at me again. As I get closer, he whines, performs an odd cross between a spin and a jump, whines again, and paces. Then I detect the object of his anxiety.

A torn black garbage bag rests on the ground by the water. It's wet, surrounded by shards of ripped plastic. For the first time I notice Calvin is wet, and also see a sliver of black plastic at the corner of his mouth. I put it together in a New York minute. While I was sleeping, he went swimming without permission. Bad enough on its own, but while in the water, he retrieved a bag of floating garbage someone threw in the pond. Another big slip-up. No wonder he's so upset. I put on my stern face.

- What have you gotten into?

Playing with Garbage is a more serious infraction than swimming. I look directly at the trash bag. For the second time this morning something odd catches my eye. In fact, it's what I could swear almost looks like another eye, staring back at me out of the torn side of the bag.

It's curious how the mind works when confronted by what appears to be the impossible.

I flick through alternatives with strobe-light speed: a discarded doll, a mangled mannequin, a birthday balloon, a Halloween mask, anything, anything, anything but what lies hidden in the dark recesses of my imagination.

Calvin backs away, lowers his head, and growls as I crouch within reach of the bag. I don't want to touch it, but I can't stop myself. I insert my fingers into the hole Calvin has already torn open and cautiously pull back the ripped edges. I am holding my breath as the grotesque contents inside the black bag are revealed.

A severed human head stares at me, lifeless eyes open, mouth frozen wide mid-scream. This is not the worst shock. I feel myself leaving my body, floating upward, looking down on myself from above. I see Calvin, sitting, head cocked, looking up at me. I see myself crouching, reaching, gaping slack-jawed. I see the face of a dead man gazing up at me out of the bag.

A dead man I recognize. A dead man I know.

III. GADGET

It was noon when Gadget opened his eyes and looked around without moving. Best to figure out where he was before getting out of a strange bed. The lavishly decorated room looked like a hotel but not one he immediately recognized. Classy, though. Very classy.

The naked figure tangled in the sheet and passed out next to him was breathing. A good sign. It meant things had not gotten too out of control last night, although he did remember vast quantities of alcohol and a virtual cornucopia of drugs. He tried to recall the sex but no clear pictures came to mind. That wasn't unusual. He'd have been on top, of course, doing the fucking, no discussion required or even allowed. Gadget was no bonking bottom butt boy. He carefully lifted the sheet on his side of the bed and slowly slid his legs over the mattress. Slinky silk sheets. Delicious. This hunky Eurotrash had style. Where did they meet? Gadget couldn't remember that either. Bar? Darkroom? He didn't think so. It would come to him—or not. He didn't care and it didn't matter as long as the guy was still breathing.

He scanned the room for his clothes. The first order of business was always to get dressed, in case the need for a hasty exit arose. There—next to an obviously expensive green leather armchair. He had a flash of his knees on the arms of the chair, pounding into the mouth of his seated trick, rush of amyl nitrate speeding his heartbeat, fueling his desire. He liked chairs. Chairs were fun. There was a lot you could do in a chair. Smiling, he silently slipped into his black briefs, black socks, black jeans, black T-shirt, black trainers. He had been dressed for the night. Maybe they had met on the street? Didn't feel right.

Aha. Wallet on dresser. Trusting and stupid, his two favorite traits in a man. He painstakingly unzipped it and found 645 guilders in mostly large bills. They hadn't discussed money, he never discussed money, but he knew the missing cash would not be reported. You could always depend on Eurotrash to keep their mouth shut about getting ripped off after a night of drunk and disorderly. Still, it was a big wad to carry around bar-hopping or cruising.

That's when Gadget remembered. The whole night came flooding back like a runaway freight train barreling down the tracks in reverse at breakneck speed. The sex, the bed, the sex, the chair, the strip, the high, the drugs, the cigars, the mini-bar. The hotel, the walk, the park, the sex, the bench, the pick-up, the rose garden. The package.

Goddamnmotherfuckshitpisscuntscrew!

Gadget thought his head would explode.

Who's stupid now, you fucking idiot?

He stuffed the bills into his pocket and glanced at the peacefully sleeping man in the bed. The asshole had no idea how lucky he was, how sorely tempted Gadget was to leave him an aromatic parting gift. No, worse. He wanted to bash his head into a bloody pulp with the heavy glass ashtray that had somehow appeared in his hand.

This is your fault, you fucking faggot fudgehole!

But Gadget controlled his rage and moderated his heavy breathing. He gently set the ashtray back on the desk, plucked his leather jacket from the floor, and stole soundlessly out of the room.

❖

Gadget had no intention of attempting to retrieve his well-hidden swag in broad daylight. He was not a complete fool. But a sunny summer afternoon in the park attracted many visitors, and it would be wise to keep an eye on it from a safe distance until the evening hours. Then he could walk it to one of the larger ponds not far away in Rembrandtpark. Add some rocks or bricks to ensure the bag sank into the muck, never to be found. That was the plan.

As soon as Gadget entered the rose garden, he knew he'd made a horrible mistake.

At the far end near the pond, a huge crowd of gawkers had gathered behind red-and-white crime scene tape and police barricades. Some people stood on park benches to get a better view. On the other side of the pond cyclists stopped their bikes on the path and stared.

Police cars, an ambulance, and other emergency vehicles were parked helter-skelter in an adjoining field. Men in black diving gear explored the bottom of the pond with long poles, dredging up old bike frames and other less identifiable trash, which police officers pulled onto the grass for further inspection. Other policemen interviewed people in hushed tones. The scene was eerily quiet, no music drifting from nearby cafés, no laughter of children in playgrounds.

Gadget fumed in anger and frustration. Next time he would keep his mind on the fucking task at hand. Next time he would not be distracted and led astray by his cock.

Next time, Gadget, next time!

How could this happen? He refused to believe he was totally to blame. He needed to know what unexpected twist of fate had thrown a spanner in his usually well-oiled works. Casing the spectators, he spied a pair of rubbernecking queens standing by the trees at the other side of the gay beach.

So much for sunbathing today, faggots.

Gadget maneuvered himself around the perimeter of the crowd to stand beside them.

- What's going on?
- We heard they found some guy's head.
- Yeah. Floating in a trash bag.
- No shit.
- Right? Fucking freaky.
- Shit, yeah.
- Somebody said it was a dog.
- A dog's head?
- No, a dog found the head.
- Pulled it out of the water.
- A goddamned golden retriever.
- No shit.

Shaking his head in feigned disbelief, Gadget started to move away. He did not want to get too chummy with these two morons, risk being noticed, or remembered, or thought of as overly curious.

Move along, move along, nothing to see here.

Serious cash was burning a hole in his pocket anyway, a guaranteed hot time tonight. Put this entire pathetic episode behind him. He'd had his fun. His slate was clean. It was time to take a break, take a shower, take a walk, a walk on the wild side. But a dog? A fucking dog? What kind of a fucking dog pulls a trash bag out of the water?

A dead fucking dog if Gadget had his way.

CHAPTER FOUR

I. CALVIN

calvin happy running jumping / tall grass blowing jumping more
sniffing scenting pissing marking / happy calvin more&more
dekker sitting quiet happy / watching calvin jumping more
flowers smelling windsong blowing evermore&evermore

II. DEKKER

I watch Calvin run and leap through the tall grass and purple clover, the yellow buttercups and delicate Queen Anne's lace, events of the morning forgotten, if they registered at all.

It's a dog's life. The expression used to refer to the miserable existence of working dogs back in the sixteenth or seventeenth century. The meaning has evolved to refer to the carefree life dogs enjoy today, pampered as most are by their owners. One way or the other, Calvin and I are both living a dog's life, like the old silent movie with Charlie Chaplin as the homeless tramp and his white dog, Scamp. Come to think of it, they have a run-in with the police, too.

It was a lot easier lying to them than I thought it would be. Not lying exactly, but certainly withholding pertinent information. Why would it occur to them to ask if I knew the head in the bag? And if I told them, wouldn't that make me their number-one suspect? That's not what I was thinking at the time, before I called over one of the groundskeepers working in the rose garden, before police arrived on the scene, cars pulling up on the grass, sirens blaring, sending Calvin into another frenzied fit of barking. By then I'd safely secreted the keys into my pocket, secure in thinking they belonged to the victim.

A victim I'd known, whose address I knew. Because I'd been in his house on more than one occasion.

A pair of white swans glide across the far side of the pond in this quiet corner of Rembrandtpark, disappearing behind the plume of water created by a center fountain. Rembrandt is more famous than the poet Vondel but this park is less frequented, has more areas of wild, uncultivated beauty. A large dragonfly entertains me, performing lazy figure eights, wings glistening in the afternoon sunlight.

I lie back on the grass between two tall trees, some sort of elms that must have survived the pandemic of the 1960s. Their leaves flicker in the breeze, creating kaleidoscopic patterns against the clear cobalt sky. The only sign of urban life is the distant hum of traffic I hear from the highway, the occasional jet I see heading toward the airport.

Cal and I could easily have walked here from Vondelpark but I'd left my knapsack containing our daily rations of food and water in the jeep. I wanted to move it to a more remote parking spot anyway. Calvin loves riding in Jax, sitting in the passenger seat, head hanging out the window, lapping at the wind in his face. I think he even likes curling up in the back and sleeping there. I, however, have had enough of this nomadic existence, more than enough. I only had to think about last night. Had I come close, literally, to the end of my rope? I've been thrown a lifeline, or the possibility of one. I just have to figure out if and how I can take advantage of it.

I reach into my pants pocket and pull out the key ring, which I'd given a thorough cleansing in the pond. I finger the keys one at a time. There are four. One is a four-sided key normally used for a deadbolt and another is a standard flat key. Front door and back garden door? Am I correct to assume he lived in the same house? It seems likely but I can't be certain. Easy enough to confirm later, once it gets dark. Just walk by and read the nameplate. If there is a nameplate. What if there are two names on it? What if he lived with someone? There's also a car key in a black plastic cover etched with a VW logo. Interesting. The last of the four is an old-fashioned skeleton key, indicating something less important. A storage closet? A garden gate? An old armoire or maybe an antique safe deposit box? My mind drifts into overly imaginative territory. I'm trying to remain calm, cautiously optimistic, but it's difficult to control my growing excitement.

I can picture the street although I can't remember the name. It runs along the last and widest of the concentric canals encircling the city. It's near the bridge where de Clercqstraat changes its name to Admiraal de Ruyterweg, at the edge of an old neighborhood called the Baarsjes, a run-down and not particularly safe area. I lived nearby in a flat of student rooms when I first arrived in Amsterdam. He could have sold the place for all I knew and moved somewhere else. Where would I even begin to look?

My thoughts are interrupted by Calvin, who licks my face and plops himself down beside me, nosing into my jacket pocket for one of the dog treats he knows I'm hoarding. It's almost time for his dinner but I give him one of the biscuits anyway. He chomps away in his exaggerated manner, as if it was a large juicy bone instead of a meager bite of baked bone-shaped meal.

I stroke his thick white coat, nearly dry since his last swim in this much cleaner pond. A yellow ladybug crawls from his neck onto my hand. I've never seen a yellow one before. I count the white spots on its back, like my grandmother taught me. She said seven brought you luck, and seven it is. The pretty little insect opens her shell, flutters her wings, and flies away.

Fly away home, your house is on fire, your children are gone.

That nursery rhyme always terrified me as a child. It seems tame after this morning.

I've had some interesting birthdays in my life, but none so bizarre as this one. I used to brag about having the longest day of the year to celebrate. Today the sun will not set soon enough. It won't be dark until well after ten o'clock and I don't want to wait that long for some preliminary reconnaissance. I grab my bag, pull out Calvin's dish and a can of dog food. He jumps up, tail wagging in anticipation, greeting the unexpected treat of an early dinner with unadulterated delight.

III. GADGET

Grapes, cherries, bell, lemons. Push. Oranges, lemons, pears, pears. Push. Strawberries, seven, seven, cherries. Hold sevens and push.

Seven, seven, seven, pears. Twenty points. Save and push. Cherries, lemons, grapes, melons. Two points. Gamble. Five points. Save and push. Bell, oranges, bell, grapes. Save bells and push. Bell, bell, bell, bell. Two hundred points. Jackpot. Pay out. Push.

Gadget was in the zone, the winning zone. Flashing lights, spinning wheels, clinking coins pouring into the tray. The cumulative effect drove the receptors in his brain insane, bouncing off each other like a game of neuropsychiatric pinball. Better than any boring nicotine buzz. Stimulation equals relaxation equals Gadget at one with the machine and all is good in the universe.

Lemons, oranges, plums, melons. Push. Cherries, cherries, pears, pears. Five points. Gamble. Lose and push. Oranges, seven, strawberries, seven. Hold sevens and push. Cherries, seven, grapes, seven. Two points. Save and push.

Knowing when to gamble or not was key, and when in the zone Gadget always knew, almost always knew. Tonight he knew, always. Except when that old dude stood right beside him and watched, practically breathing down his neck, annoying the shit out of him. Gadget hated old dudes, scraggly white hair, bellies that hung over their belts, stinking of cheap cologne to mask their old-dude smell. Always the same stupid line.

- Are you winning?
- Huh?
- Are you winning?
- Always winning. Fuck off.

The old dude looked confused, acted all offended, stumbled back to the bar. It didn't take much to blow off the old dudes, but it threw him off his stride all the same. Not for long. Now he was back, back in the zone, flying on a pure adrenaline high, no additives necessary, money in his pocket to take the edge off his crazy-ass day. Then lay low for a while, that's the ticket.

Until next time, Gadget. Next time.

He threw back his head and laughed like a lunatic, didn't give a shit if people stared. Fuck 'em if they don't get the joke. Gadget laughed again and he kept on laughing, laughing until his stomach ached, laughing until tears streamed down his face, tears of pure joy. Blindly, he pushed the button once more.

Seven, seven, seven, seven. Jackpot.

IV. Calvin

standing turning curling down&down / time for sleeping
bluebear finding biting licking / bluebear soft&warm
quiet jax quiet outside / window steaming /
    darkness outside / darkness in
sleepy dekker softly breathing / calvin waiting /
    always waiting dekker sleeping
sleeping coming drifting darkness / ever waiting / evermore

V. Dekker

Lying with the seat reclined as far back as possible, body quilted in my hideous but comforting winter jacket on this mild midsummer night, I think about how easily one adapts, accepts, takes for granted the most unusual circumstances. It must be how people endure severe natural disasters, hurricanes that batter coastal towns, tornadoes that randomly tear through trailer parks, sudden mudslides that bury remote villages. You see pictures of the aftermath on television, men and women with blank faces or confused expressions, children dazed or crying, and you wonder how they deal with it. Family members lost, possessions gone, their lives turned upside down and inside out. The reality is cruel but simple. You do what you have to do to survive. You pick yourself up, you sift through the rubble, and you keep on keeping on, whatever it takes, however you can, whichever path offers the least resistance. You might feel depressed, but depression is a luxury you cannot afford, not if you want to make it through to the other side. That's the way it is for me, anyway. I'm not ready to give up, not today. I have to stop thinking that the light at the end of the tunnel is just another train.

❖

I found the house without difficulty. It was only a fifteen-minute walk from where I'd parked, nestled between an old warehouse and a more recently built block of apartments. First we walked past on the other side of the street, along the canal. It's not one of the beautiful, wide-front dwellings with tall windows that line the canals in the city center, exemplifying its Old World charm. It looked more like a dilapidated gingerbread house imagined by the Brothers Grimm. Barely two stories high with a long, steeply peaked roof on one end and a small turret-like room on the other. The windows were dark, curtains pulled closed, blinds shut. The first time I saw it years ago I thought it was delightful, but on this particular evening it cast a gloomier impression, almost derelict. I began to wonder if anyone lived there at all.

We walked to the end of the street, a cul-de-sac actually, with stairs that led up to a main avenue and the bridge. Calvin wanted to climb the stairs, continue on, and was confused when I turned around to walk back the way we came. He has some very set notions when it comes to walking the streets. One of them is: when given a choice of direction never retrace your steps, which I have to admit is not a bad mantra for life in general. Too often I let him take the lead, but a sharp jerk on his leash let him know that I was in charge and we'd go my way whether he liked it or not.

Walking back slowly, we stuck to the sidewalk so I could get a good look at the front door. As we passed, I spotted the brass plate bearing a single name etched in a delicate antique font. *V. Mackenzie*. I also noticed the house number was thirty-three. Happy birthday to me.

I took Calvin on a long roundabout route back to the jeep, hoping to tire him out. We walked the scenic Admiralengracht, a short canal that cut through the neighborhood and led to Erasmuspark, a pretty square of green in an otherwise drab area. Calvin caught sight of a rabbit and chased him into the shrubbery. We passed the outdoor municipal pool at the other end of Rembrandtpark, as well as an extensive garden plot where children from a local school planted vegetables. The sun was finally setting as we strolled the winding paths through the length of the park toward Lucas Andreas Hospital, behind which I'd parked Jax on Nachtwachtlaan.

❖

Night Watch Lane. How ironic. No more watching tonight. I'm exhausted and I sense Calvin is, as well. He's curled up in the back with his beloved Blue Bear, the only toy I let him keep from his once-extensive menagerie. His last present from Willy.

Does he remember? How many dog years before a memory fades

and is forgotten? Once lost can it be retrieved, recollected at a certain place, beckoned by a special touch, evoked through a taste, summoned with a sound, or suggested in a scent?

I take a deep breath. I can no longer detect the slightest trace of Willy, but I imagine Calvin can. Comfort enough.

PART TWO: THE CANAL-HOUSE

"Come back often, hold me in the night when lips and skin remember."

—C.P. Cavafy, *Come Back*

Chapter Five

I. Dekker

I watch the house for a week, walking by at different hours of the day or night. There is no sign of any change, no opening of curtains, no appearance of crime scene tape on the entrance, no police or other outside interest of any kind. On the opposite side of the street, a bench faces the canal on a small patch of grass and I spend a full day sitting there with Calvin to get a more complete picture of the surroundings.

The cul-de-sac is quiet, with little foot traffic. The most regular denizens seem to be young working mothers with toddlers in tow or infants in strollers, making use of a day-care center on the ground floor of the apartment building next door. They come and go in a rush, too intent on their charges or focused on getting to work to register anything out of the ordinary, street-wise. Few bicycles pass, preferring to veer off into a little lane behind the house that takes them straight to the main intersection without having to dismount and carry their bike up the stairway at the end of the block.

Directly across the canal, on a small green plot along the water, a collection of sheds and outbuildings surrounded by a white picket fence make up a *kinderboederij*, or children's farm, what we call in the States a petting zoo. Ducks, exotic chickens and a brightly colored rooster, some well-fed rabbits, a handful of goats, a couple of sheep, and a lone Shetland pony reside there. Tall trees line the street behind the farm, ensuring the house is hidden from the scrutiny of apartments in buildings across the canal.

This island of rural tranquility in the midst of an urban landscape is oddly relaxing. It reminds me of the farm where I grew up, the farm

I sold after my grandmother passed during the winter holiday of my senior year at Camden College. The farm that provided the funds to get me here in the first place.

❖

When I announced my intention to explore the literary passion of Vincent van Gogh and how it related to his painting, my classmates assumed it was a strategy to travel around Europe. I could have written my thesis without leaving the campus library, much less the country. But Camden encouraged students to travel abroad for study, work, or simply to broaden their horizons. Literally. Although most of my normal academic expenses were covered by scholarships, there was no way I could afford such a trip. Until my grandmother slipped on the icy front porch steps, broke her hip, and contracted pneumonia. She might have survived one condition, but both were too much for her frail body. She died peacefully in the hospital between Christmas and New Year's.

A car accident had left me in the care of my grandparents, an orphan at the age of four. When I was in high school, cancer had taken my grandfather, and with him my unwished-for future as a farmer. Death again proved a turning point in my life, sending me off in a new direction. Long story short, I delayed returning to Camden while I sorted the loose ends of my grandmother's paltry estate, quickly selling the house and everything in it for a song, or more like a symphony to my impoverished ears.

I went back to school briefly to talk with my advisor and pick up my few belongings. There was nothing else to keep me there. I saw a couple of classmates before I left and we promised to stay in touch until we met at graduation, but I knew we were just going through the motions. There would be no letters or postcards, no commencement celebrations or happy reunions. I took the bus to Boston, caught the next flight to Amsterdam, and never looked back.

❖

Calvin stares up at me with his questioning look.

- Time for a change of scenery?

He stands and shakes his whole body in agreement. He knows how to lighten my mood, or at least give it a swift kick in the pants.

I remember a day I was morbidly depressed. I also remember why, but push that thought into a cloud-hidden corner of my mind. I sat on a park bench. Calvin sat facing me with a tennis ball in his mouth.

I'm not in the mood to play today, I communed with a shake of my head.

He cocked his head, stood up, dropped the ball directly into my lap, took a couple of steps backward, and stared straight into my eyes.

Just keep throwing the ball. I'll keep bringing it back.

Dog Zen translation: *One foot in front of the other, one step at a time.*

A good walk is what I need right now to clear my head and Cal knows it. We'll continue our surveillance later. As we start down the street, a colony of seagulls screech into battle for crusts of bread someone has thrown into the canal.

II. Gadget

A murder of crows flies over a golden wheat field under an ominous black and blue sky. That's what the painting should've been called. *A Murder of Crows.* Gadget hated museums but it was his mother's idea, and Gadget was nothing if not a good son. Fortunately, he'd slept for days before her call woke him yesterday afternoon. Her watercolor class had planned the excursion, and as always, her last-minute suggestion that he join them insinuated more demand than invitation.

He met her at the train station at ten o'clock. On the tram he eyeballed a grimy backpacker into giving up his seat so she wouldn't have to stand. At the museum he paid for both of their admission tickets. After they finished the tour they would have lunch in the Museum Café. He would accompany her on the train back to his childhood home in the east of the country. He would stay for the weekend and help her change the wallpaper in the dining room, a yearly ritual. His attendance was mandatory. A small price to pay for the relative autonomy she granted him when he left school.

Gadget may have been a good son but he had not been a good student. He was clever enough, according to his teachers, but prone to sudden violent outbursts that were never tolerated at home. His mother, a stricter taskmaster than his teachers, presided over his household chores with a well-worn leather strap and the more menacing threat of the dark garden shed.

At an early age Gadget was taught to control his outbursts. Never cry, never shout, never laugh. In school he discovered that shouting was not punished, crying was rewarded with gentle hugs, teachers and students laughed together. This confused him at first, but he soon learned to act one way in school and another at home. It became more difficult as he grew older. The quieter he remained in the presence of his mother, the more unruly his behavior became in the classroom.

A teacher suggested that Gadget talk to their priest. He might get to the bottom of the boy's problems. Get to the boy's bottom was a more accurate way of putting it.

The priest's dark confessional became the equivalent of his mother's dreaded garden shed. The harder Gadget tried to forget his ungodly sessions with the priest, the more his violent conduct escalated in school. Then one afternoon Gadget hit another child so hard the doctor had to be called. A week of being shuttled between his mother and the priest, the shed and the confessional, was all the punishment needed to mend his schoolboy foolishness. He found the evenness of temper, the necessary lack of affect required to survive school, the priest, and his mother, until he reached the age of sixteen and was finally permitted to leave them all.

Staring at the painting, Gadget felt cracks beginning to emerge in his veneer of calm. He wasn't sure he could last a full weekend with his mother and her more-than-passive aggression. It was always the same. At first he would almost enjoy the mindless routine, the steady rhythm of the wallpapering.

Measure, cut, paste, and hang. Measure, cut, paste, and hang.

Mother would preside over him like a prison guard. When the first wall was completed, she'd examine the seams with her magnifying glass, search out the minutest divergence from matching the intricate pattern. When a flaw was found, she would rip the long, narrow sheets from the wall and force him to begin the whole process again.

By the end of the day, his shoulders were tight, his arms ached, and his fingers were cramped. No matter. He had to start all over. And again the next morning.

Measure, cut, paste, and hang. Measure, cut, paste, and hang.

He'd need help from the weed he had tucked in his pocket. Or maybe something stronger. He should have thought of that earlier. There would be no alcohol in the house, of course, and it would be tricky to sneak out, even after his mother was asleep. His head started to throb just thinking about the days to come. When they finally came to an end, someone would have to pay for his suffering, pay dearly.

Measure, cut, paste, and hang. Measure, cut, paste, and hang.

CHAPTER SIX

I. DEKKER

- Stay. I'll be back in five minutes.

I illustrate this with my hand, palm forward, fingers splayed, directly in front of Calvin's face. He understands three durations of time. One minute, one finger, is the shortest period. He will not have to wait long. Two minutes, two fingers, means he should sit since he has to be a bit more patient. Five minutes, five fingers, is the longest stretch of time. He has learned he might as well lie down, close his eyes, and take a nap because whatever I have to do takes precedence over what he wants. He knows five minutes will not last forever but it can seem like it. Calvin doesn't like five minutes, especially five minutes alone inside Jax, even with the window cracked open for fresh air and Blue Bear to keep him company. There's nothing he can do about it but it must be endured.

I don't like leaving Calvin alone in the jeep any more than he does. What if something outside startles him, he starts barking, and some well-meaning passerby calls the animal protection authorities, who break in and take him away? I'd have a lot of explaining to do, the last thing I need right now. I don't feel I have a choice tonight. This is something I better do alone. If all goes according to plan, our days and nights of living and sleeping in the jeep will be over, like a bad dream that fades into obscurity once morning comes.

I have everything I think I might need. A small flashlight loaded with fresh batteries that I bought at the Guilder Store, a Swiss army knife with several blades and utensils that I can't imagine will be useful, except to give me an illusory sense of security.

Yesterday I surreptitiously tried the key when the street was deserted, and discovered with palpable relief that it not only fit into the slot but turned easily, releasing the locking mechanism with a soft click. I turned the key back, locking the door again, and moved on before someone appeared and noticed a shabby shady character acting too paranoid to be ignored.

A thick cover of clouds has turned the warm, humid night darker a bit earlier than usual for this time of year. Halfway to the house it starts to rain. I take this as a good omen since it means less chance of anyone out for a midsummer stroll along the canal. It's not really a neighborhood suited for evening walks unless you happen to be on the prowl for trouble, specifically your drug of choice. There are no bars or nightclubs in the area, only a small night shop a few blocks away that stocks essentials like milk and bread, munchies and cigarettes, dog food and condoms. As the rain comes down harder, I pull down the brim of my black Yankees baseball cap to protect my face.

On the corner up ahead I see the lights of a snack bar I'd forgotten about, but it appears empty of customers. I cross to the other side of the street, just in case. I'm trying to act casual but my nerves are jangling like the jittery bamboo stalks of an Asian wind chime.

Keep it together, Dekker, you're almost there, almost home free.

Or rather the opposite, I hope. Stupid joke. My stomach is tied up in apprehensive knots, my palms damp, and not from the rain. I'm sweating all over.

Please please please let me get through this night without falling to pieces.

I turn left when I get to the canal. The house is only a block and a half away. I slow my pace, hoping to slow my heartbeat as well. I literally feel the blood pulsing through my veins, fingers tingling, jaw tensing shut, feet pounding the pavement, and all of a sudden I'm in front of the door, a couple of steps below street level.

Time stands still and the nervous energy that fueled my courage drains from my body, like the Cowardly Lion quaking before the great and powerful Wizard of Oz. What was I thinking? This is the worst idea in the world. There's no chance I can get away with this. I will go directly to jail.

Do not pass Go. Do not collect two hundred dollars.

I cannot control the random rambling rubbish in my brain. What brain? I haven't got a brain.

I'll miss you most of all, Scarecrow.

The key ring is in my hand. I have no idea how it got there, how I got here, what to do next. I'm frozen to the spot like the Tin Man in the orchard, unable to move a muscle.

Oilcan. Oilcan.

I want to scream. Without comprehension or forethought, my hand levitates toward the lock of its own volition and inserts the key.

I'm standing in a pitch-black hallway before I remember the flashlight. I wait for my eyes to get accustomed to the darkness while I picture the interior of the canal-house in my mind. I've thought about it every waking hour, so my memory of the place has been fine-tuned, telescoping the years since I was last here.

Through the door on the left is an open-plan sitting room, dining area, and kitchen. To the right a door leads to the small bedroom, behind which is a second door to the compact bathroom. Along the hall is a stairway to the second floor, but I was never up there. Watching the house from outside, I've imagined a small study in the turret and an attic for storage under the roof. At the rear of the house, there is a neatly trimmed garden with a high wooden fence closing it off from the back street.

I pull the flashlight from my pocket and flick it on. The beam on the stairs casts eerie shadows along the narrow hall. I step toward the closed door, which leads to the living room, and put my hand on an ornately carved wood doorknob. I freeze when I hear a shuffling sound, like someone walking through autumn leaves. It makes no sense but I keep absolutely still. Again. A rustle of papers?

Someone is inside the darkened room.

I'm not sure whether to call out or turn around and get the hell out of there. Before I can decide, a loud voice breaks the silence.

- Hello, motherfucker.

I gasp, horrified, and almost piss myself as I fall against the wall and drop the flashlight. The hall plunges into darkness again. My body shakes, my mind reels.

Impossible. Simply impossible.

The voice I heard was unmistakably his, the voice of a dead man.

II. Calvin

rabbits here rabbits there / rabbits jumping high&low
rabbits racing calvin hunting / finding playing scaring no
rabbits growing calvin barking / rabbits growing more&more
rabbits chasing scaring calvin / calvin hiding nonono
calvin waking rabbits gone / dekkergone&willygone
bluebear licking gentle kissing / calvin sleeping more&more

III. Dekker

What an idiot!

I'd completely forgotten about the parrot, a sleek African Grey called Bastard with an extraordinary talent for mimicry. Recovering from my initial shock, I enter the living room and see the covered cage near the curtained front window. I carefully remove the black-and-white Palestinian scarf and find the bird crouched at the bottom of his cage. He looks ruffled and listless but manages a weak string of profanities. He must be starving.

I sweep the flashlight beam around, spot a box of sunflower seeds and a bag of peanuts on a nearby shelf. I drop a handful of nuts through the bars at the top of the cage. He immediately grabs one and starts to remove the shell with his beak. I sprinkle some of the sunflower seeds in for him as well. I have no idea how much food a parrot needs but figure he has enough to keep him busy for the time being. I reach my hand inside and pull out the empty water dish hooked to the side of the cage.

As I stand at the kitchen window filling the dish with water from the tap, I watch the falling rain illuminated by a streetlamp. The back garden is dark and doesn't appear to be overlooked by nearby dwellings. I set the dish on the counter, and before turning off the water, let it run over my hands and wipe the sweat from my face. I catch sight of my reflection in the glass. I have not shaved for weeks and my beard is full, itchy, but the cool water feels good on my skin.

I pick up the dish and take it back to the cage. I consider setting it on the floor in case the bird is too weak to climb, but I don't want to pass my hand within reach of his beak. I know nothing about parrots, tame or otherwise, and am not about to risk getting bitten. I hook the dish back where it was and snap the cage door shut, whereupon Bastard deftly pulls himself up the bars and drinks. Not so weak after all. Another survivor. I came with the single-minded intention of saving myself, and end up saving a parrot. I wonder how he and Cal might get along.

The main reason I decided not to bring Calvin with me on this initial visit was that I had no idea what I might find, least of all a starving parrot. I had imagined, expected, a gruesome scene of gore and body parts. As I look around, the room seems in perfect order, much as I remember from the first time I was here. The kitchen area is spotless, flowers on the dining table have barely begun to wilt, and nothing seems out of place in the front lounge. Perhaps the bedroom has a more grisly tale to tell.

No, as it turns out. The bed is unmade and a few clothes are piled carelessly on a chair. Otherwise the room is tidy. Likewise the bathroom. The light-color carpet on the stairs is clean. No sign of bloody footprints to indicate a scene of carnage on the upper floor.

Whatever happened to Valentine Mackenzie did not happen here.

We met as most gay men meet, in a bar. My primary objective for coming to Amsterdam might have been to investigate the inner life of Vincent van Gogh, but I fully intended to explore my own inner life as well. In high school, I had little more than a vague notion of what it meant to be gay. A faint stirring of unidentified desire while working with shirtless farm hands during the summer haying season. Brick's ambiguous secret in the film *Cat on a Hot Tin Roof*. Who wouldn't be insecure with a wife as beautiful as Elizabeth Taylor? College had opened my mind to a new world of possibilities. I had never acted on my newly understood desires but was determined to change that now that I was in what people called the Gay Capital of Europe.

The problem was I had never been in a gay bar, had no idea what to expect, how to behave. Camden brought me out of my introverted shell and I no longer had difficulty striking up a conversation with a complete stranger. Yet I was intimidated by my inexperience, my total ignorance of the rules of engagement.

When gay classmates talked about cruising and pick-ups and hanky codes, it was like they were speaking a foreign language, a language I had to learn. I read books like John Rechy's *The Sexual Outlaw*, graphically detailing the life of a gay hustler, and the coming-of-age novel *A Boy's Own Story* by Edmund White. I was desperate to fill the gaps in my knowledge but only succeeded in becoming more confused. I came to the conclusion the only way to solve my sexual *Sturm und Drang* was simple. Go to a bar, order a drink, wait and see what happens next.

It's almost funny to look back now, knowing how easy it was, how quickly I learned. Of course I was popular and got more attention than I knew how to handle. I was a fresh face in a scene that grew tired fast, fresh meat in a market where turnover was key, quite literally a freshman, a boy-toy, a cub, a chicken, a cherry ripe for picking. I may not have known the language but I was a quick study, learning by trial and error. There were many errors, some more serious than others.

Valentine Mackenzie was one of the early mistakes. I learned lessons in the limits of yes, the etiquette of tactful disengagement, and the sensitive parameters of discretion. He was a few years older than me and made the first move, offering to buy me a drink. Why not? He was attractive, slim but well-built, with dark hair and neatly trimmed beard.

As he handed me a bottle of beer, he said it was his day, Valentine's Day. I didn't believe him when he told me that was his name. Making up names was common practice then, perhaps still is. I've no idea.

- I can't call you Valentine. It's too weird.

- Call me Mac. That's what everybody else calls me.

- Mac, then. I'm Dekker. Thanks for the drink.

- My pleasure. American?

- Yes.

- Just visiting?

- Sort of. I'm a student, writing my senior thesis.

- On what subject?

- Um…Art. And literature. And van Gogh.

- Van who?

- Van Gogh. The painter?

- Oh, him. Van *Goff*.

He was having a bit of fun with me. That was fine. Bar talk was best kept light and breezy. I asked him if his accent was Scottish and he told me he grew up in Scotland but had a Dutch mother.

- That's funny. My mother's family was Scottish and my father's was Dutch. We're opposites.

- That we are. And you know what they say.

- Ha ha. Right. Opposites attract.

- Do they now?

He wasn't wasting any time, and I had already decided I wouldn't mind going home with him. We had another beer, neither one of us wanting to appear too eager, both of us feeling hornier by the minute.

- Let's go.

I didn't ask where, just followed him out the door and down the street. He hailed a taxi, we got in together, and he gave the driver his address. I tentatively touched his leg.

- Save it.

He curtly brushed my hand aside. We were headed in the same direction as my student room but I decided not to mention it.

The cab stopped at the corner near his house. He paid the fare and we got out. He unlocked the door and ushered me in. I'd never been in a Dutch home like his, an actual house as opposed to an apartment. He told me he was lucky, had inherited it from his uncle. Before he could get past me in the narrow hall, I moved toward him, mouth slightly open, ready to be kissed, a cue that he ignored as he took my hand and led me into the sitting room.

It wasn't my first time, but it was certainly the strangest night of sex I ever had. If you can call it sex. Mac was into role-playing. He was the prisoner. I was the guard. No actual handcuffs. He held his arms in the air, wrists together, as if he were suspended from a high bar. Although he took the passive role, he actively directed me, perhaps because I was so hesitant.

- Take off your shirt. Unbuckle your belt. Leave it on. Walk around me. Insult me. Threaten me. Rip off my shirt. Stroke my nipples. Softly. Barely touching. Take off my boots. Take off my socks. Circle me. Insult me. Call me your bitch. Spit at my feet. Take off my belt. Whip me with it. Not so hard. Again. Am I your bitch? Pull down my jeans. Pull them off. Insult me. Tell me I'm bad. Deserve to be punished. Tell me. Take off your shoes. Your socks. Your jeans. Stand behind me.

Close. Closer. No touching. Pull off my shorts. Threaten to fuck me. Don't touch me. Don't touch me. Pull out your dick. Show me. Show me. Oooh, it's a big one. Tell me. What will it do to me? What a big dick. Jack off. Don't touch me. Tell me. Don't touch me. Jack off. Don't touch me. Tell me. Are you coming? Don't touch me. Fuck me. Don't touch me. Coming. I'm coming. Don't. Tell. Come. Now. Now. Now.

That was pretty much it. Afterward, we cleaned up, he gave me a robe, got us a couple of beers, and said I was welcome to sleep with him. No cuddling. No spooning. No touching in bed at all. He slept. I did not.

I was awake to hear a rooster crow early the next morning. He made coffee and, uncovering the birdcage, introduced me to the beautiful Bastard, also inherited from his uncle. The bird greeted me with the perfect imitation of a flushing toilet. I left feeling a little polluted myself.

Despite my reservations, Mac and I had a couple more sessions together. The next time involved stripping down for an interrogation and binding his balls tightly with coarse string as he jerked off. Still no extraneous touching and no kissing, not even good night when I opted out of staying until morning.

I don't like thinking about the last time. Clearly with each encounter he was pushing the boundaries, testing my limits. He spread a black rubber sheet on the floor and told me to piss in his mouth. That was as far as I was willing to go. As I dressed, I told him I couldn't do this anymore. He continued to beg me, perhaps thinking I was still playing out the perverse drama, teasing him, making him wait for it. Maybe he did know, just pretended to believe I would return, to save some shred of dignity, if that was possible. As I left he was still lying prone on the rubber sheet, pleading.

\- Shit on me. Shit on my chest. Shit on me.

❖

I hadn't seen Valentine for years. Maybe he began to frequent more extreme bars in the red-light district, maybe he always had. It was a scene I never explored. I'd had my taste of fetishism, learned the language, and discovered I was a vanilla kind of guy.

I rarely thought of those curious encounters, or of Valentine.

When I did, I wondered if he might have moved away or even died. He seemed to have disappeared completely. I shudder thinking of his final role, and am startled as Bastard channels his voice again in the darkness.

- Fuck me. Don't touch me.

Chapter Seven

I. Dekker

I let the water run as hot as I can stand it, turning the bathroom into a steamy sauna. I stand under the shower until my body turns pink from the heat and harsh scrubbing necessary to remove thick layers of grime and sweat, especially crusted around my ankles and between my toes. I shampoo the grease from my long shaggy hair, twice, then again, scratching my scalp vigorously each time, removing sand, dandruff, and flaking skin. I can't remember when I last showered, felt clean. I could stand here forever.

My face appears in the mirror as I wipe the condensation from the surface with my hand. I barely recognize myself, even with wet hair slicked back, looking shorter, the way I used to wear it. My face is hairier, beard longer than ever before. The blurry image I see makes me think of a young Grizzly Adams. Not so young anymore, to be honest. I see something else, as well, something I can't quite put my finger on, something familiar and yet unfamiliar at the same time. I pull some weird faces, not as ugly as a gurning champion, but enough to distort the image in the mirror and possibly latch onto that elusive something I'm trying to see. Nothing. Nix. Nada. I relax my features and a flicker of recognition glimmers for an instant, not of me, of someone else, before it vanishes as quickly as it appeared. Who was that? What is my subconscious trying to tell me?

Then it hits me, like light reflected from another source brings something new into focus. Could it be? I'm not sure. I need proof. Stark naked, I dash from the bathroom, down the short hall to the bedroom, flip the light switch on. A quick glance around tells me, no, it wasn't here. I turn the light off and cross to the lounge. It's still dark and I don't want to risk turning on a light that might shine through the curtainless kitchen window. Where did I leave the flashlight?

Bathroom. I race back to retrieve it, slamming my knee painfully into the doorjamb.

Take it easy, Dekker. Stay cool.

Flashlight in hand, I limp back to the lounge, sweep the room with the shaft of light, settling on a wall of polished wood bookcases. Yes. On one of the shelves, I find what I'm looking for, a strip of four passport-sized photographs, the kind you take in a photo booth. Mac is alone, making faces at the camera. I bring them back to the bathroom and tuck them into the frame on the side of the mirror.

My eyes shift back and forth between the photos and my reflection. I mimic the different expressions on Mac's face, as if trying them on for size. Not a perfect fit, but closer than I could have imagined. We were about the same height and build, same hair color. Those details I remember. I can't tell the color of his eyes from the black-and-white images, but that won't matter. What matters is that we look like brothers, not identical twins, but maybe fraternal. If I shave my head, closely crop my beard and trim it goatee-style as in these pictures, maybe? Was I just seeing what I want to see, need to see?

I need time to process this because it's totally insane, a crazy idea that couldn't possibly work, not with anyone who really knew him. Mac and I were nothing alike, had almost nothing in common, but as the concept swims around in my head, possibilities begin to take shape. The premise is not to become Mac, but to pass for Mac, in his neighborhood, at least until I can figure out some more permanent solution for my screwed-up situation. Sure, there will be details that need to be worked out, problems to be solved. I don't expect it'll be a piece of cake to step into someone else's shoes. But if the shoe fits?

❖

Not only did the shoes fit, so did his whole wardrobe. I check myself out in the full-length mirror on the bedroom door and am more than a little blown away by the totality of the transformation.

Newly shaved head, trimmed mustache and beard, tight white T-shirt, crisp clean black jeans, Doc Martens boots. I'm hot, if I say so myself.

Soft early-morning light begins to seep through a small gap between the drapes. I need to get moving. Calvin might freak out if I'm not back before sunrise. I put the cover back over Bastard's cage and leave the place pretty much as I found it.

Outside I cross the street and stand at the edge of the canal for a moment, take deep breaths of cool fresh air. I have not slept, should feel exhausted, but I'm on some kind of natural high.

A colony of gray and white gulls with black wingtips land on the water and begin bathing together. I've never seen this behavior before. Each in its own rhythm, they flap their wings in high-energy splashing displays, repeatedly dunk their heads underwater and come up shaking, preen their chests with orange beaks, lift inches above the water with hovering hops, tail-feathers wagging, orange legs dangling, plop down again, and create circular rings of small waves, ever expanding, which intersect each other on the surface of the water. Refreshed, the gulls fly off as one, calling into a new day.

II. Calvin

calvin startling waking barking / rabbits gone&gone
dekker surprising dekker here
dekker smelling sweet not dekker / smelling bath&soap
- Hey there, Calvin. Glad to see me?
dekker hugging calvin close / calvin growling bighugs happy
outside jumping shaking wagging
dekker smiling more&more
- Gotta surprise for Mister Calvin.
gooddog calvin begging presents / tearing paper ripping sniffing
wagging happy body wagging / jumping dekker laughing more
happy calvin / evermore&evermore
- Take it easy, Cookie Monster.
stopping jumping shaking sitting / waiting cookie waiting more
dekker cookie finding holding / calvin pawing waiting

dekker throwing calvin catching / chomping chewing
happy calvin
wagging happy evermore&evermore

III. Dekker

Calvin and Bastard stand motionless, engaging in a stare-down, daring each other to be the first to avert their gaze, flinch, or even blink, in so doing admit defeat, submission. Clearly it is a test of two strong-willed creatures, both with dominant personalities. Bastard has the knowledge that comes with age, unyielding patience of a life lived in the solitary confinement of limited space. I wonder if his wings are clipped. Calvin has the advantage of youth, endless endurance, his life lived as top dog, only dog, a position he is unwilling to relinquish.

However, Calvin will by no means underestimate his avian adversary. He is familiar with the cleverness of birds. He once attempted to chase a crow off his self-proclaimed turf, in the same way he barks away herons standing serenely along the edge of canals. The crow was not so easily intimidated. It flew to a low branch, just out of Calvin's jumping range, taunting him with raucous caws and dramatic wing flapping. When Calvin turned his back on the bird, it swooped toward him, past him, and settled on the grass, waiting for Calvin's next barking charge, before lifting quickly into the air and alighting on another branch. Calvin jumped and barked, the crow cawed and flapped. They quarreled and chased each other like hyperactive children in a playground. The fiercely fought skirmish lasted nearly an hour before the crow tired of the game and flew off, leaving Calvin to bark with relish at his hard-won victory.

Calvin's first reaction upon discovering a parrot in the room was as I expected, a frantic fit of barking.

Birds don't belong inside. Birds belong outside.

Not surprisingly, Bastard responded with ruffled feathers and high-pitched squawking, interspersed with the occasional obscenity. It took some stern words and calming hands to settle Calvin and make him shut his noisy trap. I laid it all out for him in simple terms and gestures, nose to nose, repeating key words so he would understand.

- This is Bastard. Bastard's our new Friend. Calvin's new House is Bastard's House. Bastard lives Here. We live Here, with new Friend Bastard. In Bastard's House. Calvin's new House is Bastard's House. Bastard and Calvin. Friends.

He may not have been totally convinced, but I knew he'd got the idea when he mumbled a disgruntled growl and licked my face, directly on the lips.

Shut up already.

I gave the thick fur under his neck a vigorous scratching with both hands.

- Good boy. Now, take a rest.

He ignored this advice, walked back to the cage, sat in front of it, and commenced the staring match.

Much to my surprise Calvin backs down. He barks one last warning at the stoic Bastard, walks away with practiced disinterest, and curls up on the sheepskin rug in front of the decorative fireplace. A tentative truce has been reached, and I trust them to keep it that way while I rustle up something for breakfast.

IV. Calvin

calvin gooddog newfriend bastard / sniffing
cooking dekker making
calvin gooddog newfriend bastard / waiting watching trusting no
sniffing something smelling bad / calvin looking seeking hunting
upstairs going stopping sniffing / sniffing more&more
dekker danger warning dekker / going down&down
finding dekker danger barking / dekker angry
- Lay down, Calvin. Lay down now.
calvin quiet watching guarding / waiting something bad

V. Dekker

The place looks completely different flooded with sunlight after I open the heavy black-and-gray damask drapes that hang over the large picture window facing the street. The furnishings are an eclectic mix of antique and modern pieces. An Art Deco carved oak sideboard with a marble top contrasts sharply with the contemporary chrome and smoked glass dining table. The dated but functional white kitchen appliances versus brushed aluminum accessories from IKEA. A chic black leather sofa is paired with a vintage brown leather club chair. A 1970s veneer coffee table, old wooden bookcases, and a modern entertainment console. What the décor might lack in any unified style is made up for in its comfortable, inviting ambience, although anywhere would be comfortable and inviting after weeks of living in the jeep.

Calvin easily adjusts from outdoor to indoor living again. He snores lightly, asleep on the throw rug he has claimed as his own. Bastard still eyes him suspiciously, but silently, from within his cage. I've decided to allow him time to get used to our being here before making any further friendly overtures.

Meanwhile, I need to do some more investigating. There is no sign of any personal papers or correspondence in the lounge, the kitchen, or the bedroom. No bills to be paid, no bank statements, no information of any kind that might be helpful in avoiding curiosity or concern about Mac or his home.

I head upstairs, the only part of the house I've yet to explore. I was correct about the turret, which provides just enough space for a small office. The desk faces a window, covered with closed blinds. I open them, revealing a wonderful view of the canal and the children's farm across the water. On the desk sits a computer and a stack of trays, full of paperwork and mail, much of which look like bills and printed material from the bank, as well as the conspicuous blue envelopes indicating correspondence from the tax office. File box organizers, the contents of each neatly labeled, line a couple of wall shelves.

A cursory look through the most recent papers reveals Valentine Mackenzie up to date regarding his bills. He has a sizable bank balance, and no apparent matters pending with the tax authorities. I breathe an initial sigh of relief and sit at the computer, pressing the start button to see if I will need to locate a password. That would be a no, I discover, as icons begin to fill the screen. With the latest Windows 95 operating system installed, Mac is also technologically up to date. This is all I want to know for the time being, so I switch the power off. A drawer at the side of the desk contains his passport, identity card, and the document I most hoped to find, a copy of his car registration. I tuck that into my shirt pocket and leave everything else in the office as I found it.

On the opposite side of the upstairs hallway is another door, which turns out to be locked. Probably a storage attic under the roof, I remind myself. The keyhole looks as if it will be a fit for the old skeleton key on the ring that I left downstairs. Plenty of time to see what's inside later. I'm more interested in the other key, the one with the VW logo.

During the week I cased the area, I saw several Volkswagens parked on nearby streets. I'm hoping one of them belonged to Mac, one with a parking permit since this neighborhood is no longer a free-parking zone. I didn't want to risk setting off a car alarm by randomly trying the key in each door, which could have been dangerous, even at night. His car registration will solve that problem, with its license plate number clearly printed on it. I'll know exactly which car he owned. I'm not sure what I'll do with this information, but the more I know, the easier it will be to figure out the next step.

I start down the stairs and see Calvin sitting at the bottom, waiting for me. It's odd he didn't come up and find me. Maybe the strangeness of new surroundings has him a little unsettled after all.

CHAPTER EIGHT

I. GADGET

Oldenzaal, Hengelo, Goor, Lochem, Zutphen.

He clocked the towns and villages at each station, checking his watch, noting the hour and minute of arrival and departure. He didn't need to look at a schedule. The stops and times were locked in his memory from years of making this journey, there and back, over and over again. Just as his anxiety grew as the train traveled farther and farther away from Amsterdam, the angst diminished on the return trip, as the countryside rushed past the window in a blur of rural woodlands and fields crisscrossed with irrigation ditches, solitary farms, and hamlets of houses, too insignificant to deem worth a train stop.

It was always the same for Gadget. The malevolent thoughts and sadistic intentions that built up in anticipation of his home visits had been crushed, beaten out of him by a power more potent, a force more dominant than his own. He was left feeling drained, exhausted, a pathetic whisper of himself. There was barely enough energy to think of retribution or revenge, much less the ability to carry out such an undertaking. He needed to retreat to his bed, pull the worn duvet tightly around him, and hibernate, like a bear crawls into its cave for winter, until his strength was fully restored.

Brummen, Dieren, Rheden, Velp, Arnhem.

He has never been able to sleep on the train, but staring out the window put Gadget into a kind of hypnotic trance, allowed his thoughts to drift into a recurring daydream. He no longer remembered the first time it surfaced, but it never failed to calm his habitual episodes of restiveness.

❖

It always begins the same. Gadget carefully arranges the body of a small child, a little girl who appears to be about six years old, dressed in a frilly white pinafore. He never sees the act of killing her, but knows he is responsible for the murder. At the top of a hill, he props her upright against a lone tree. It is difficult to get her head in the correct position because her neck is broken. It is extremely important that she face west, staring toward the horizon, although he has already removed the eyes from their sockets and put them in an olive jar for safekeeping. In the background music plays, some old pop hit about seeing clearly now. It is the beginning of his finest creation.

The second killings involve two children, this time a little boy and a little girl. Again, Gadget does not remember the murders, only the arrangement of the bodies. At the edge of an orchard on a misty summer night, he hooks their arms over the top of a white fence so that they appear to be leaning against it. Their heads are bent toward each other, the little boy's lips touching the little girl's forehead in a chaste kiss. The hands of each child are Krazy-Glued over the ears of the other, lending the tableau an innocent sweetness. But the music this time adds a disturbing element with a discordant version of something Cher sang in a movie, something about his kiss.

The last victim is a little boy, who lies on his back in the middle of a field, arms outstretched, palms of his hands facing upward, knees slightly bent, feet together, head angled slightly toward his shoulder. Naked but for a pair of perfectly white underpants, he is a childlike parody of the crucified Christ, albeit horizontal instead of vertical. Black tape covers his mouth. The music is a choral lullaby Gadget remembers from his childhood.

When at night I go to sleep, fourteen angels watch do keep.

His completed masterpiece is a triptych, a macabre variation on the old Japanese proverb depicted by the Three Wise Monkeys. *See no evil. Hear no evil. Speak no evil.* He surveys his handiwork, arms crossed in paradoxical imitation of the little-known Fourth Monkey. *Do no evil.*

The vision does not end here. The entire sequence begins again, only this time the victims are all adolescents. Everything else remains the same, the tableaus, the music, even the pace of the reverie leading to its gruesome conclusion. Then it starts all over yet again with young men and women as the murdered subjects. For some reason that he cannot fathom, the figures never age further, never become older than he is now.

He has no idea what the fantasy means, or why it soothes him.

❖

Wolfheze, Ede, Maarn, Bunnik, Utrecht.

Not long now. Almost home.

Gadget read somewhere that a famous headshrinker said you were all the characters in your dreams. That was bullshit. He was no victim, and he was no little girl. He was the murder artist, nothing less and nothing more. And when he got his strength back, nothing was going to keep him from his next creation.

II. DEKKER

Of many odd idiomatic expressions in the Dutch language, one of the strangest must be *ijsberen*, turning the noun *polar bear* into a verb. The idea of an animal being an action isn't entirely uncommon. In English you might cow someone into submission or hound someone mercilessly. The Dutch term refers particularly to the bear's behavior in captivity, when it paces back and forth or in circles, in the confined space of a cage. For some reason I can't quite grasp, that always bugged me. There it is again, *bug* me. But now the Dutch expression makes perfect sense because I'm polar bearing all over the place, cannot sit still, cannot concentrate on any one thing for more than a few minutes at a time. It's like I'm stricken with a severe case of attention deficit disorder. I wouldn't have been surprised to see Calvin acting agitated on this first evening in unfamiliar surroundings, but he's calm and relaxed while keeping a watchful eye on Bastard, who hangs upside down from his highest perch, watching Calvin. I'm the one who's a bundle of nervous energy, unable to contain my bewildered, conflicted emotions. What's wrong with me?

I light a cigarette and sink into the leather club chair, throwing my legs over one arm, resting my neck on the other. This feels comfortable, familiar. I could get used to this. So far, everything has gone without a hitch.

It didn't take long to locate the black Volkswagen Golf, parked just a couple of blocks away. I unlocked the front door, told Calvin to jump inside, and after only a moment's hesitation he did, settling automatically into the passenger seat. I sat behind the wheel, closed the door, and looked around, half expecting someone on the street to start yelling for the police. There was no one in sight except a bicyclist who passed by without a second glance. The clean interior had a new-car smell, and I opened the glove compartment to find the original registration and insurance papers, all up to date, in a leather organizer. There are also a couple of maps and manuals, a flashlight, and an expensive pair of Ray-Ban aviator shades in a black leather case. Mac clearly had a thing for leather.

I tried on the sunglasses, checking them out in the rearview mirror. Very cool.

I closed the glove compartment, put the key in the ignition, and started the car. The engine came to life easily and sounded in great condition, a helluva lot better than Jax. The gas tank was almost full but I decided not to take it for a spin. Better to leave it here in this convenient spot, safe and sound, with its neighborhood parking permit, just in case a fast getaway was in the cards. Not only was I acting like a criminal, I was thinking like one.

The rest of the day was uneventful. Walk Calvin. Stop at the market for some basics. Stop at the pet store for some Calvin stuff. I perused a book about parrots, read they like to eat fresh fruit and raw vegetables, in addition to their staple diet of seeds and nuts. I considered buying the book but it cost more than I wanted to spend. Cash is still tight. Maybe another time. Stop at a fruit and vegetable stand for some Bastard stuff. Loaded up with all this foodstuff for me and Calvin and Bastard, we headed back to the house. A little less paranoid as we approached the door, I still breathed a deep sigh of relief once inside.

After peanut butter and jelly sandwiches for lunch, polar bearing. Maybe it's some kind of sugar rush.

I pull myself out of the comfortable club chair, crush my cigarette out in the glass Art Deco ashtray, and check the street through the picture window. Nothing. I cross the room and peer into the back garden. Nothing. I don't even know what I'm looking for.

A wave of exhaustion overtakes me, and I collapse on the sofa, the inevitable crash. Calvin gets up from his rug and joins me, stretching out to his full length, cuddling alongside my body, the way we used to take naps in our own home, before everything went so drastically haywire.

❖

- You might want to meet Willy Hart.

The museum curator told me the artist specialized in self-portraits, had an interesting take on the connection between art and literature, a psychological approach. He might give me a different perspective, add some needed depth to my thesis, which had begun to stall in the doldrums of banal art history research. How the relationship between artist and subject…blah, blah, blah. Why the depiction of specific books in paintings…blah, blah, blah.

Hart was preparing for a major exhibition at an important gallery. He didn't seem overly enthusiastic about talking to me, didn't know what I hoped to glean from his work, but he agreed to let me come to his studio for coffee and a short chat. He didn't have a lot of time to waste right now, especially for some foreign student's art project.

I was already intimidated by our brief telephone conversation, but the feeling intensified when I read an article that mentioned him in the catalogue of a recent Van Gogh Museum exhibit. It focused on the tortured artist's work in relation to his precarious mental states.

The colors of van Gogh's paintings reflected his changing moods began the piece. Pretty basic, I thought. Then it started discussing this guy Hart's work and how his paintings were informed by a psychological condition called synaesthesia. He perceived the sound of words, and even individual letters, as specific colors. He heard something and, in the same instant, saw its color, the color of its sound. I couldn't quite wrap my brain around the concept. Did he see colors all the time, like on some permanent hallucinogenic trip? Did it only happen when he heard words out loud, or was thinking them enough to trigger the phenomenon? Was it something he could turn on and off at will?

On the next page, four of his works were displayed and the effect was striking, bizarre. Together they looked like one of Warhol's lithograph portrait series, as if painted by Picasso or Miró. The central figure was always Hart himself, each done with pretty much the same color palette. In all of them he held a book, the title of which was the title of the painting. That was what made each one unique. There was no literal figuration of the book's story or theme, just an amazing background of colors, vibrant and explosive, or muted and serene. They were fantastic, mesmerizing, and although I had no idea how his work might fit into my thesis, I didn't care. I wanted to meet Willy Hart, talk with him, find out all I could about his creative process. The artist scared me but I was in love with his art.

What I didn't know was the reason he agreed to meet with me. Over the telephone, Willy Hart had fallen in love as well, fallen in love with the colors of my name.

❖

I leap off the sofa, setting off a noisy chain reaction. Calvin barks excitedly at the sudden movement, which sets off Bastard, feathers flying, letting rip with a series of perfectly mimicked toilet flushes, telephone rings, doorbell buzzes. The last sound causes Calvin to start another round of loud barking. It takes a few minutes to calm them down, bribing both with dog biscuits, apparently also a tasty treat for parrots, much to Calvin's dismay.

The momentary panic at least achieved the goal of getting my mind off the past and back into the present. It's time to do a more thorough search of the paperwork and files in the office upstairs. While I'm up there, I might as well check out the attic.

I grab the key ring from the ceramic bowl on the dining table and dash up the steps, Calvin following close on my heels this time. It's always been his routine to tag along wherever I go in the house. He'd follow me into the bathroom if I let him. He's still hyper after the latest excitement, me jumping off the couch and Bastard going mental.

Big whoop!

As I guessed, the skeleton key is a match for the lock. The wooden door sticks a bit as I try to pull it open, probably due to the summer heat. A good jerk and it comes free, the hinges creaking. Maybe it's not been opened for a while. I detect the scent of candle wax, leather, and something I cannot identify, a coppery metallic odor. Calvin stands beside me, growling softly.

- What's up, Cal?

He goes quiet and sits, but his body remains tense, his eyes and ears alert. The room is pitch black. Either there are no windows here or they've been covered. I try to think what it looked like from outside. No, I don't remember windows, not along the street side of the roof.

I feel along the wall near the door for a light source and find a round dimmer switch. I rotate it and the room is dimly illuminated from track lights at the top of the A-frame ceiling.

At first I'm not entirely sure what I'm looking at, as I take a couple of hesitant steps through the doorway. It's a room, yes. But not for storage.

The walls and peaked ceiling are covered in what appears to be black leather. The floor covering is black as well, a thin black rubber matting. An odd cross-shaped bench stands in the center of the room. Custom-made racks hold an array of whips, chains, walking sticks, riding crops, and other less identifiable instruments. At the far end of the room there appears to be some kind of leather chair or swing hanging from chains attached to the ceiling. Wall sconces with candles line both side walls. Everything looks new or in near-perfect condition. Leather smooth and shining, metal sparkling, floor spotlessly clean. Mac had raised his fetishism to the highest level. He had designed, built, and furnished an obviously expensive attic dungeon for his extreme sadomasochistic fun and games. And sex. Goes without saying.

The more I look around, the more details I notice. Small speakers are fixed high on the wall at either side of the door, perhaps connected to the sound system downstairs. There is a small cabinet in one corner with an assortment of dildos, cock rings, lubricants, rubber gloves, condoms, and other paraphernalia. In another corner a compact, well-stocked fridge serves as mini-bar, as well as storage for several varieties of poppers and an unhealthy selection of pills. On one side of the room, a narrow mattress lies on the floor. On the other side handcuffs are attached to the wall. Some sort of shackles attached to the bench, as well.

On the far wall hang a couple of framed prints of what look like medieval scenes. Monks, soldiers, and spectators bear witness to grotesque acts of violence. An arctic shiver runs down my spine. One of the prints depicts a beheading.

What the hell had you gotten yourself into, Mac?

I nearly jump out of my skin when Calvin barks from the open doorway.

- You're right, boy. This is fucking creepy.

I cross back to Calvin, take a last glance around, turn off the lights, and close the door. Some secrets are best kept locked away. Mac's secret is safe with me. Whatever wild scene he was into ended very badly. This was one aspect of his life I have no intention of investigating further.

CHAPTER NINE

I. CALVIN

calvin stopping seeing finding
lookit dekker lookit humpbuddy / lookit dekker calvin wanting
tail wagging happy finding humpbuddy waiting streetoutside
big&soft big&ready big&furry big&mine
    - Calvin, no. Garbage, Calvin. No No No.
calvin sniffing licking tasting / humpbuddy biting mine&mine
helpit dekker helpit home / dekker looking smiling laughing
    - Really, Calvin? Really? No.

calvin wagging yes&yes / calvin happy more&more
lookit dekker humpbuddy perfect big&big
dekker touching grabbing lifting
    - Maybe. Maybe now.
calvin&dekker helpit home / lifting pulling pushing dragging
calvin stopping pissing happy / mine&mine / home&home
dekker laughing calvin barking / happy&happy /
    more&more&evermore

II. VALENTINE

The young monk knew he must be punished, even before he committed the sin. Mere thoughts alone were enough to cast his immortal soul into eternal damnation. His customary rite of nightly self-flagellation would not be enough. His lithe body must be bent, broken, forced to submit to the expert crack and slash from the whip of the Holy Castigator. The novice knelt on the cold stone floor of the chapel, performing a pretense of prayer for guidance, for he knew where he was about to go, what he was about to do. Valentin had known since Gelasius whispered into his ear during Vespers as they passed in the candlelit cloister.

- Meet me in the loft after Compline.

He waited nervously in his cold, unadorned cell until a deeply profound silence descended within the monastery walls. He hurried his bare feet soundlessly down the stairs, along the open arcade, and past the enclosed garden. He slipped through the gate and across the grass to the barn housing the livestock. He paused to rest, breathing in the sweet musky scent of cattle and freshly harvested hay. But he did not tarry long, for their assignation must be completed before the strike of the arcane Midnight Office bell roused the excessively devout older priests.

Valentin climbed the ladder to the dark loft. As he reached the top, strong hands reached under his arms and pulled him through the open trap door. Gelasius always arrived first, more reckless and eager, unafraid of the dire consequences should they be caught. He swung Valentin onto a soft bed of fragrant dry fodder and stood above him, pulling his sackcloth robe over his head, revealing himself in all his magnificent nakedness. He knelt over Valentin's chest and thumbed the sign of the cross over his mouth, whispering.

- Lord, open my lips.

- And my mouth will proclaim your praise.

Valentin opened his mouth and received the bulbous throbbing head of Gelasius's swollen cock on his tongue, gently as the Holy Host, body of Christ. He felt the shaft grow harder, lengthening into his throat, forcing him to breathe through his nose. The intoxicating stench of cock and balls filled his senses as Gelasius thrust as deeply as Valentin could bear without gagging, slowly withdrew, and thrust again, gradually increasing his to-and-fro rhythm. Valentin could not see his rugged face, but imagined Gelasius gazed toward Heaven, eyes burning bright with ecstatic fervor. He had seen the expression before. Gelasius pulled his gleaming wet member from Valentin's hungry mouth and whispered again, his voice harsher, raw.

- God, come to my assistance.
- Lord, make haste to help me.

Gelasius arched his sweat-covered body as his Rod of Aaron spurted a hot stream of baptismal blessing across Valentin's angelic countenance.

III. DEKKER

It wasn't exactly Tolstoy, I giggle to myself, but it does shine a whole new light on the term Christian anarchy. I wonder if he meant it to be amusing. The short story is one of many I find in numerous files on the office computer, all homoerotic, all featuring a character called Valentine, or some variation thereof. This particular file, labeled *Val&Gel*, appears to be a series of episodes detailing the unabashed sexual adventures of the two young monks. What I have yet to figure out is whether Mac wrote for his own pleasure or if he submitted the stories somewhere for publication. Was it possible he made his living writing porn?

If true, it's oddly serendipitous that I should discover this today, which began with Calvin spotting the gigantic cuddly toy, a red squirrel someone had left out on the street for the trash. He decided adamantly to adopt it, bring it home for a new hump buddy. I was reluctant to give in to his demand, but ugly as the monstrosity was, it didn't appear to be in bad condition. Probably a prize from a street carnival that looked more appealing hanging in the booth than it did when Papa got it home. So we carried it back together, although Calvin's contribution was more hindrance than help. Immediately upon arrival he broke it in, leaving me free to come upstairs and start searching through the material stored on Mac's computer without distraction.

Aside from the numerous files of porn stories, I find computer games, mostly combat or sports, but also some kind of graphic adventure game called Myst, where the player takes on the role of The Stranger and explores different fictional worlds called Ages. I've never been a fan of gaming, and at the moment real life is strange enough. But I can see how it might have fueled Mac's inclination for role-play, and even how it could contribute to his, dare I say, creative writing.

I'm hit by another synchronistic resonance. I've not been through all of Mac's files, but have skimmed enough to recognize him as the main character in all his stories, if sometimes in name only. It's a pornographic version of literary self-portraiture. When I met Willy, he only did self-portraits, as well. Strange. I'm not sure what to make of it. Probably means nothing.

Willy pretty much stopped doing self-portraits after we met, after Jason Dekker became the muse that inspired him.

Not me.

My name.

At least, that's how it started.

❖

- Have you ever modeled before?

I shook my head no, slipped out of the robe, and tossed it over the back of the chair. I had taken a few figure-drawing classes at Camden, dropping the course when I realized I had no artistic talent whatsoever. So I thought I knew what to expect. I hadn't counted on feeling so nervous, so embarrassed. Not with the nudity. I had no problem showing off my body to another man, especially one as attractive as Willy Hart. It was the idea of posing that made me uncomfortable.

- I'm not sure what I should do.

- Just relax. Take a seat, sideways with your arm over the back of the chair. Don't look at me. Look toward the wall. Let your mind wander free, like meditation. And relax.

Some canvases leaned haphazardly in the corner of the studio, whether unfinished or deemed unworthy of exhibition, I couldn't tell. Most of them faced the wall but I could see tantalizing edges of color here and there.

At the end of our first all-too-short meeting, Hart had handed me an invitation to the opening of his exhibition, with a nonchalance that almost seemed an afterthought. Of course I attended. We exchanged a few words, me trying not to gush about his work, he vaguely distracted by the swarm of friends, potential buyers, art critics, and other guests vying for his attention. I didn't stay long, feeling well out of my league with this upmarket crowd. Before leaving, I looked around the gallery and saw him deep in conversation with a distinguished white-haired gentleman wearing an expensive suit and silk cravat. I decided to leave without saying good-bye, certain he wouldn't even notice. We barely knew each other, after all.

Two days later, I was surprised when he called. He apologized for not spending more time with me at the opening and invited me back to his studio for lunch the following day, if that was convenient. He said he had some further insights that might be relevant to my thesis, as well as thoughts about another project he wanted to discuss with me. I had nothing important planned for the next day, I told him. I was intrigued. To be honest, I was flattered by this unexpected attention.

Lunch was a simple meal of vegetable soup, fresh baguettes with cheese, and a bottle of excellent white wine. He charmed me into doing most of the talking, asking questions about where I grew up, how I had gotten interested in art history, what drew me to Impressionism. I was more interested in hearing what this new project was he had mentioned, but didn't want to appear too eager by asking him outright. Maybe he'd had second thoughts about discussing it with me.

I couldn't have been more wrong.

- How is your thesis going?

His question caught me off guard. In the three days since we'd spoken, I did have a major breakthrough, a direct result of being introduced to his work and talking with him about it. But I didn't want to come across too sycophantic. Nobody likes a gusher. So I tried to play it casual.

- Better, I guess. Too early to say for sure, but I got this new idea. I read a poem. It's hard to explain. Something about the connection between what van Gogh read and his life.

- Not his work?

- Oh, that'll be in there, too, but this personal thing. I never thought of it before. After speaking to you, then finding a reference to this poem in a couple of his letters, it just hit me. It's probably stupid.

- Perhaps not. Tell me more.

- Okay. Vincent is twenty-two, living in Paris. He writes to his brother Theo, mentioning a poem by Alfred de Musset. French Romantic? It's about this guy who goes through his life shadowed by a mysterious figure dressed in black, who looks enough like him to be his brother. He never really knows who the man in black is, or why he always shows up at times of great sadness. Until, that is, the last line of the poem, when the stranger says: *My friend, my name is Solitude.* Right? Fast-forward thirteen years. Vincent is going crazy in the Yellow House at Arles, with Gauguin, when he mentions the poem again, in another letter to Theo. A week later he chops his ear off, and eighteen months after that he shoots himself in a field. I don't know. He's thinking about the same poem when's he's just getting started, and when it's almost all over. It's like he felt alone his whole life. If I could connect those particular dots, maybe in some kind of framing story. I don't know. Sorry. I'm rambling.

- No. It's interesting. Give the idea some time to grow. It's the right season, yes? In fact, perhaps we should indulge in the good weather. Let's take a walk.

I was feeling light-headed, not used to drinking wine so early in the day. More likely, not used to spilling my guts to someone I hardly know. Some fresh air would be good, I told him. I still hoped he'd tell me about his own new project. Sun sparkled on the water of the grubby canal outside his studio. Trees were beginning to turn green. The city had changed almost overnight, emerging from the dark shadows of chilly winter into the gentler, brighter light of spring.

- I have a better idea. You came by bike, yes? We'll take a ride instead. I'll show you one of my favorite places in Amsterdam.

I wasn't sure what to expect. We cycled together on the narrow city streets, over picturesque canal bridges, through the charming antique quarter, and into the park. Stopping for a moment, Hart pointed out a statue of the great seventeenth-century Dutch poet Joost van den Vondel, whose great masterpiece, he told me, was his play *Lucifer*, which inspired Milton's *Paradise Lost.* I thought this might be what he wanted to show me, but he jumped back on his bike and continued through the park. I followed, pedaling like crazy to catch up.

He seemed a different person while cycling, stronger, more animated. He pointed and yelled as we passed the Picasso fish sculpture, when he spotted an old lady hanging bird feeders for the parrots, and when he saw a pair of white swans floating on a pond, necks entwined in a heart shape.

I had never seen Amsterdam in quite the same way before. I saw the city through the eyes of an artist. It was as if I were watching a film, a film in my head directed by Willy Hart.

We reached the end of the park, crossed the tramlines, crossed yet another postcard-perfect bridge, and turned left to cycle along a wider canal than those in the city center. Hart pulled off at a bend in the road, stopped, jumped nimbly off his bike, and leaned it against a tree. I did the same, with considerably less grace. Apparently, we had arrived at our destination.

- It's an old graveyard called *Te Vraag*, which means *to question.* In the late fifteenth century, Emperor Maximilian the First stopped here to ask directions to Amsterdam, or so the story goes.

Hart knew a lot about the place, since an artist/gardener friend had been appointed caretaker and was restoring the cemetery, which had fallen into disrepair after many years of neglect. A wooden footbridge led to the tall wrought-iron entrance gate across a small canal. Just past the gate stood a pretty white gazebo, formerly a mortuary. Now it displayed a vase of fresh flowers from the garden and, Hart pointed out, a new commemorative poem every week.

A short way down a tree-lined lane, another gate had been erected with pillars salvaged from an old theater that was destroyed by fire in the 1700s. An inscription on a plaque that hung overhead read *Memento Mori*, Latin for *Remember you must die.* I always thought it was an interesting turn of phrase for the genre of Dutch still-life painting that portrayed symbolic objects representing the theme of mortality. Its use here seemed downright sinister.

I thought it no less strange this was the favorite place Hart wanted to show me. As we walked around, the beauty of the spot was undeniable. Narrow dirt paths cut through the thick ground cover of ivy, dotted by hundreds of newly blooming white narcissus. There were large drooping elms, slender weeping willows, and a rather majestic chestnut tree. Neatly trimmed rectangular hedges created a pattern of sarcophagus-like shapes among the gravestones. Hart called it a green necropolis, a verdant city of the dead, which looked more like an overgrown archaeological site than a final resting place. He gestured to a bench, and we sat together in silence, immersed in the tranquil atmosphere, accompanied only by birdsong.

I felt a vague pang of nostalgia as I realized how much the place reminded me of the old cemetery next to my grandparents' farm. Among my few fond childhood memories was playing hide-and-seek among the gravestones with my dog, Tracey, my best friend and only playmate. I had not mentioned any of this to Hart. There was no way he could have known. Why had he brought me here? Once he started to explain, his words tumbled out in a passionate monologue like a spring flood rages down a mountain, and there was nothing for me to do but listen.

- The first time we met you asked me why I only painted self-portraits. I wasn't completely honest with you. I told you that from an early age I felt my synaesthesia was a gift, something I was not meant to share, not willing to share. People often asked me to do their portraits but I was unwilling to apply my gift to others, to be exploited by their vicarious desire to peer inside my head or satisfy some curious whim. I was being selfish. It was all about me, me, me. I was painting me because it was my experience, mine alone, and in the beginning I did not even want to show my work to anyone else. Until I realized that if I did not show the paintings to anyone, wasn't my work just some sort of creative masturbation? What kind of art is that?

He paused for a moment. I sensed his question was rhetorical and remained silent.

- So I began to let people see what I was doing. By then it had become a habit, a habit I did not feel the urge to break or modify in any way. People began to become interested and paintings began to sell. Galleries wanted to exhibit me, museums started to ask about me. Someone coined the expression *A Hart by Hart*. I turned myself into a brand, not unlike what Rembrandt did three hundred years ago. At least that's what art critics began to write about me. I was the new Rembrandt. I was the new van Gogh. I didn't know what I was. I didn't care. I just painted. For the first time I could live off my work. I didn't want to think about it. Until you started asking your questions, questions I had not thought about for a very long time.

I almost began to apologize but he didn't give me a chance.

- Then I saw everything hanging in the gallery, I stood in the middle of a room filled with images of me, me, me. I became embarrassed, ashamed of myself, of my huge idiotic ego being fed by the system, the exhibitors, the buyers, the critics, the sycophants. A bookstore chain offered me a large amount of money to put my work on their shopping bags. Can you imagine? My face, my painting, my art, endless copies printed onto paper bags by a factory assembly line. It's crazy, no? Do you want to know what's even crazier? I was about to give in to this crass commercialization of what once meant something to me, meant more to me than life itself. I was talking to the company director when I looked across the gallery and saw you leaving. I got this idea in my head that it was you, Jason Dekker, it was you who could save me from myself. I said your name aloud, and your colors blazed as you walked out the door without looking back, leaving the colorless crowd behind you. I wanted to follow you, follow your light and shade, your thalo green and your burnt sienna, your pale cadmium yellow and your royal Tyrian purple, your fading trace of Venetian red dust. I want to paint these colors, your colors, but I am not sure how to do it. I've been using the same colors for so long, painting the same pictures for so long, pictures of me, me, me, nothing but me, and I am not sure how to approach something new, something bright, original and fresh, something to be remembered, something. Someone like you. If you are willing to help me, sit for me, be patient with me, I want to try. What do you say? Yes. Say yes. Yes?

What else could I answer?

As we left the cemetery together, I saw that another Latin phrase was painted on the opposite side of the plaque hanging from the entrance gate, now the exit gate.

MEMENTO VIVERE. Remember to live.

❖

Willy never painted another self-portrait. Despite his exhibitor's fear this would extinguish all interest in his work, once the art world caught on, the value of those paintings skyrocketed, commanding prices rarely seen by a living artist.

Willy always insisted he didn't care one way or the other. It wasn't entirely true, but it made good press. Now he was painting me, always me, only me. This work would sell almost equally well. Especially when word got around that soon Willy Hart would not be painting anything at all.

IV. GADGET

Luck is what happens when preparation meets opportunity, that's what they say anyway. Gadget was making a pretty good case for being the luckiest guy on the planet. Unlike the man following him up the ladder of the construction site, although he probably thought he was lucky, too. They had met only a couple of hours before, and Gadget had fished enough information from the drunken Canadian from Vancouver to determine he was a good catch, once he got the talkative fuck to shut his trap and focus on the present. Not to mention the immediate future of undoubtedly hot sex with a very tasty trick. Gadget grinned at the irony. The immediate was the only future this dumbass lumberjack was gonna see.

He had planned well for this night. He scoped out the location by day when the unfinished building was crawling with activity, and by darkness when it was as still as a tomb. He had executed a dry run the night before, found the best route to the uppermost floors, stashed an inconspicuous bag of gear that might come in handy, and explored alternative ways down should unexpected trouble arise. Yes, Gadget had done all the necessary preparation so he would be ready when opportunity knocked.

Almost all, that is. He wished he had remembered to retrieve the excellent razor-sharp double-edged sabre he had taken from the canal-house and secreted away under thick shrubbery in a small sidewalk garden plot a few blocks away. He didn't really need it tonight, but maybe later. Maybe even later tonight.

Next time, Gadget. Next time.

The about-to-be-mounted Mountie stopped to catch his breath after Gadget helped him up the last rungs of the ladder. There was one more floor under construction above them, but the outer walls weren't in place, leaving it too exposed. Someone might look up and see shadowy figures moving about. That would not do. Besides, this floor was high enough for an exhilarating view through the window openings and a less-than-exhilarating fall. Gadget had chosen it well.

His bag of tricks was right where he left it. He hung the coil of rope around his neck, turned the roll of silver duct tape into a bracelet, and tucked the fully loaded pneumatic nail gun under his belt.

Enough to get us started. He stood, turned to the winded whinging wimp, and pulled a bottle of poppers from his chest pocket. Their eager eyes met. Gadget knew his eyes were his best feature, piercing and charismatic. Tonight they glistened in the moonlight.

- Ready for some fun?

Chapter Ten

I. Dekker

Calvin stands stock still in the middle of the room as Bastard watches him from the top of his cage. Contrary to his name and vocabulary, the bird turns out to be remarkably tame, even affectionate.

When offered slices of apple or banana, he delicately took them from my fingers through the bars of his cage. I began to leave the cage door open so he could venture out, allowing him to reach his parrot playground of perches, climbing ropes, and swinging rings. His unbridled excitement and antic acrobatics revealed a playful personality. So I braved an invitation for him to climb onto my shoulder. I leaned toward him slowly, eyes averted, and waited until he was ready to trust me. It didn't take long, and we happily walked around the house like Long John Silver and Captain Flint. Before returning to the cage, he leaned into my neck and gently nibbled my ear, surprisingly not an unpleasant sensation.

However, Calvin is not delighted by these developments, particularly the growing friendship between me and Bastard. Accustomed to being the center of my attention, especially in the last few months, he is unwilling to share the spotlight. Certainly not with a bird.

What are you thinking, Dekker?

It may also be that Bastard has learned he can always get a barking rise out of Calvin by imitating the doorbell, a trick Calvin is uncharacteristically slow to catch on to, increasing his animosity.

Bastard is perfectly aware of the toll his actions are taking, literally strutting back and forth on his perch when Calvin returns from the hall, his brow furled in frustration. I think they would make a very funny pair of animated adversaries, not unlike Road Runner and Coyote.

I sense something unusual going on today, though, some silent communication impossible for me to fully understand. Sure enough, Bastard starts to climb down the side of his cage, using both talons and beak. By way of a knotted rope hanging from the bottom, he continues his descent all the way to the floor. I'm ready to intervene if necessary, less afraid Calvin might mount an aggressive attack than hoping to avoid feathers and fur flying should the two actually get into a physical squabble. Bastard eases himself to the floor, ruffles his feathers, and looks at Calvin. Calvin barks once, but neither gives up ground.

Bastard takes a couple of steps in Calvin's direction. Calvin cocks his head suspiciously and takes a step backward. This appears to be the signal Bastard was waiting for. He walks confidently toward Calvin, stops, looks up at him, and cocks his own head in curiosity. Calvin must seem much bigger this close, but it doesn't discourage Bastard in any way. He walks past him and, to my amazement, begins to climb up Calvin's rear leg, grabbing fur firmly in his beak until he can stand comfortably balanced on the dog's back.

I expect fireworks to explode any minute, but Calvin stands like a statue, transfixed. Bastard carefully sidesteps along his back until he reaches the collar, and then begins to gently preen Calvin's coat. I hoped the two would eventually tolerate each other so I could leave them alone without concern. But this was more than anything I could have imagined. It was something you might see on *Funniest Home Videos.*

Calvin heaves a deep sigh and sits, unsettling Bastard enough that he must grab the collar for balance. Calvin eases himself down onto the floor, in total submission to his African housemate. After a few minutes, the parrot slides down the side of the dog and trots back to the rope as Calvin places his head between his paws.

Perhaps my ears are playing tricks on me, I'm not sure, but before Bastard starts his climb back up to the cage, I could swear I hear him speak.

- Good dog.

II. Calvin

calvin upstairs bastard downstairs / calvin up not down
sulking lying scenting badroom / guarding badroom / now&now
calvin letting bastard winning / gooddog calvin letting winning
calvin gooddog / all&all
dekker sitting clicking fingers / tapping clicking more&more
waiting dinner waiting watching / guarding badroom now&now
calvin waiting watching guarding / badroom smelling
    fading slow
waiting dinner / evermore&evermore

III. Dekker

Calvin wants to go out.

I know this because earlier he asked for dinner, moving his empty dish around on the kitchen floor, pretending to eat the last invisible crumbs from yesterday. I fed him.

He already asked for help with his latest hump buddy, the huge squirrel with a tail as fluffy as his own. He uses the sleeve of my sweatshirt as a kind of foreplay, nuzzling it, biting it, until I get off the couch and hold the squirrel upright against my leg so he can start humping it. Once he gets going I leave him on his own, maneuvering the once cuddly, already cruddy animal beneath him, this way and that until he climaxes. It takes a while before his swollen dick returns to normal and he can move again.

He has asked for water, which he does by simply standing in front of me and staring me straight in the eye. It took me a long time to figure out this demand. The stare doesn't waver, there's no shake of the head or movement to the door. Finally I get it.

Empty water dish. How much clearer can I be?

I gave him water. So now I know he must want to go out because there's nothing else he might be asking for this late at night. I get off the couch again, and this time he heads for the umbrella stand where his leash is kept. By the time I get to the hall he's waiting, leash in mouth, tail wagging.

Outside a strong wind blows wispy clouds across a bright full moon. I realize this is why I have been anxious all evening, agitated, with an unreasonable desire to go to a bar and get shit-faced. The Cancer side of my cusp is powerfully affected by the pull of the moon. On those rare occasions when I actually know in advance the full moon is approaching, I lock myself inside as one would a nascent werewolf. Too many nights lost to too much alcohol have proved this necessary. It was Willy who first noticed how much hotter I was when a full moon shone through the skylight of our bedroom.

I don't want to think about that tonight, must not must not must not think about that tonight. I lock the door and automatically start walking left toward the little park. I stop when I realize Calvin is not ahead of me. Turning around, I see him standing poised to head off in the opposite direction.

I don't want little park, Dekker. We went to little park this morning. I want canal walk.

- Fine. We'll do the canal walk tonight.

Calvin leads the way, tail bouncing happily.

I won. I won. I won.

We have not walked the Admiralengracht in a few days. It's a little farther away than I prefer to go at this hour, but it's a mild night, apart from the wind, and I feel like being outside. Even though there's no street traffic, Calvin waits for me to catch up at each corner.

- Okay.

We cross together. People who see this are impressed by how well trained he is but it wasn't difficult to teach him not to cross the street alone. He doesn't even chase his ball into the street, always waits at the curb for me to retrieve it for him. He didn't bring a ball tonight.

No ball for canal walk.

In front of the snack bar at the corner, a pair of Moroccan youths pretend to fight, egged on by a couple of friends. Calvin stops and growls at them.

Bad boys. Bad boys fear Calvin. The leash he carries in his mouth muffles a bark.

The youths stop their horseplay, back off a bit. I don't know what it is about Arabic culture that makes them so fearful of dogs. Okay, Calvin is almost fifty kilos of growling menace right now, but I've seen similar reactions to puppies.

- Come on, Cal. Let's go.

He shoots them one last warning look before following me.

Arriving at the canal, Calvin drops the leash for me to carry and begins sniffing the grass that borders the water. It must be full of messages left by his canine neighbors but almost immediately he is distracted by a sound, a soft plaintive woman's voice.

- Aaaaaandy. Andy. Aaaaaaandy.

Cal looks around, ears alert, and spots an old woman across the street. I think she must be trying to find a lost cat because no one calls a dog so quietly. The anxiety in her voice upsets Calvin.

Where is Andy? Must find Andy. His head darts up and down the canal, searching. He sniffs under parked cars. I assume he's hunting for another dog since he has little interest in cats.

- Calvin, let's walk. The lady is looking for her cat. You'll just scare it away.

Calvin is still concerned as we head off along the canal, but within a few meters the old woman's voice is lost in the wind.

We reach the next bridge, cross over, and begin to walk back down the other side of the canal. Ducks line the edge between two docked boats until Calvin spooks them into the black water. Ripples reflect the moonlight.

Calvin stops, stands rigidly at attention for a moment, then takes off at a quick trot. Up ahead I see Sela, a gorgeous Siberian husky, almost as big as Calvin. We've encountered her a couple of times, and she's always friendly. But Calvin has little interest in her. He once snapped at her nose when she continued to ignore his threatening growls.

Tonight is different. Maybe it's the full moon. Or more likely, Sela is nearly in heat. I assume not fully or her handsome young owner would have her firmly in tow on a leash. That's another thing about the full moon. Almost every man suddenly looks more attractive.

Sela takes charge of this encounter and Calvin is reduced to a pathetic, lovesick puppy. All signs of his machismo norm vanish as he attempts to get a good sniff of her rear end. She teases him mercilessly, twisting her body away from his prying nose after a few seconds, and then hugging up against him seductively. She never allows him enough time to assume the position, running circles around his growing frustration. Calvin gives her a sharp bark, and for a moment she appears receptive, rolling onto the grass, belly up, smelly fanny fully exposed. As soon as Calvin is close enough to give her a good lick, she rolls away and jumps quickly to her feet.

Come and get me, big boy!

Calvin is left with his tongue hanging out, drooling like a sex-starved tourist in the red-light district. He looks at me with a forlorn expression.

Could you help me out here, Dekker? Please?

- Sorry, Cal, you're on your own.

By now Sela's dad has caught up with her. I always remember the names of the dogs but never their owners, especially when they're as obviously straight as this young hunk. With some difficulty, he manages to get the leash clipped to her collar.

Calvin uses this opportunity for a last futile attempt to get a good lick of Sela's ass. It's her turn to snarl him off, obviously annoyed with her boss's intervention. I grab Calvin's collar and begin to drag him away, tail between his legs in despair. He actually starts to whine like a child.

Please, Dekker, please, she smells so good, Dekker, please.

- How about a little dignity, Calvin, huh?

When Sela has been led far enough away, I release him. He takes one long look back at his nearly beloved, raises a leg to piss a love note, and we continue our walk along the canal.

- Aaaaaaandy. Andy. Aaaaaaandy.

The old woman is standing on the bridge we normally cross to get back home. Her long gray curls are windswept and she looks so frail I fear she might be blown into the canal. She grasps the railing tightly and continues to call out for her missing cat. Calvin has lost interest in her plight, avidly tracking a trail left behind by Sela.

- Aaaaaaandy. Andy. Aaaaaaandy.

It sounds like a mantra, more chanted than called, as if part of a nightly ritual. An unnerving thought insinuates itself into my psyche. Perhaps Andy has been lost for more than a few hours. Perhaps Andy has been missing for days or weeks, months or even years. Perhaps Andy was not her cat but her husband. Maybe she doesn't do this every night, only those lonely nights when she feels his absence like an amputated limb, when his voice is heard in the rattle of the wind on the window, when his heart beats in the ticking of the old clock on the wall, when she reaches for an empty space on the bed.

- Wiiiiiilly. Willy. Wiiiiiilly.

I pass the bridge quickly, trying to block out the old woman's voice. I must not must not must not think these thoughts tonight, tonight of all nights. Not while the moon is full and Calvin in love and Andy lost and Willy gone and Dekker on the verge of losing his mind. I stumble along the canal until I reach a bench, midway to the next bridge, collapse on it, my whole body shaking.

Minutes or hours later I open my eyes. Calvin sits in front of me, leveling his ever-inquisitive gaze into my face.

What's up? We don't sit on a bench in nighttime.

I look back toward the bridge. The old woman is gone. The streets are empty but the moon is still full. I decide to take a roundabout route back to the house. I don't want to hear her haunting cries again this night.

Two blocks from home, I see her crouch by a parked car. Her voice is barely a whisper as she coaxes a frightened white kitten into her arms. I'm convinced this is not Andy. This is some stray she found to replace the empty basket in her heart. If not Andy, any cat will do. She disappears around the corner, ghost cat in her arms, two lost spirits in the mist.

❖

I climb the stairs to the office. This afternoon I saw that Mac got an email from the editor of a website specializing in literary gay porn. I use the word *literary* in its loosest sense. Most of what I found there was crap, with no aspirations to the loftier term *erotica*. But now I realize he was actually getting paid for writing his Valentine material, which if I'm honest, is a cut above most of the stuff I skimmed through. Apparently, the turnover is pretty fast because the editor complained he'd not heard from Mac in a couple of weeks, expected a new story, *ASAP*.

I don't need any repercussions from some missed deadline, although I doubt the editor of a website based thousands of miles away would report the disappearance of one of his contributors. But you never know. Stranger things have happened. It wouldn't hurt to keep some money rolling into his account, in case I get up the nerve to use the bankcard and PIN code I found. My own resources are almost gone.

I'm still afraid I'll wake up one morning with the police breaking in, looking for a crime scene.

Maybe enough time has passed. Maybe I should commit myself to the whole crazy scheme that began when I lied to the police, broke into the house, looked in the bathroom mirror, and saw what I thought was a passing resemblance. If Mac is to continue to live, Valentine must continue to write. I've read his stories and I think I can imitate his voice. Maybe not as precisely as Bastard, but enough to satisfy an eager editor. I've read his notes about the next story, the story he would never write, a story set, ironically, among criminals and murderers.

I take a deep breath. I'm as ready as I'll ever be. I turn on the computer.

Calvin pokes his nose through the doorway, carrying his cherished playmate in his mouth. He curls up in the hallway holding Blue Bear between his paws, licking him tenderly.

As I wait for the computer to boot up, I look out the window through the open blinds. The moon has disappeared from the night sky. Across the water, through the thickening mist, under the soft warm glow of the streetlights, I can barely distinguish the outline of the little barn where the pony and goats sleep.

I will not sleep this night. I will lose Dekker and become Valentine. I will write his fantasies and forget the old woman's delusions. I will dance with Valentine's demons, and with any luck, exorcise Dekker's ghosts in the process.

I pull the blinds closed and turn my attention to the computer, bring up a new document, and begin to type.

IV. Gadget

This was fucking spooky and it had nothing whatsoever to do with the mist. Gadget stood on the street and stared up at the now darkened window. Impossible. He didn't believe in fucking ghosts. He wasn't even superstitious.

As he walked toward the canal-house, he was certain he saw a light shining from the upstairs window. He got closer and saw a shadowed figure behind the open blinds before they abruptly closed shut. It looked like the guy but with the light behind him, his face was totally obscured. It couldn't be the guy. It must be some figment of his drug-infused brain. It shouldn't be anyone, the house should be empty. It hadn't been that long, had it? He wasn't sure.

He was tempted to ring the bell, just to see what would happen, prove to himself that it was just his hopped-up wacko-jacko imagination, but he was well and truly freaked out. No way was he ringing any bell.

He remembered a garden in the back, with a fence along the street, too high to see over. Maybe he could catch a glimpse through the slats. If everything was completely dark from that side, case closed. He was a fucking lunatic.

He rounded the corner beyond the old deserted warehouse and walked casually up the sidewalk to the fence. Through a narrow crack he saw dim light coming from what he thought must be a kitchen window.

Goddamnmotherfuckshitpisscuntscrew.

He had not left any lights on, he was fucking sure of that. Somebody had been in the house since he left it. The police, maybe? Sure. That was possible. Now his brain was working better. They could have identified the guy somehow, could have found the keys he'd stuck in the bag with the motherfucker's head. They wouldn't find anything inside the house. He had made damn sure of that. He was no fucking amateur. But something didn't feel right about this, not right at all. He needed to come back, check things out in the light of day. He wasn't gonna hang around here anymore getting spooked in the dark.

As so often happened when Gadget was distracted, he completely forgot the main reason he'd come in the first place. The most excellent fine-looking razor-sharp sabre remained hidden a few blocks away, exactly where he'd left it.

Chapter Eleven

I. Valentine

Moonface couldn't believe Johnny got mowed down on Valentine's Day. Of all the dumb luck. He opened the Friday edition of the *Chicago Herald Examiner* to the photo page. There was Highball, cowering under a car, looking straight at the camera. That German shepherd loved Johnny May. He couldn't go nowhere without that dog.

Johnny was no gangster. This was a case of wrong place, wrong time. Sure, he did car jobs for the Bugs Moran gang, but just for the dough. He had a wife and seven babies to feed. He'd do about anything for hard cash.

That's how Moonface met him, just another ordinary Joe willing to service the slummers for a couple of bucks at the K-9 Club. But it wasn't like that between Johnny and Moonface. They weren't no pansies, dressing up in fancy gowns for the Fairy Ball at the Black and Tan Cabaret, or hanging around Bughouse Square looking for a pickup. What happened between them was different, real. Moonface smiled as he remembered how it used to be, back when he thought things might turn out some other way than they did.

He could tell right off the bat that Johnny was new to the game. The club was packed, filled with blue smoke, cheap alcohol, and raucous laughter. The musical acts were all pretty second-rate, but that didn't keep everyone from having a good time. Johnny was hanging around by the Gents', waiting to catch an interested eye before following them inside. He was never in there long and he always came out alone, so

Moonface had the idea he wasn't having much success. It was kind of strange because Johnny was a good-looking kid, tall and gangly, but high cheekbones and a pouty mouth, usually a good draw. Moonface snaked his way through the crowd and sidled up beside Johnny. He leaned against the wall and gave him a knowing wink.

- Not having a good night?

- Just a bunch of lowlife cheapskates here tonight.

- You got that right. I seen you around but we never actually met. I'm Valen Moon, but everybody calls me Moonface.

- Johnny May.

- Good to meet you, Johnny May. I suppose you could stand around here all night wasting your time, nickel-and-diming it. But if you happen to be interested in some serious cash, I know about a gig that pays real good.

- I'm all ears.

- So is this place. Meet me outside in five and I'll tell you all about it. Gotta cigarette?

Johnny shook a Lucky out of his pack. Moonface tucked it behind his ear and elbowed his way to the door. He was sitting on the curb down the block when Johnny joined him a few minutes later.

- So what's the story?

- It's a private lounge up near Crystal Lake. They call it the Officer's Club, but I don't think it's exactly military. There's this glass box set-up, with a bed inside. We just do what we been doing, but with each other. The men watch us through the glass.

- Fuckin' degenerates.

- Yeah, but the pay makes it worth it. A hundred bucks cash for the night.

- A hundred? What kinda chump you take me for?

- Not a dumb one. But hey, it's no skin off my nose if you're not interested. I know plenty who'd do it for less.

Johnny made a big show of thinking it over, but Moonface knew he had him at a hundred. They arranged to meet Friday afternoon to go over the details beforehand. Moonface was a little concerned Johnny might turn chicken but, sure enough, he showed up right on time. He did look a little nervous, though.

- You know, this gig is like a performance. I was thinking maybe we should do a dry run, just to make sure we're on the same page.

- You mean here? Now?

- You bet. And the shy virgin face you're pulling is good. Those horny homos will eat it up.

Moonface took Johnny's hand and pulled him to the bed, where they sat. Neither one of them was sure what to do first. For all his bravado, Moonface was a little nervous, too, but for different reasons. He actually liked this kid and was getting a hard-on just thinking about seeing him buck naked. He began to unbutton his shirt, and Johnny mirrored his actions. Moonface slid Johnny's shirt from his shoulders. Johnny did the same for him. Moonface leaned in to give him a kiss, and Johnny pulled away.

- Whoa!

- Relax. It don't mean nothin'. It's just for the show.

Moonface put one hand behind Johnny's neck, gently urging their mouths together, while his other hand stroked the kid's smooth chest, moved downward, felt a growing hardness beneath the gray flannel. A piece of cake, Moonface thought, or better yet, a slice of cherry pie. He placed his hands under Johnny's ass, and the kid stood up facing him. Moonface slowly loosened the belt, undid each button, and slid Johnny's trousers to the floor. He wasn't wearing underpants and his long stiff young dick practically popped into Moonface's mouth all by itself. Johnny may have been only on the receiving end before, but he had no problem switch-hitting into the more active role. Well-practiced as Moonface was, he had trouble keeping up with the kid's quick rhythm, deep-diving down his throat, making him gag. A little more finesse would be required for tonight, but they could talk about that later. Moonface didn't want to interrupt the wild abandon of this first hot-blooded encounter. He knew it wouldn't last long.

Sure enough, the kid had no control and was shooting his huge load down Moonface's gullet in hard, choking spurts. They'd have to work on that, too. There was plenty of time before tonight's performance, and plenty more nights to practice, if Moonface had anything to say about it. As far as first impressions went, he was hey-diddle-diddle over-the-moon happy.

Johnny never shared that feeling. At least not until he had the cash in his hand. They did the gig every Friday for a month, until management wanted fresh faces, new meat. Johnny bought Highball with a cut from his last pay, much to his wife's annoyance. Moonface and Johnny drifted apart. But sometimes Moonface stopped by the garage, and that German shepherd was always tied to the bumper of Johnny's truck, watching him work, waiting for a pat on the head. He wondered what was gonna happen to Highball, now that Johnny was dead as a doornail. He liked the dog, too. Just not as much as he liked Johnny, or as much as Johnny loved that dog.

II. GADGET

A fucking dog! He had not been waiting long before the front door opened and that white monster retriever jumped out, holding a leash in its mouth, followed by another big shocker. Wasn't this just a day for surprises? His ghost in the window turned out to be a guy who looked like his guy, dressed like his guy, even walked like his guy. But most definitely a different guy, a living guy, a guy with a fucking dog.

Gadget was totally gobsmacked. He could not work it out. Did his guy have a twin brother he didn't know about? It just didn't make sense. Was this guy pretending to be his guy? What the hell for? Had Gadget suddenly beamed into some alternate reality? Seemed as likely as any other possibility he could come up with.

They set off down the sidewalk, and Gadget followed at a safe distance. Up the stairs, across the main street, down the stairs on the other side, along the path between the high-rises and the gardens that bordered the canal.

The fucking dog led the way confidently, wagging tail held high, smelling bushes before pissing all over them. Dogs didn't give a shit where they pissed, or where they shit, for that matter. Gadget hated stepping in dog shit, another good reason to have all the filthy beasts put down. Put down, right? Gadget sneered. Only a dogfucker would come up with a lame expression like that. Slit their dirty bastard throats, that was more like it.

Gadget was getting too worked up. He stopped for a minute, took a deep breath, and inhaled a whopping dose of fresh dog poop. Almost made him barf. Could this fucking day get any worse?

The mystery guy and his hairy hound stopped at a small triangular park with lots of benches circling a dried-up fountain. There was a fair number of people around, most with their own dogs that played together, sniffed each other's asses, or rolled around in the grass. The guy sat at the edge of the canal, ignoring his mutt, letting it do whatever the fuck it wanted.

Gadget sat on the back of a bench, as far from everyone else as possible but still able to keep an eye on his target. This was not the time or place for direct action. Gadget needed more intel, needed time to think, needed to come up with a plan. A plan for what? Gadget had no idea.

Then he heard a loud splash. Across the grass, the guy's white monster had jumped into the canal and was swimming around in slow circles. Head held above the water, the animal looked more like a polar bear than a dog. The guy heaved a ball out into the canal and the beast took off after it.

Suddenly a swarm of images flew into Gadget's brain like bats from a black hole in hell. The white dog, the park, the bag, the rose garden, the pond, the head, the trick, the dog, the police, the faggots, the white dog swimming, his head was spinning, the dog's head, his guy's head, his head, his head was about to explode.

The fucking dog. It had to be the same fucking dog.

III. DEKKER

The message is short and to the point: *Too many words. Cut boring background. Add sex scene in club. Nobody cares about the dog.*

I have to laugh. I didn't think I had done a total hack job for my first effort, but I made a classic error. Too much back-story before the main action, especially true for porn, I imagine. It would be easy enough to fix and I wouldn't make the same mistake again. However, I'm relieved the editor responded quickly and freely accepted the story as the work of Valentine, Mac's *nom de plume*. An inspired choice for an author of homoerotic tales. It may have been his given name, but I have a hard time thinking of him as anything but Mac. Valentine and Mac are two different people to me, but I begin to understand how they could coalesce into one. There's a literary term for that. French, I think. Something Proust did? I don't remember. Not important.

What's important is that I've made a tentative step toward reinventing myself, perhaps a sign I'm beginning to accept the possibility this peculiar plan might work. I still don't believe I could permanently live Mac's life, but it's a place to begin, a place to figure out what the hell I'm going to do next.

It's also a place where I can finally relax. The stress of the last months has taken a toll on me. If I went to a doctor, I'd probably be diagnosed with depression, sent to a shrink, and put on medication. I don't need a therapist or pills. I've stared into the abyss, as Nietzsche wrote, and the abyss stared back. I've held my nerve and fought off the demons. But I also know I'm not out of the woods yet. Most people forget the beginning of Nietzsche's quotation. *Whoever fights monsters risks becoming a monster himself.* Or words to that effect.

Willy always wore a necklace, a thin silver chain with a hematite pendant. He said warriors carried such a talisman into battle for protection, called it a stone for the mind, with powers to fight negativity. His was beautiful, titanium gray with a vermilion streak, like most crystals from blood ore. The last time I saw him he tried to give it to me. I told him to hold on to it for a while, not realizing I'd never see him again. I wish I had it now, but I have my own talisman.

A Native American myth venerates a Creator who fashioned the world and men, accompanied by a dog. An Iroquois story tells of a dog that guards the bridge over which the dead must cross, barring any soul who was cruel to a dog in life. Across my native land, many tribes believed white dogs to be sacred, bestowed with magical powers of healing and protection from harm.

Calvin is my healer, my protector, my talisman. As long as he accompanies me, I neither fear monsters, nor fear becoming one.

Chapter Twelve

I. Dekker

Rembrandtpark is an excellent place to write. It's never crowded. There are plenty of wooded areas, open fields, and canine park-pals to keep Calvin occupied. And from the bench where I sit with my notebook, the view is quite inspiring. A short distance away, a very attractive young man puts his well-muscled body through its paces at one of the exercise stations. He wears baggy black gym shorts, a tight white sleeveless T-shirt, and running sneakers without socks as he does chin-ups on a high bar. He's showing off, clearly, but that's fine by me. He has a physique worth flaunting and if he keeps it up, he might find himself in Valentine's next story.

It's been a long time since I've been turned on by watching someone, even longer since I've been interested enough to think about sex. When I've hung out in a bar recently, I may talk to good-looking men but that's as far as it goes. I'm there with one aim: to lose myself in the haze of cigarette smoke and alcohol, to drink myself stupid enough to forget. Forget the past, forget the present, and forget the fact that I see no future. The last thing I want to think about is how different my life was with Willy, how I lost him, and consequently how I lost myself.

I haven't had a drink since the night of my birthday, the night my own story could have ended. I still don't remember much of it, which is scary enough. But one thing I know for sure. If my tequila-soaked brain imagined a sweet reunion in the great hereafter, I was more than a few cards short of a full deck. Willy would have been extremely pissed off with me and would've held nothing back. He'd have given me a wicked tongue-lashing before he picked me up and threw me headlong out of the light. Willy was fearless, in his art and in his life, and he expected no less from me.

❖

When the paintings selected for the series that came to be called *Colors of Darkness I* were ready for exhibition, Willy asked me to move in with him. I was already spending more time at his place than I was at my own, but for him it had been important that some distance remained between us until he finished everything. Our relationship had grown gradually, much like the long, measured process Willy employed to create his art.

First, there was the extended period of modeling for his countless pencil sketches on paper. Figure drawings in various postures and poses. Portraits in profile, front view, and even the back of my head. Close-up detail studies of every body part: my neck, my shoulder, my elbow, hands and fingers, my legs, feet and toes, my chest and my stomach, my ass, my cock.

The next phase, which lasted nearly as long, was color experimentation. Finding the right combination of oils, pigments, resins, and solvents to make base colors. Mixing and blending these on palettes, ever increasing the range of tints and tones. Brushing different hues in broad haphazard strokes, first on white paper, then on blank canvas. I didn't understand why he needed me in the studio for this part of the process but I didn't ask questions. He didn't need me naked anymore. He must have memorized every hair, birthmark, curve, and crevice by then. Physically, at least, I held no secrets from him.

Intense as the work during this period was, we had downtime, as well. We ate together, took long walks together, talked and got to know each other. It surprised me to find we had more in common than I'd thought possible. We read the same books, liked the same films. Our tastes in music differed, his strictly classical and mine New Wave, but it was never a problem. We went to an occasional concert or movie, but never socialized with each other's friends. Not that I had any, aside from a few student colleagues and bar buddies. However, he seemed to deliberately keep me from meeting anyone in his inner circle. No one ever stopped by the ground-floor studio or visited his apartment upstairs, at least not when I was around. I didn't mind. I liked whatever our relationship had become. Not boyfriends, certainly not lovers, but intimate, more intimate than I'd ever experienced.

Then came what Willy called the merging process. He hung the sketches and color tests on the walls or from clotheslines stretched across the studio. He spread them out on the floor. He matched them on easels, tried various combinations, rejected most, and put some aside in a large leather portfolio. I found my role during this process a little strange, but again kept my thoughts to myself. He asked me to wander aimlessly around the studio saying my name out loud, over and over. Jason Dekker. I am Jason Dekker. My name's Jason Dekker. Jason Dekker. For hours at a time, without falling into any repetitive rhythm. It was harder than it sounds.

I asked if I could put my voice on tape so I wouldn't actually have to be there. Nope. Jason Dekker had to be heard, Jason Dekker had to be present, in the flesh. I dealt with it, got used to it, as I had with the modeling. This was a kind of modeling, too, I guess. Just not any I'd ever heard of.

One day he told me to stop. The merging was done. Well, not entirely.

Willy crossed the room, took my face in his hands without another word, and kissed me full on the lips. I was startled, but not enough to keep me from giving back as much as I took, with no fear of giving more or giving too much. Our hands explored our bodies, we held each other tight, as if we might never let go. When we did, Willy Hart took Jason Dekker's hand and led him upstairs for the first time, into his bedroom, his bed, his body and soul.

In the weeks that followed, the task of applying paint to canvas and creating perfect works of art was simple and seamless compared with the difficult preparations beforehand. The same was true with our relationship. Without the usual flirtatious banter or sexual innuendo most gay men indulge in, our long courtship dance produced an unconditional compatible union.

When he finally disclosed what he wanted to show with his series, I understood why he kept me in the shadows, away from his art world friends and associates. It was them he was keeping in the dark, never revealing that *Colors of Darkness I* was his synaesthetic anagram of

Jason Dekker. All the colors of all the sounds were on vivid display. Except for the Venetian red *J*, which would remain a secret, held close to his, and only his, heart.

❖

The athletic young man, limber limbs shining with sweat, pulls the damp T-shirt over his head, uses it to wipe his chest, under his arms, across his flat stomach.

I force myself to look away, not wishing to be caught staring with my mouth gaping open, practically drooling, like Calvin salivating after Sela in heat. But I sneak another peek as the exceptional model of male musculature tosses his shirt nonchalantly over his shoulder and starts to jog down the path in our direction.

Calvin lies at my feet, head raised, ears alert, watching the approach with interest.

As the guy gets close, he bends forward to give Calvin a friendly pat on the head, raises his eyes to meet mine, and mutters a soft-spoken compliment.

- Beautiful dog.

Instead of returning the compliment, Calvin turns on his mean-face, baring teeth and emitting an intimidating growl.

The young man lurches backward, arms pinwheeling in almost comical cartoon fashion.

- Whoa!

- Hey, Calvin!

I yelp with as much admonishment as I can muster, under the circumstances.

- He was just gonna say hello.

To me, I telepathically command him to understand as I ruffle the raised fur on his neck.

He was going to say hello to me.

II. GADGET

Everything was going according to plan, Gadget thought as he almost fell on his ass. Except for the fucking dog. He made a quick recovery, gave an embarrassed little chuckle, and flashed his most captivating smile.

- That's some crazy dog you got. Does he bite?

- No. Sorry about that. He's usually very friendly.

- Oh, really? I hadn't noticed.

- Sometimes he just likes to show off.

Good. Gadget had turned the tables, and it was the guy's turn to be embarrassed. Was he blushing, as well? Gadget had a knack for reading people. The guy thought Gadget was the one showing off. All those chin-ups. Yes, sir, he was back in charge.

- I know the type. The human type, anyway.

- Right.

- Will he mind if I sit down? I was going for a run but I think I need a breather after all that excitement.

- No problem. He'll be fine.

The guy picked up his knapsack from the bench, slipped the notebook he was holding inside, and set it down beside the dog.

Gadget sat, leaning back, stretching his very long, very sexy legs.

- Damn. Forgot to bring a bottle of water. I'm parched.

- Have a swig of mine, if you want.

The guy bent down and pulled a plastic bottle from his bag, offered it.

Gadget took the water with a nod, unscrewed the cap, chugged down all of what was left, and tossed the empty bottle backward into the bushes. The dog, who had not taken his eye off Gadget, immediately took off after it. That was better, just the two of them.

He smiled his irresistible smile.

- Guess that's why they call them retrievers.

III. Calvin

running seeking searching bushes / hurry calvin fast&fast
badman talking dekker smiling / calvin trusting no&no
searching bottle searching sniffing / smelling badman no&no
meanface calvin growling digging / searching bottle more&more
bottle finding up&up / jumping leaping
    bottle falling down&down

dekker talking badman smiling / nono dekker no&no
calvin biting bottle holding / letsgo dekker wanting home
dropping bottle biting knapsack lifting taking
letsgo dekker home&home

IV. DEKKER

I have no idea what has gotten into Calvin. I've rarely seen him in such a state. He stands on the path we normally take home, holds my knapsack in his mouth, and tries to bark at the same time, resulting in muffled woofs. Funny, yes, but odd. It's never his idea to leave the park. On a late sunny afternoon I usually have to bribe him with the promise of dinner to get him to leave without forcibly putting him on the leash and dragging him away.

The young man, whose name I did not quite catch, is laughing. He has a good sense of humor, considering our inauspicious introduction.

Thank you, Calvin.

I'd like to sit here and talk to him some more. Although there is this nagging thought at the back of my mind that he's too good-looking, too young, too charming, which combined spell *trouble* with a capital T. His laid-back style is infused with a practiced pretentiousness that suggests a hustler mentality. I've observed this in action many times in bars but never been faced with it so directly. If true, he's way off the mark trying to hit on me.

Calvin makes another muffled attempt at a commanding bark. I give the guy an apologetic shrug.

- Looks like my escort is ready to go home.

Did I just say escort? Jesus, Dekker, shut the fuck up.

- I should take off, too. Which way you heading?

- Toward the Baarsjesweg.

- Me, too. I'll walk with you.

Interesting. He stands, stretches and pulls his T-shirt on. Calvin looks perplexed as we walk toward him together. Then, with a big shake of his body suggesting a disparaging *harrumph*, he turns and trots off ahead of us in the direction of the park exit without looking back.

- Does he always get his own way?

- Not always.

- I'll bet. Looks like he has you well and truly whipped.

- Are you calling me a pussy?

- If the shoe fits.

Okay. He's playing with me, that much is clear. It's an aggressive flirtation that could get irritating very quickly. I refuse to take the bait and turn our conversation to more neutral territory.

- Are you a student?

- What makes you think that?

- Well, your age. And you seem smart enough.

- Maybe I'm older than I look. I take pretty good care of myself, in case you didn't notice.

- Oh, I noticed.

- So how old do you think I am?

- Early twenties.

- Sweet.

He smirks with a low chuckle. If he is older than he looks, I can't be off by much.

We catch up to Calvin, who is waiting for us curbside. He crosses the street as soon as we arrive, without waiting for the customary *Okay.* I bend over to pick up my knapsack, which my grumpy friend has dropped onto the sidewalk, clearly not in one of his help-dog moods. As I do, I receive an unexpected slap on my ass.

- Told you. Whipped.

Not Okay. This is too cheeky from someone I've just met. It might be acceptable at night in a bar after a few drinks. On the street in broad daylight, in a neighborhood not known to be particularly tolerant of gays? I don't think so. On one hand, I don't want to make a big deal of it. On the other hand, I'm not willing to let it pass if we're engaging in macho one-upmanship. I give his arm a friendly punch, not too hard, but solid enough to say *Watch it, buster.*

- Whoa. I'm just fooling with you.

- Yeah, well, not cool.

- Point taken, sir.

He performs a quick, sarcastic salute. The eye contact he makes with me is so direct, so intense, it feels almost as if I've never looked anyone in the eye before. He's all charming smiles again as we follow Cal across the street.

We don't speak for the next couple of blocks. At each corner I hope he will say a quick good-bye and head off in another direction, but he continues to tag along, like a lost puppy. We reach the footbridge over the canal a few blocks from Mac's house, where he pauses a moment, leans on the railing, and heaves a pensive sigh.

- I'm not a student. I'm not smart. I don't know what I am. I work through a temp agency. Shit work, but I don't know what else I'd rather be doing. Except watching television or playing video games. I go to the bars, but guys just look at me like I'm a trophy to win for the night. They circle me with hungry eyes, like sharks closing in for the kill. That's me. Gay shark bait. Nobody wants to be friends, have a conversation or a laugh, like you. Aw, fuck it. I don't know what I'm talking about. Sorry. I shouldn't unload all this bullshit on you. I'm gonna go. Nice to meet you. Sorry.

He starts to move away but after a couple of steps, grabs the railing unsteadily, stops and turns back. He looks as if he's about to cry.

Beyond him Calvin sits at the other end of the bridge, waiting. None too patiently. He issues a sharp bark.

- Calvin. Hold your horses.

Without thinking, I hear myself say that Cal and I don't live far from here. Maybe he'd like to come back with us, sit in the garden, have a beer or something. Almost as soon as the words are out of my mouth, I want to retract them, make some feeble excuse, remember an appointment, anything. Before I can formulate a reasonable-sounding pretext, he smiles and accepts the invitation, says he could really use a cold beer. We are already walking together. He throws an arm around my shoulders as if we're best mates.

V. Calvin

calvin walking growling walking / badman following
    calvin home
dekker talking badman walking / dekker walking badman home
stopping sniffing / something smelling / badroom badman
    smelling same
sniffing bushes pawing digging / something under smelling same
lookit dekker lookit / finding present under bushes
dekker lookit / smelling same

VI. Gadget

Son of a bitch! The fucking dog found his stash.

Gadget could not believe this was happening. It was all going so well. He sensed his mark was losing interest, having doubts, putting up a wall of distrustful silence between them. So he pulled the little-boy-lost routine out of his bag of tricks and it worked a treat. As usual. Some men were a sucker for a good sob story, and he had plenty in his repertoire. He didn't even need to turn on the waterworks. Once in the house, he would get the guy talking, find out what the fuck he was doing there, and get whatever information he needed before making his next move. He wasn't exactly sure what that was yet, but there was time to figure it out, and in the meantime he could have some fun.

One thing he hadn't counted on was the fucking dog.

The animal tugged the carved handle of the sheathed sabre free from the shrubbery. The guy knelt down to get a look at what his fiendish hellhound had found. With some resistance, he took the treasure from the fucking dog's mouth, felt the hefty weight of the thing, and showed it to Gadget.

- Look at this. Calvin finds the damnedest things.

- What is it?

- Looks like some kind of old sword.

- Cool.

- Who would bury something like this here?

The guy pulled the blade partway out of the sheath. It glinted, catching a ray of the afternoon sun.

- It looks sharp. Dangerous. What if some kids found it?

The dog wagged its tail and made a quick move forward, as if to reclaim its prize. But the guy stood, holding it aloft.

- No way, Calvin. He probably thinks it's an umbrella or something. He likes to carry stuff. Calvin, no. *Garbage*.

- Garbage?

- Just a word he understands. It means leave it alone. I'm not throwing this away. It might be worth something.

You got that right. Definitely something worth hanging on to.

Once more Gadget could turn this to his advantage. He was nothing if not resourceful.

CHAPTER THIRTEEN

I. DEKKER

Calvin heads immediately for his water dish in the kitchen, and what's-his-name asks to use the toilet. I direct him down the hall. After admiring the sword's intricately carved handle, I stash it in the umbrella stand by the door.

I grab a handful of peanuts to keep Bastard occupied. He thanks me with his usual gracious *Fuck you* and sets about shelling his treats. I leave the cage door open so he can get to his climbing perches and start for the kitchen to grab a couple of beers from the fridge.

My guest returns, but before I have a chance to offer him a can, he asks if he could take a quick shower first.

- I kinda stink after my workout in the park.

- Uh, sure. No problem. Clean towels are in the wicker basket under the sink. Take your time.

- Thanks, man.

Seems a little presumptuous, I think, setting his beer on the kitchen counter and opening my own. I'm beginning to recognize this as typical behavior from him. Meet someone, drink all his water. Chat a bit, you're best buddies. Come to his house, jump in the shower. Next thing you know he'll expect me to suck his dick. I've already decided nothing like that will happen today. We'll have a drink, talk some more, and I'll send him on his way. Maybe we can meet up again. Or not, depending on how things go.

I swallow a big gulp of beer, pull my notebook out of the knapsack, and take it upstairs to the office. I may as well check to see if the editor has sent an email about the rewrite. I'm sure my new friend is a leisurely long hot shower kind of guy.

II. Gadget

He didn't flinch as the cold spray hit his body. Gadget liked the brisk shock to his system that opened his mind, steeled his resolve. Then he ran the water until it was boiling hot, tingled his skin, got the circulation going. Then cold again, then hot, seven times in a row. It unblocked the body's flow, left him invigorated, all his senses alert, fully alive.

He took pleasure in a vigorous towel-down and shook his head. His long, dark hair flung excess water all over, but he didn't care. His hair looked good wet, shaggy and shiny and curly. It was something men liked. He intended to fashion an eye-catching distraction, craft a clever bit of misdirection to mask the magic of his next act.

Gadget took the plush black terry-cloth robe off its hook and slipped into it, pulled it closed but didn't belt it, ready for the accidental, inviting reveal. He could already feel a slight swelling of anticipation that he knew would impress. It always did.

He stepped out of the bathroom and froze, felt his privates shrink in fear.

The white monster stood blocking the end of the hallway, fangs bared, gaze unwavering, growling viciously, ready to attack at the slightest provocation.

Gadget didn't dare move forward. Instead, he took a step back, only to hear the growl intensify. Retreat was not an option.

He flashed on the crazy vision of a fucked-up Wild West showdown, a standoff on Main Street, unarmed and naked, staring down the double-barrel shotgun of the local sheriff. Only this was not funny. Not funny at all.

He hated the thought of sounding like a wimp, but he couldn't think of anything else to do except call for help. He barely managed a thin vocal exhalation of air. That totally pissed him off.

Fuck it all to hell.

Gadget took a deep breath and yelled at the top of his lungs.

- Call off your dog. I think he wants to fucking kill me.

III. DEKKER

I jump up, race down the steps, and stop halfway. Calvin stands in the hall by the foot of the stairs, tail pointed, hair along his back raised, growling as I've never heard before. I look over the railing. At the back of the hallway near the bathroom door, the young man stands in a robe, shaking, eyes wide-open, face pale. I bite my lip to keep from laughing. I'm the only one who finds anything funny about this situation.

Without giving an inch, Calvin's eyes dart up to meet mine.

I've got him. What do you want me to do? Say the word and he's mine.

- Calvin, stop. What's wrong with you? Be nice. Go lay down.

I give his neck rough scratches to calm his raised hackles and let him know my stern voice is not a serious reprimand. I point him in the direction of the living room.

He acquiesces, and with a last warning glance down the hall, goes to his rug in front of the fireplace and sits. More for extra recovery time than anything else, I give a commanding point toward the floor. He lies down, albeit reluctantly.

I turn back to the hallway and catch the young man pulling the belt of the robe tightly around his waist, clearly embarrassed. He looks at me sheepishly, but a hint of thinly veiled anger is evident below the surface.

- I don't think your dog likes me.

- I'm really sorry about that. I went upstairs and I guess his territorial instinct went into overdrive. Maybe it was the robe.

- The robe?

- My robe. He's only ever seen me wearing it. Maybe that's what set him off.

- No. He was waiting for me when I came out. How'd he know I'd be wearing your robe?

He was right and, if I'm honest, it was a pretty lame excuse. In Calvin's defense, this was a strange situation. Usually he has time to get used to new friends but this whole chain of events is out of his comfort zone. Not to mention his odd conservative streak regarding things being just as they're supposed to be, according to his strict canine constraints.

- I left my clothes on the floor and they got wet. I didn't think it would be a big deal to borrow your robe.

- It's not. It's fine. Really. But you do look like you could use that beer now.

IV. Gadget

Gadget tried to smile, hoping it looked less like a grimace than it felt. He followed the guy into the lounge, saw the fucking dog keeping a close eye on him, and hugged the wall as he continued to the kitchen. The guy handed him a beer. He popped the top and chugged half of it down in one go. He needed more than a goddamn beer.

- Have a seat. Relax.

- Here is fine.

The guy had moved toward the comfortable-looking leather sofa, but Gadget sat at the table, a welcome barrier between him and the hellhound. The guy joined him, sitting on the other side and blocking the view of his beast. He could still feel it watching him, waiting. He needed time to regroup. *Small talk.*

- Nice place.

- Thanks.

- How long you live here?

- Oh, a while now. I inherited it from a Dutch uncle.

A Dutch uncle, my ass. His guy couldn't be this guy's uncle. That was a no-brainer. This guy was acting all squirrelly now, like that big funky cuddly toy in the corner. *Change tracks.*

- What's upstairs?

- Just a small office, more like an alcove, really.

- Seems like there'd be more. Under the roof?

Gadget knew exactly what was under the roof, but he had to be careful. He didn't want to give himself away.

- There's an attic, but I don't use it. Too dark.

- Are you kidding? This is Amsterdam, man. You could rent a fucking closet to a student or somebody. Run some electricity up there for lights. You could make some extra cash.

- It's got lights.

Gadget saw the guy shut up before spilling any more. He took another gulp of beer. *Try a lighter touch.*

- Of course, you'd have to get permission.

He paused a beat.

- From your dog.

The guy started to laugh and Gadget joined him. That was more like it. The laughter was infectious. They couldn't stop, both laughing their fucking asses off, like it was the funniest joke they ever heard. Gadget could stop if he wanted to, but this was working great. The guy had tears running down his face, he laughed so hard.

All the tension that had built up between them vanished. Gadget had this guy right where he wanted him, like a bird eating out of the palm of his hand. The guy finally got control of himself, wiped his eyes with his hands, and breathed a big sigh.

Gadget took another sip and notched up the charm again with his pearly white smile.

- So. Are you going to give me the grand tour, or what?

V. Dekker

- There's really not all that much to see. The garden.

As I open the back door, Calvin jumps up and charges outside to investigate. That will keep him occupied for a while.

- Nice.

The kid, whatever his name is, barely glances in the direction of the garden as he stands and moves toward the hall. He looks toward the front entrance and pushes open the bedroom door before I get there. He's blocking the way in, so I stand behind him. I can smell his hair, still wet from his shower. He cocks his head back and forth, not unlike the way Calvin does.

- Very small bedroom, obviously.

- Obviously.

- But big enough.

- For what?

He winks suggestively over his shoulder. My face reddens with an involuntary blush.

Jesus, Dekker.

He chuckles, edges past me, brushing his back against my arm, and launches himself up the stairs two at a time. It's clear who's leading this tour, I think, following behind him, following his behind.

Dekker, stop.

I'm unable to control my sudden unconscious desire to see him naked. Maybe not so unconscious.

Upstairs, he leans against the office doorjamb, his loose robe, Mac's loose robe, ever so slightly open. I avert my gaze and slip by him into the tiny office, which feels all the more claustrophobic when his athletic body fills the low narrow doorway.

- You work here?

- Yes. I do some writing.

- You're a writer? What kind of writer?

- Stories. Short stories.

- Cool.

Neither of us speaks for a moment. An uncomfortable silence for me but he seems relaxed, deep in thought, almost in another world. He doesn't look at me as he raises his arms, links his fingers together at the back of his head and stretches his torso from side to side, seemingly unaware that the robe is completely open, fully exposing his considerable attributes. Just as casually, he pulls the robe closed and turns his back on me.

- And this must be the attic.

Shit.

Although the door was locked, I had removed the skeleton key from the ring and left it in the keyhole. I hear him try the handle, then turn the key, opening the door.

My mind races. How am I going to explain the *empty room* is actually a well-equipped sex dungeon?

- You were right. It's dark.

Before I can respond, he finds the wall switch and the dim lamps flood the room with bright blinding light.

PART THREE: THE ATTIC

"All knowledge, the totality of all questions and all answers is contained in the dog."

—Franz Kafka

Chapter Fourteen

I. Calvin

wind whipping face ears nose / sniffing all so fast&fast
window open dekker driving / music blasting fur flying
trees passing sun flashing / eyes closed / seeing nothing
wind&wind more&more / evermore&evermore

II. Dekker

Driving helps me think but it's not working, not today. The Volkswagen is a smooth ride compared to the Suzuki. No comparison at all, in fact, strengthening my idea to hold on to this baby and sell the jeep. I love Jax, would be sad to see him go, not least of all because he was a gift from Willy. It just makes more sense to keep the sleeker, mint-condition VW, if everything goes according to plan. At the moment that's a huge if, because the plan is in grave danger of imploding and I have no one to blame but myself.

How could I have been so stupid, so reckless, so utterly out of my mind?

Calvin, head hanging out the open window, blissfully laps at the backrush of summer breezes. You have to envy a dog. No regrets from the past, no worries for the future, always content to live in the Now and make the most of whatever that means.

I once observed a particularly wretched homeless guy begging on the street, his dog cuddled in his arms. I didn't give a shit about the man. I felt for the dog. Now I understand how misguided I was, and not because of my own homelessness. The dog didn't need my pity. He was content to live in the sweet embrace of his one-and-only, then and probably now. Whether I knew it or not, Calvin was teaching me about living in the Now long before that day.

That's why Willy gave him to me.

❖

It was the best of days, it was the worst of days.

I asked Willy where we were going. I should have been suspicious right away when he said it was a surprise. Willy kept a lot close to his chest but he didn't do surprises. We'd been together for a couple of years when I learned that the hard way. I made the mistake of throwing him a birthday party. When he walked into the darkened studio, all the friends and invited guests from the gallery's mailing list yelled, *Surprise!* He looked at me, eyes burning with betrayal, turned around and walked out. I ran after him, tried to cajole him into returning, but he wouldn't speak to me. He pushed me out of his way and kept walking. I'd never seen him so angry, and for the first time since we met I feared I might lose him. When he came home late that night, I started to apologize but he shut me up by kissing me fiercely and leading me to the bedroom. We never talked about it, then or ever. Message sent and received. Willy didn't like surprises.

We drove through a neighborhood in southeast Amsterdam of high-rise apartment buildings with large landscaped areas of grass and trees. Appealingly green by day, its high crime rate made it dangerous by night. I couldn't imagine why we were here when Willy pulled into a parking spot.

An elevator took us to the seventh floor and a rough-looking heavyset Dutch man opened a door down the hall. I could tell Willy didn't know the man as they chatted briefly, but my attention was drawn to the two beautiful white golden retrievers who stood by his side. The man introduced them as Rocky and Gizmo and ushered us into the apartment.

I heard squealing from behind a closed door by the kitchen, where Gizmo stopped as Rocky led us to the living room. I shot Willy a questioning look. He grinned but said nothing.

The man entered the room, arms full of white balls of fur, which he set gently on the carpet. Four terminally cute puppies immediately began crawling around the floor, sniffing, exploring, and playing together. Gizmo and Rocky watched in protective parental fashion. The man brought in four more, adding to the frenetic energy that filled the room.

- Which one?

- You're joking.

- We have first pick of the nest.

- Pick of the litter?

- Nest, litter, whatever you say.

- Are you kidding me?

One of the pups bumped into my sneaker and started chewing. I was spellbound, unable to absorb what was happening. The man asked Willy if we wanted a boy or a girl.

- Definitely a male.

The owner lifted the puppies two at a time, checking their privates, and took the three females back to their nest. Gizmo followed closely behind him. The five remaining boy-pups looked exactly alike, each one as cute as the other. The one gnawing at my shoelace seemed a little chubbier, maybe just because he was so close. The man returned with a bowl of what looked like vanilla pudding and placed it on the floor.

- Sometimes you see a difference by the way they eat.

The puppy at my feet raised his nose, sniffed the air, and lost all interest in my footwear, heading directly toward the bowl as fast as his oversized paws could carry him. He lapped up the food with ravenous glee, pushing his brothers aside as they tried to join him. Only eight weeks old and the greedy little bugger had personality to spare. I pointed. The man grabbed him by the scruff of the neck and handed him to me.

kicking, yelping, complaining

I held the wriggling fur ball to my face. We looked into each other's eyes and he licked my nose, smelling of sweetness and sheer joy. I turned to Willy, who was laughing, nodding in agreement.

That night we lay in bed, Calvin snuggled between us, softly snoring. And Willy told me the rest. His visits to the doctor, the tests, the results, the diagnosis, the ulterior motive behind his uncharacteristic surprise.

❖

Calvin loves running up and down and between the sandy dunes.

I hadn't intended to drive this far, didn't even realize where we were headed until we arrived. Calvin got excited as soon as he sniffed a whiff of the sea. When I parked and let him out, he ran toward the shore, but I called him back. Once he had a taste of the ocean, it would be nearly impossible to coax him away until he exhausted himself. He kept running in that direction and I kept calling him back, a game of imaginary tug-of-war he enjoyed more than I. Content to explore the dune grass for half-buried hidden treasure, he has brought me two raggedy tennis balls and one that looks almost new.

I stand, brush the sand from my pants, and give Calvin a shout. It's time to get back and figure out what to do about our unexpected guest. Part of me wishes he would never wake up. That might be tricky to handle but it would be easier than any alternative. If he has come out of his comatose state, he'll still be there. I made sure of that. What next? I have no better idea than when I left the house hours ago. Every option I imagine has potential for disaster.

Calvin returns, panting hard, tail wagging happily.

I crouch down and give him a big hug. He growls his approval, but if I hold on for too long he'll bark me off. Nose to nose, I look deeply into his amber eyes.

- You knew. You knew and you tried to tell me and I didn't listen. If I had we wouldn't be in this mess. Another fine kettle of fish I've gotten us into.

Calvin returns my intense gaze, but remains silent. No comment necessary.

III. Gadget

He woke up in the dark, did not know where he was or how he had gotten there. His head hurt, pounded, as if he'd been on an epic binge. Had he been drinking? Something stronger, more lethal? He didn't think so but he wasn't sure. He could not remember.

He tried to move but his wrists and his ankles were restrained by something cold, metal. Cuffs of some sort. That felt wrong, in some profound way he could not put his finger on. He listened for some sound, any sound that might give him a clue as to his location.

Nothing. The silence was complete, absolute.

The distant crowing of a cock broke the tomblike stillness.

Was he dead? Was this hell? What had he done to deserve such punishment? Maybe he was dreaming. It might explain the muddled fog that enveloped his brain, confused his thoughts, pulled him once more into a murky shroud of obscurity.

Before he slipped back into unconsciousness, a fleeting thought filled him with dread. He had no idea who he was.

CHAPTER FIFTEEN

I. DEKKER

I listen at the door, motionless, but hear nothing from inside.

Be careful what you wish for.

Do I really want to deal with a dead body? Perhaps he is still just unconscious. Just unconscious. Right. That would be so much better. Damn.

Maybe I should have bundled him into the car and dropped him off at a hospital emergency room. There would've been questions, calls to the police, more questions, questions I wouldn't be able to answer without incriminating myself. Was there an equivalent to the Fifth Amendment in this country? I don't know.

The assault was clearly a case of self-defense. What about the rest? Covering up a crime, impeding an investigation, even accessory after the fact. At any rate, everything would come out. And what then? What now?

For the hundredth time I try to envision the events of the last twenty-four hours, hoping they will make more sense. It all happened so fast that some of it is merely a vague impression, some of it simply surreal, a nightmare scenario loosely held together with a significant helping of clever guesswork. Or the paranoid imagination of a homeless crackpot gone over the edge.

❖

- I thought you said the attic was empty.

- I think I said dark. It was like this when I moved in. My, uh, uncle apparently had some interesting proclivities.

- Pro what?

- He must have been into some kinky shit. I didn't know him that well.

- Interesting.

The nameless young man looked around the room with interest, brushed his finger across the rack of implements. He took a black leather mask from its hook on the wall, put it on, and wandered farther into the room. The effect was unnerving. Maybe it was the robe, but a sudden vision of Mac materialized, casually introducing a guest to his dungeon, a teasing glimpse of games to come.

Despite the stifling heat from the sun on the roof, I experienced every cliché I could think of from the lexicon of horror writing. My blood ran cold, an icy chill crept up my spine, hair raised on the back of my neck. Seriously. Creepy didn't begin to cover it. If this was a movie, I'd be the first to yell at the screen.

Get the hell out of there, you idiot.

I wanted to ask my masked intruder to leave but couldn't seem to form the words. He gazed intently at the framed print of the beheading of St. Valentine. Was he chuckling under the mask, just audible enough for me to hear? He turned and faced me from across the room, leaned into the hanging sling, and pushed off the floor with his feet. He spun in slow circles, head thrown back, laughing with gleeful abandon like a kid in the playground. I found a reasonable semblance of my voice.

- Let's go back downstairs. Have another beer. It's fucking hot up here.

- It is. Fucking hot.

He didn't move from the sling, just tilted his body back and continued to spin, legs outstretched. For the first time, I wondered if he might be high. It never occurred to me when we met after his exercise session, but he was acting peculiar. Perhaps he'd get the point with some gentle physical persuasion.

I walked around the unusual cross-shaped bench in the center of the room. Avoiding his long legs, I grabbed one of the chains to stop the spinning. He performed a graceful dismount. Sliding the mask to the top of his head, he surprised me with an abrupt exaggerated kiss on the lips.

- Hey!

- You should try it. It's fun!

- No, thanks. Let's—

- Aw, come on. You'll like it. Really.

I continued to protest as he took firm hold of my shoulders and forced me into the sling. He was laughing but I didn't find it the least bit funny. As we grappled, I lost my footing, grabbed the suspended chains to keep my balance, and more fell than sat, far enough back that my feet couldn't touch the floor.

He spun me around much faster than he'd spun himself. I hung almost upside down, with the leather seat near the back of my knees. I tried to pull myself upright against the centrifugal force, which was making me dizzy and nauseated. I hate spinning fairground rides for this exact reason, but his strong arms held me down and kept me in perpetual motion. The walls of the room whizzed past, creating a sensation I can only describe as a kind of horizontal vertigo.

As quickly as it began, it stopped, but only for a moment. He let go and the twisted chains started to disentangle, spinning me in the opposite direction.

It wasn't as endless as it seemed. He must have lost interest. The back-and-forth spins gradually lost power, and I pulled myself upright, light-headed and reeling as if I'd had too much to drink in too little time. I began to bend forward to keep from fainting when I sensed a swift movement from behind. Something whooshed in front of my face, around my neck, yanked me back. The asshole had slipped the belt from Mac's robe and was choking me with it.

What happened next is difficult to put into any kind of coherent account, like a dream where conventional notions of time become distorted in a simultaneous combination of slow motion and fast-forward, where action appears in a series of freeze frames, where images are created by sound as much as by sight. Dalí could have painted it better than I can describe it.

A growling, snarling, a protesting yelp, a shrill shriek filling the room.

A bellowing *motherfucking cocksucking* echoing off the walls.

White streaking, wind rushing, mouths opening, fangs flashing, shapes shifting.

Wings flapping, telephone ringing, hands flailing, terrycloth chafing, throat stinging.

Beast leaping, fowl flying, teeth gnashing, doorbell chiming, heavy breathing.

Calvin barking, Bastard screeching, human screaming, figures falling.

Black robe opening, head cracking, rooster crowing crack of dawn.

Bench bouncing, body crashing, Mac swearing, heads rolling.

Clock ticking, blood sticking.

Hourglass melting, raindrops pelting.

Willy snoring, sleeping, dying.

Candles flickering, blades flashing.

Calvin hovering, watching, guarding,

Bastard mumbling, thoughts tumbling.

Soft gray feathers floating in the air like dandelion parachutes on a summer afternoon.

❖

I was in a state somewhere between panic and shock, and acted on gut instinct. The amount of blood freaked me out until I remembered that head wounds bled more profusely than other injuries. Might he have fractured his skull when it impacted the bench? I didn't know. I didn't care. I just wanted to make sure he wasn't going to attack me again when he came to.

That's when I saw the rings secured to the floor at either end of the mattress. I slid his inert body onto the mattress and secured his wrists and ankles with the cuffs attached to the rings. There must be a key somewhere, but that wasn't important for the time being.

Once he was immobilized, I got Calvin and Bastard back downstairs. They were both pretty shaken up, no less so than I. How or why they came upstairs together when they did, I couldn't begin to comprehend. I was just grateful they had or I wouldn't be around to think about it. I gave them both some treats. For Bastard, some leftover spaghetti I'd learned was one of his favorites. For Calvin, a stick of chewy rawhide I knew would keep him busy for a while.

I was beginning to think more rationally. I wrapped some ice cubes in a towel, got some warm water and antiseptic from the bathroom, and went back upstairs. I found the break in the scumbag's scalp, cleaned it as best I could, and ripped a T-shirt into strips to wrap it tight. He probably could have done with a few stitches. I was not about to attempt that, though the thought of causing him pain held enormous appeal.

❖

He lies where I left him, under a light sheet. His breathing still sounds normal, same as before I took Calvin for a drive this morning. I don't know if he's unconscious or in a coma. Or what the difference is, for that matter. Almost twenty-four hours seems a long time to remain out cold like this. He should probably be on some kind of hydrating drip or something.

No, he belongs in a fucking hospital, not trussed up in an attic sex dungeon.

- What the hell am I gonna do with you?

I kneel down beside him, heave a deep sigh, and gaze intently at his face. The ones who spell *Trouble* always look so harmless when they're asleep, so innocent, so vulnerable. Like Sleeping Beauty, waiting for the spell to be broken, to be brought back to life with a gentle kiss. I'm nearly tempted to pull a Prince Charming, when the murderous son of a bitch opens his eyes.

II. Gadget

Faces emerged from the shadows, fuzzy around the edges, features indistinct. He blinked his eyes, tried to get them to focus. The faces merge into one. Yes, just one face staring at him, a man's face, with a concentrated look of concern. Or anger? Maybe both at the same time. Then it was gone. The face simply vanished. Whose face? He had never seen that face before. Where was he?

Before he could remember, the man returned with a glass of water, put a hand under his head, his head that hurt, hurt a lot, lifted his aching head and raised the glass to his lips.

- Drink this. Slowly. You're dehydrated.

He had not realized how dry his mouth was until the cool liquid hit his tongue. He swallowed with difficulty but wanted more. The water took all his attention. He forgot about the unrecognized face, the unknown location. He was thirsty. He wanted to reach for the glass but discovered he couldn't move his arms. At first he thought he was paralyzed. No, he could move his elbows, bent at either side of his head, but his wrists were bound by some kind of restraint. He tried to move his legs but his ankles were also held by something cold, something metal. For a moment he felt panic, danger, then he was taking another sip of water and the sensation diminished. He had questions, so many questions, but was tired, too tired to formulate them, much less put them into words. He managed one.

- Sleepy.

- I know. You had quite a bump to your head.

The voice was soft, gentle, but not one he recognized. He was drifting off again. He didn't want to slip away into the darkness. It frightened him. He wanted to stay here, stay with the gentle voice, the fading face. There was so much he did not understand, so much he needed to know. But despite his best efforts, his heavy eyelids fluttered, closed, and he returned to the darkness.

CHAPTER SIXTEEN

I. DEKKER

It's weird how quickly the nursing instinct kicks in again, especially under such bizarre circumstances. Some freakazoid I pick up in the park tries to strangle me by way of a sex sling, gets knocked out by the guns-a-blazing canine-avian Butch and Sundance duo, and *abracadabra*, I turn into fucking Mother Teresa.

Wherever you are, Willy, I hope you're laughing your ass off.

I'd be doing the same if the whole thing weren't so insanely screwed up.

I check his forehead with my hand. It feels a little warm but it's hot as hell up here anyway. I consider crushing a couple of paracetamol tablets into the next glass of water. For now, I go to the office, open the window, unplug the small desk fan, and take it into the attic to get some of the stale warm air circulating. I assume he'll be out for another good stretch, and I'm not about to sit here holding his homicidal hand.

I leave the attic door open so I'll hear him if he wakes up screaming. The thought brings a payback smile to my face. I head downstairs to check on my unlikely heroes. Calvin sits calm but alert at the bottom of the steps, looking up at me, leash in his mouth.

- I didn't forget you, Mister Calvin. Give me one minute.

I point one finger, scratch his head, and stick mine through the doorway. Bastard placidly preens himself on his highest perch, a sign he's happy to be left alone.

Fuck you very much.

I dash to the bathroom, Calvin's hint striking a chord, and after a quick piss, stand at the sink to wash my hands. Black gym shorts and white T-shirt are neatly folded on top of the wicker basket, sneakers lined up with precision by the wall, triggering a thought that I lose before it takes hold. I stare at my ragged face in the mirror and Valentine Mackenzie stares back.

This is your fault as much as it is mine. We're in this mess together. I could use some input. You're good with stories. Write us out of this one. I'm not asking for happily-ever-after. I know that's not your thing. Just give me an all-for-the-best-in-this-best-of-all-possible-worlds, my Panglossian doppelganger.

Calvin barks me back to reality. My one minute is up. Who says dogs can't tell time?

II. Calvin

pissing pissing pissing pissing / pissing long&long
walking sniffing walking pissing / pissing more&more
sunshine warming grass inviting / rolling rolling rolling
dekker laughing calvin rolling / biting grass barking sky
dekker sitting quiet thinking / willygone long&long
badman waiting hiding waiting / waiting more&more
calvin goodboy calvin ready / two fingers five fingers more
evermore&evermore

III. Dekker

The nurse thing is nothing new for me, of course. Only we didn't call it nursing. The term was *caregiving*. It's not something you learn, something you choose. It's something you do because you have no other choice. The process is so gradual you don't realize when it begins.

You take short breaks during a walk because he is tired, out of breath. You let him lean on you. You continue to the store alone while he sits on a bench with Calvin. You carry the groceries. You suggest more naps. You do all the housework. You sit with him in the studio.

You distract him when he's too weak to mix the paint, stretch a canvas, pick up a brush. You call the taxi and take him to the doctor. You pick up the medicine and make sure he takes it. He forgets and you remind him. He gets angry and you let him. He cries and you console him. You dress him. You feed him. You bathe him. You wipe his brow. You wipe his ass. You wish he was dead. You put him to bed. You put your arms around him. You cannot live without him. You listen to his breathing. You watch him sleeping. You wake before him. You begin again.

Caregiving. Such an insipid word, unworthy of all it contains, but it's what you do. You and so many others like you. You don't know them. But you know your rituals and theirs form a community. A communion of care. You don't feel so alone, not always, as you do what you must do, alone together, together alone. You hold his hand and watch him fade, a whisper of the man you knew, the man you loved, the man you love, will never stop loving.

Jason Dekker loves Willy Hart.

You want to say the words aloud. You need to see the colors once more. With Willy gone, the world has lost its color and all that's left is an endless spectrum of gray.

On the way back to the house, Calvin pauses for the umpteenth time to pee at one of his regular pit stops, raising his leg at a corner signpost by the snack bar.

A poster hanging in the window catches my eye, bold-print words in Dutch and English: *VERMIST—MISSING.* On closer inspection I read that a forty-year-old Canadian man on vacation from Vancouver has not been heard from for a couple of weeks. Medium height and weight, light brown hair and eyes, horn-rimmed glasses, curious to experience gay nightlife. That seems an odd detail to include, although perhaps the most telling.

Gay men flock to the so-called Gay Capital, for the bars, the drugs, the sex, the all-in-one-shit-faced-wasted-weekend deal. It was never my scene but it's well known that the amount of fun you have is inversely proportional to the amount you remember. When this guy finally emerges from the alcoholic stupor, the ecstasy trance, the hashish haze, there's bound to be plenty he'll want to forget. I feel sorry for him, maybe because we have something in common. We're both lost in Amsterdam, and no map I know will help us.

Willy's family didn't want us at the funeral, but I read where it would be held in a newspaper obituary. They wouldn't let us in the chapel, but we waited outside and could hear faint strains of the music. I don't know why that seemed important.

After the memorial service, we followed the somber procession to the burial site. No one spoke to me, not even his art world friends who had met me on numerous occasions. I didn't care, didn't have anything to say to them anyway. As the casket was lowered, Calvin started whining softly. I won't say for certain he knew what was happening. It might have been a reaction to the collective sorrow that filled the spring air.

We walked away before the crowd began to disperse. The new grass along the path had not been trimmed. I remembered a Walt Whitman line that Willy quoted at the old cemetery he took me to when we first met.

The beautiful uncut hair of graves.

My gloomy reverie was interrupted when I heard my name, my first name, which always sounded strange. I turned to see one of Willy's brothers hurrying down the path to catch up with me. The same brother who told me in the hospital that his family had barred me from visiting Willy anymore, one week before he died.

He had more bad news. But this time it came as no surprise. There would be no more angry, tearful scenes. I had forty-eight hours to leave Willy's house, our home, and I better not remove anything I couldn't prove was mine, or the police would be called to have me arrested or deported or whatever other humiliation they could think up.

He was, of course, referring to the remaining paintings, particularly those for which I had modeled, the paintings of me. Willy's agent had a record of each and every piece of work and they would all be worth a small fortune now. Any attempt on my part to keep even one would be considered grand larceny. Although Willy and I were legally registered as living together, that was simply for immigration purposes. His death terminated any and all rights I had to remain in his house, or even stay in the country, for that matter.

Fortunately, the jeep was in my name. For the rest I was, as they say, well and truly fucked.

Chapter Seventeen

I. Dekker

- *Waar ben ik?*
- You're at my place. You had a nasty fall.
- *Wie ben jij?*
- I'm Dekker. We met at the park. Remember?
- No. I don't think I do.
- You were exercising, jogging.
- My head hurts.
- Yes, you fell. Bumped it on a bench, pretty hard.
- I fell?
- Um, yeah. You fell.

I'm not sure how much detail to go into at this point. He still seems dazed and confused. At least he's talking. That's an improvement. I guess. Interesting that the first questions he asks are in Dutch, before he switches to English when I answer. Can I assume that means no serious brain damage?

I give him another sip of the water laced with pain relievers. Yesterday I was worried he might never wake up. Now I have a new Pandora's box to contend with. I've come to the conclusion I need to take things one step at a time. I don't have much choice. It's like living on a need-to-know basis.

In the Now, as Zen Dog Master would say.

I've put some chicken soup in a plastic container. I don't know if he's ready to eat anything, but just in case, the classic cure-all is standing by. He whispers something else but I don't quite catch it. I lean in closer.

- Did you say something?

- What's my name?

- Ah, now that's interesting. I was just about to ask you the same question.

He closes his eyes, furrows his brow, and frowns, a look that seems to suggest deep concentration.

I'm suspicious this could all be an act, although it seems unlikely in his current condition. At the very least, he must be suffering from a concussion, which would explain the unconsciousness and the headache, as well as his disorientation. It could even cause some memory loss, if I remember correctly. I'm not certain but will look it up on the computer later. At any rate, it seems improbable that he could be cognizant enough this soon to deliberately fake symptoms. Why would he?

He opens his eyes again, tries to move his arms, and realizes he cannot.

- Why?

- It's better you don't move around too much until we're sure your head is better.

- You're a doctor?

- Um, no. I'm not. I called the doctor and he said this is the best thing to do for now. To keep you still.

To me this sounds like the obvious lie it is, but he appears to accept it without reservation and doesn't continue to struggle. Might be a good idea to try to distract him from thinking about it too much.

- You haven't eaten for a while. Would you like to try some soup?

He nods. I open the container and carefully lift a spoon of the warm broth to his mouth, which he opens wide like a baby bird. Since I gave him the first sips of water, I've placed a pillow under his head to make it easier for him to swallow. I can't tell if he's enjoying the simple meal, but he slurps down a fair number of spoonfuls before indicating he's had enough. He licks his lips, and I dab his chin with a napkin. Under the circumstances, I'm more than a little weirded out by this courteous gesture. Not for the first time, I wonder what the hell I think I'm doing.

- Dekker?

- Yes.

I don't know why but it sounds odd to hear him say my name.

- I don't understand. What happened?

- I told you. You fell.

- No. I mean, I know. You told me. But I don't remember. I don't remember anything. My mind is blank. Nothing there.

- That can happen when you hit your head. Nothing to worry about right now. Give it time. You just need to rest. It'll all come back to you soon.

That's what I'm worried about. How soon would he remember? And how much? I don't have a fucking clue.

- Stay with me, Dekker?

- I'm not going anywhere. Try to sleep.

He heaves a sigh of exhaustion and closes his eyes as a tear rolls down his cheek. I have to admit, that's more disconcerting to me than anything. In less than a minute he seems to be asleep again, but I sit by his side and watch him. I watch him much more intently and for much longer than necessary, until a voice from my childhood whispers in my ear.

Danger, Will Robinson. Danger.

II. Gadget

Darkness. He reached inside and all was darkness. There was nothing to hold on to, no path to follow, no past to guide him, no future to point toward. It was the strangest sensation, this overwhelming sense of endless gloom in vast uncharted territory. It was not normal. It terrified him.

The man with the gentle face came and went, took care of him. Dekker. An odd name. Or was it?

At least Dekker had a name. When he tried to conjure his own name, nothing emerged from the darkness, no trace of identity, no semblance of self. Dekker was kind but he would not tell him his name. Said he would remember.

Why not help him remember? If he was a friend, Dekker should help him to remember, help him out of the darkness.

Sometimes he felt another presence, lurking in the shadows behind him, watching him, saying nothing, never revealing who it was, what it was. He could hear soft breathing, a jingling of keys, faint footsteps fading away, gone. And there was a second voice, not Dekker, another man, who sometimes shouted from below, shouted curses. Cursing him? He didn't know. When Dekker came, he never remembered to ask.

What did it matter? Dekker would not tell him. He would remember. That was what Dekker kept saying.

When, Dekker? When will the darkness depart?

III. CALVIN

upstairs walking soft / watching badman sleep
silent watching / evermore

IV. DEKKER

I cannot leave him lying up there on the mattress indefinitely, hands and feet cuffed, totally dependent on me to provide him with food and water. The head wound is healing, the pain relievers seem to be working, and he is conscious for longer periods of time now, asking more and more questions I don't know how to answer. One question more frequent and more troubling than the rest.

Who am I?

I've done some research on the Web. I found a list of circumstances and symptoms that signal calling an ambulance immediately. No big surprise that my patient fit the bill to a T. I figured that much out already. Apparently, short-term memory loss is common after a head trauma that results in a severe concussion. So is something called perseverating, or repeating the same question over and over again, despite being told the answer. Check and check again. Both these things fall under the heading of anterograde amnesia, a term I didn't know. I had heard of retrograde amnesia, the kind where you forget everything you ever knew before the trauma. This is more rare, but how long it might last depends on the severity of the injury. Well, obviously. But not particularly helpful. Just to confuse matters more, there are a bunch of variations that include both types to lesser or greater degrees.

In the words of my Parrot Master, *Fuck me*.

I'm still not convinced he remembers nothing. I understand him drawing a blank on the events leading up to his headfirst dive into the bench, although I'm the one who should be suffering post-traumatic stress. He was the one throttling me, and I was closer to blacking out than I care to think about.

I know what it's like to wake up after a night of heavy drinking on an empty stomach with no memory of the hours before last call, none whatsoever, no matter how hard you try to recall some detail that might bring the whole sordid evening back. But to have no memory of who you are, what you do, where you live? For the slate to be wiped clean of your entire past history because you bumped your head? It seems too far-fetched, like something out of a film.

Right. Like the one about the homeless guy whose dog pulls a head out of the pond so he can take over the victim's house and life and end up on a date with the killer. That's so much more plausible, isn't it?

I'm not sure exactly when the pieces of the puzzle fell into place, when I realized our meeting in the park was not accidental, but part of a near-perfectly plotted plan. Nothing else makes sense, and the more I run the scenario, frame by frame, the clearer the story becomes.

For whatever twisted reason, he killed Mac and then set his sights on me, an unexpected loose end to be eliminated. Maybe he saw me and Calvin in the park that morning with the police and had been stalking us ever since. Maybe he intended to retrieve the keys himself and use the attic as his own personal kill site. Maybe he's killed before and will kill again. Maybe he was the latest model in gay serial killers, intent on breaking John Wayne Gacy's record of thirty-three victims. Once my imagination gets going, it's hard to stop. Adding up all the evidence, circumstantial as much of it is, no other conclusion makes sense.

For fuck's sake, Calvin figured it out before I did.

So now I've got a murderer locked up in the attic of his latest victim's canal-house, which I've broken into and claimed as my own. I don't have the foggiest notion what to do, other than take care of him until he recovers from his amnesia, remembers who he is, where he is, and what he intended to do to me. But what if he never regains his memory? Somehow that's more unsettling. How could I explain to him who he was and why he was here? Why would I even think of doing that? But I have to tell him something, some kind of reasonable explanation.

I don't know how long I've been standing here in the bedroom, holding the pair of sweatpants I pulled out of my only suitcase. Willy's sweatpants. When I took them, I knew they wouldn't be missed. But I could never bring myself to wear them. He and Willy were about the same height, and I felt uncomfortable about him lying under a sheet practically naked. I grab one of Mac's T-shirts as well and take the clothes upstairs.

Calvin lies in the doorway of the attic, as if guarding the prisoner. He looks at me, I motion him to come, and point down the stairs. He gets up silently, but for the soft jangling of his dog tags, and looks back into the room before reluctantly, but obediently, slinking past me.

Just call if you need me.

It's not wise to risk another close encounter between them, not yet anyway. Amnesia or not, Calvin is a thousand times less likely to ever trust this psycho again than I might be. Dogs are smarter that way.

Chapter Eighteen

I. Dekker

- Willy.
- Willy?
- Your name is Willy.
- Willy. Willy. Willy.

He lets the name roll off his tongue, tests it, tastes it, savors it, perhaps hoping it will arouse his sleeping memory. I cannot tell what he's thinking, but I feel an instantaneous pang of guilt. He asked, I opened my mouth, and it slipped out, involuntarily.

Once said aloud, I could not take it back.

He appeared to be asleep when I came in with the clothes. I took the little key from the drawer where I stowed it, knelt by his feet, and delicately unlocked the cuffs that bound his ankles, holding my breath, trying to avoid touching him. He remained motionless even as I gently drew the sheet off his body. The robe was bunched on either side of him, like the folded black wings of a fallen angel, exposing his white skin, dark nipples, and black hair trailing from navel to the curly nest, which cradled the considerable length and girth of his flaccid uncut penis. He was undeniably one of the most striking young men I had ever seen, and I found it difficult to pull my eyes away.

I gathered together the soft material of each sweatpants leg so I could slip his feet through them as easily as possible, first one, then the other, and carefully pulled the elastic waistband up his calves. I stopped when I got to his knees, raised them slightly, and continued to pull until I reached his ass. The back of my left thumb brushed against his cock, which quivered, swelling slightly. Although I feared it might wake him, I quickly gave the pants a final tug under his well-shaped bottom and into place around his trim waist.

I stood as he moaned softly, stretched, slightly turned his body toward the wall with bent knees. He didn't seem to wake but looked a little more comfortable. On the other hand, sweat dripped off my face, more from tension than heat. I decided to leave well enough alone and skip the T-shirt I'd brought up for him.

I returned downstairs and found Calvin again waiting by the bottom step. He'd become quite the guard dog during this ordeal, not usually a function suited to retrievers. But role-play had taken on a whole new dimension for both of us.

II. Gadget

He didn't open his eyes when he heard Dekker enter. Not when Dekker opened the drawer, and not when Dekker uncuffed his ankles. Not when Dekker lifted the sheet, and not when Dekker pulled the comfortable sweatpants up his legs. He could not keep still when he sensed the stirring in his loins, a whisper of desire. He felt the need to turn away, hide his arousal. He didn't understand why he reacted that way.

Something had changed, a tenderness broached, a suggestion of intimacy. He did not know what it meant, but it was not to be trusted. Something did not feel right about any of this.

The darkness still loomed beneath the surface and questions remained unanswered.

Where am I? Why am I here? Who am I? What is my name?

III. Dekker

- Willy.
- Yes. Your name is Willy.

- You knew.

- Yes. I knew.

- Why wouldn't you tell me?

- I thought it was part of the game.

- Game?

- Yes. We were playing a game.

- I don't understand.

- We were doing this role-playing thing. It's what we do up here, in the attic. Play sex games. It got out of hand.

I'm not surprised he looks confused. I'm confused. I didn't think this through enough. The idea was to come up with a story that supported undeniable elements, like the fact we were here together in a sex dungeon. And circumvent anything dangerously close to pivotal details, like the fact he tried to murder me. That's also the main reason to keep him from seeing Calvin again too soon. And yet less than five minutes into this perverse version of show-and-tell, I've given him the name of my dead lover and told him we were cavorting in a kinky sex scene that got out of hand.

Really, Dekker? That's what you come up with?

- You see the leather sling hanging in the corner? You, um, lost your balance and slammed your head into the bench. Right there. It was an accident.

- We were having sex?

- Well, leading up to having. Yes, sex.

An odd expression appears on his face. He smiles, almost winks.

- Am I your boyfriend?

What the fuck. Just go with it.

- Yes. You're my boyfriend.

I take the kind of deep breath one would before a bungee jump, lean toward him, and discover what it might be like to kiss an angel of death.

IV. Valentine

A romantic kiss on the red carpet in front of Grauman's Chinese Theatre was what the photographers wanted for a premiere, and Valentino was not about to disappoint them. He did not remember the name of the wannabe starlet his agent had arranged to accompany him but they were all the same, as lovely as they were cloying, disposable, never to be seen again. He pulled her into his arms, bent her skinny frame impossibly backward, and made a mess of her lipstick. That would teach the little vixen.

He was not *the* Valentino, of course, the one for whom women wept a few years back when his untimely death was announced. Not so untimely, Valentino thought with a wicked grin. Loverboy would never have survived the talkies. Valentino was every bit as dashing, wore his hair in the same Vaselino style, and the new and improved Valentino had a sexy baritone voice that would make them forget his silent namesake. They did have one other thing in common, though, Valentino and Valentino. The public might have seen them both parade a bevy of beauties in front of the cameras, but behind the scenes they both preferred to dip their wicks in rougher masculine trade.

Valentino was impatient for the gala rituals to end so the real festivities could begin. A new club was opening later that night, which promised a chorus line of boys, dancing nancies high on music-hall adrenaline and eager to please a film star. Valentino had secured a private room on the premises, stocked with champagne to get the party going.

He fidgeted through the film, dumped the debutante, and hightailed it to the nightclub where a bevy of beauties awaited him. Valentino was granted the pick of the litter, as always.

He didn't want to appear greedy, so he chose only two, one fair and one dark, tasty vanilla and chocolate treats. He liked to take his time, tease them, ply them with bubbly, encourage them to kiss each other, compete for his attention. Who has the softest mouth? Tweedledum or Tweedledee? Who can undress the fastest? Who has the biggest, the longest, the hardest?

No contest. Valentino had the dick of death, as it was known. The boys gawked with fearful amazement when he finally allowed them to reveal it in all its glorious magnificence. He let them lick it like a luscious lollipop. First one, then the other, and all together now. His slide-tromboner was too big for all but the most experienced mouths to play.

Valentino bent the nubile twosome over the table side by side, naked bottoms quivering in anticipation. He tweedled them at the same time with the long probing fingers of each hand, tested their tightness, tasted their warmth, lubricating them with his pointed serpent's tongue. When they were ready, when he was ready, ready or not, here he comes, tweedling Dee and tweedling Dum, tweedling deeper with every thrust. Tweedledum and Tweedledee cried out in pain, cried out in pleasure, and when Valentino finished inside each of them, he would not, could not choose a winner. Valentino loved opening nights!

CHAPTER NINETEEN

I. DEKKER

Psychologists say our minds are trained to resist randomness. We search for meaning, even where none exists. Maybe so. I guess those are the people who shrug and say *everything happens for a reason.* Then spend the rest of their lives trying to find that ever-elusive purpose for which everything happens. I don't buy it. I'm not claiming to be smarter than the experts who have it all figured out. I'm not even claiming to be smarter than the huddled masses yearning to breathe free. I'm not claiming to know anything, really, except for one thing. Shit happens.

Willy is asleep. It isn't easy for me to say his name, the name I stole for him, because that's what it feels like. I stole Willy's name, just like I stole Mac's house, Mac's life. He still sleeps a lot but when he wakes up, I sit with him, talk to him, feed him more stories about his life, our life together, in our house, our garden, our bedroom, our bed.

I could not leave him cuffed to the mattress upstairs, not after what happened when I kissed him and he kissed me back. For most gay men kissing is no big deal, a tactic, a form of flirtation, a foreplay maneuver, nothing more than a means to an end. I know that. I've seen it a million times. Hell, I've done it myself. So no matter how many times I run it through my head, I can't figure out what happened up there.

I said he was my boyfriend. I thought what I needed to do was prove it to him, make him believe it. I had to keep him from remembering anything else. The only way I could think to do that was to kiss him, and hold him, and whisper his name in his ear.

Willy. Willy. Willy. I missed you, but you're back, you're here, here with me, safe with me.

It didn't occur to me that at the same time I was trying to convince him, I was beginning to convince myself. Shit happens.

One big problem needs to be sorted out. More than one, if I'm honest. But one very determined obstacle that I have no idea how to overcome. Calvin is having none of it, and there seems to be nothing I can do to convince him otherwise.

When I first brought Willy downstairs, Calvin was clearly upset, growling, pacing, whining, and even barking, something he rarely does inside, except when Bastard mimics the doorbell. I had to put him outdoors in the garden with Blue Bear, tell him to chill. Later, with Willy resting in the bedroom, I closed the hall doors and let Calvin back in. He made an exaggerated show of drinking of water.

I could've died of thirst out there for all you care.

He jumped up on me, paws on my chest, and growled in my face, nose to angry nose. I tried to get him to cuddle with me on the sofa so I could talk him down, but he refused, instead sitting next to his new best friend's cage.

Bastard knows. Why not Dekker?

The situation didn't improve when I banned him from the bedroom. Calvin doesn't actually like sleeping with me, but his routine never wavers: climb into bed when I do, move to the floor once I'm asleep, and return to the bed in the morning so he's there when I wake up. The first night, to avoid the issue completely, I slept on the couch. The next morning, Willy was upset and asked me why I hadn't come to bed with him. I told him I slept on the couch with Calvin because he'd been sick. He asked me who Calvin was, and I had to invent more of our story.

I don't want to think about what will happen if Calvin hears me call him Willy.

II. Gadget/Willy

Calvin is a beauty but the dog doesn't like him. Dekker explained how he rescued him from a shelter before they met. The poor animal had been terribly mistreated. It took Dekker a long time and a lot of patience to nurse Calvin back to health, but he still has serious trust issues. Willy understood. Dekker was doing the same for him.

Although he was beginning to feel a degree of trust, it wasn't easy. Doubts kept creeping in from the darkness, taunting him, scaring him, no matter how hard he tried to shut them out. This made him want to be friends with Calvin all the more. But the dog would not approach Willy, watched him from a distance like a hawk eyeballing its prey. He growled if Willy even thought of petting him, as if he had some canine mind-reading superpower.

Dekker said Calvin would come around eventually. Willy was acting different than before the accident, that was why Calvin was behaving this way. Willy hoped so. He loved dogs. Dekker said it was one of the things that brought them together. Willy wished he could remember, but his whole life before the fall remained an empty black hole, no matter how much Dekker attempted to fill in the blanks.

At least the persistent headache wasn't as severe, and he could stand up without getting dizzy. Dekker didn't have to accompany him to the bathroom anymore. That had been embarrassing. But Dekker joked it was nothing he hadn't seen before. Dekker made a lot of jokes. Willy liked that about him. Though sometimes he sensed sadness or uneasiness beneath the laughter. He wasn't sure which. Maybe both.

That's what bothered Willy more than anything else. His brain seemed to function normally except for the memory part. He watched an episode of a television series with Dekker. He understood everything happening, but he didn't remember ever seeing it before. He asked Dekker to bring him a newspaper. He read it with no problem once the words came into focus, but there was no background to the stories. His thoughts could switch back and forth between Dutch and English. He was Dutch. Somehow he knew that. But when did he learn English? What school? Where? Did he have a family? Who were they? Did they miss him? So many questions crowded his head and Dekker didn't know all the answers.

Willy got so frustrated he wanted to scream or smash his fist through a wall, that's what he really wanted to do. He wondered why he didn't.

III. Calvin

grumpycalvin walking grumping
dekker walking slow stopping turning
    - Look, Calvin.
bigbird standing calvin running calvin barking
bigbird flapping faster flying / byebye bigbird
lookit dekker barking bigbird barking badman
byebye bigbird / byebye badman / same&same / more&more

IV. Dekker

I light another cigarette as we walk along the canal after our visit to the pet food shop.

Calvin store.

He drops the sack of his favorite bacon-flavored treats, secure in the knowledge I'll carry it the rest of the way home. He has picked up Sela's scent, is tracking her. I see her way ahead of us, too distant for Calvin to actively pursue. The distraction is good for him. He's more relaxed here than in the house, where he stays as far from Willy as possible, while still keeping a guarded eye on him.

I'm exhausted. I awoke in the middle of the night from the worst nightmare ever and I didn't want to risk falling back to sleep and have the dream pick up where it left off, as often happens to me. I no longer remember the details leading up to it, but the final image is seared into my brain.

Calvin barking frantically, locked inside Jax, engine running. The plastic hose snaked along the side, one end attached to the exhaust pipe and the other filling the jeep with fumes through the cracked open driver's side window. I screamed his name, desperate to reach him, but was held back by the strong grip of arms wrapped around my body. I couldn't see who, but I knew their voices.

It's better this way.

Whispers in one ear, then the other.

I need him with me.

Both of them whispering at the same time, Willy past and Willy present, drowning out my screams.

Let him come. Let him go.

I'm so engrossed in my futile attempt to wipe the bad memory away that I almost miss it. A new flyer in the snack bar window, next to the *Missing* poster. This one is more official, printed by the police. Two pictures. One is a photo of the smiling Canadian. The other is a sketch artist's rendering, a person of interest sought for questioning. I recognize the face immediately. Shit happens.

Chapter Twenty

I. Dekker

- I was thinking of Arles.

- Arles?

- In the south of France. We always wanted to go there.

- We did?

I did. I point it out on the map I'd taken from the glove compartment of the Volkswagen, now spread over the garden table.

- It's where the artist Vincent van Gogh spent his last months, painted with his friend Gauguin in the little yellow house.

He looks at me with a blank expression. He has no idea what I'm talking about. Why should he? He's probably like Calvin, doesn't care where we go as long as he gets to ride in the front seat with his head hanging out the window, feeling the wind in his face. What I don't tell him is that van Gogh went crazy there. I figure it's as good a place as any for me to go insane, dragging my psychopathic amnesiac reincarnated boyfriend along for company.

When it comes to the fight-or-flight response to a bad situation, I always prefer the flight option. One of my heroes as a kid was Harry Houdini, the ultimate escape artist. I used to dream up a million ways to escape from the farm. I would tunnel my way to China, or be kidnapped by a band of gypsies, or my all-time favorite, run away with the circus and join the Great Wallendas' high-wire act. Come to think of it, this isn't all that different or any less dangerous.

- It looks far.

- Maybe a couple of days to drive. Through the mountains or the wine valleys, down to the coast. It'll be beautiful.

I'm not sure he's well enough to travel. Yesterday I took him outside for a short walk with Calvin, who responded with a look of disdain.

Really, Dekker? Has it come to this?

But it'll be risky to try another walk with his face plastered in windows around the neighborhood, probably all over the city. Forget about going out to a bar or café. I've no idea where he might have picked up an unsuspecting tourist looking for a fun time, a Canadian who ended up God knows where. No, it's better to get out of town for a while until the whole manhunt thing dies down. At least until I have a chance to figure out a better solution to our rather complicated little problems. I'll keep him inside for a few more days, then we'll take the smooth-driving Volkswagen and escape south, south of the border with our dog and parrot sidekicks. A Butch and Sundance double act.

II. Gadget/Willy

There it was again. Dekker was smiling but he looked sad. Willy wished there was something he could do, something he could say, but he didn't know what.

Dekker said a road trip would do them both good, take their minds off all the stress of the past days. Dekker said maybe a long relaxing drive would help bring his memory back.

Willy hoped this was true, but he wasn't going to count on it. Something about the idea didn't feel right. It didn't feel wrong but it didn't feel right.

Willy wanted to trust Dekker, needed to trust him. He didn't have anyone else. Did he? He couldn't be sure. That painter's name sounded familiar. Vincent van Gogh. Maybe he'd read about him. He remembered some book-learned things but it wasn't the same as remembering. There was a hazy but unquestionable line between learning and memory, and he couldn't make himself cross over the border. Trying to look inside his head was like trying to see through a prison wall. No, more like banging his head against a prison wall. Because that's what he felt like doing right now, banging his head hard against a wall, banging it until he shook his memory loose, banging it into a bloody pulp. For a second he saw the image of a bleeding ear. What was that? A flash of a memory? Something he'd done? Something done to him? Something he'd read?

Some crows were making a racket in the garden.

A murder of crows.

And the thought was gone.

Chapter Twenty-one

I. Dekker

Once again I made a snap decision without thinking it through.

Road trip through France. Great! Let's jump in the car and go.

And what are we going to do about money? Accommodations for a dog, and let's not forget the parrot. And there's the question of wardrobe. My own, limited as it is, won't be a perfect fit for my newly imagined boyfriend, nor anything in Mac's closet. How am I going to explain that? A couple of tight-fitting T-shirts might pass unnoticed, but he can't spend however long we're away switching between a pair of running shorts and Willy's old sweatpants.

The funding issue is a no-brainer. Except for the fact I'm breaking the law. Again. Theft, illegal use of a dead man's bank card, whatever that's called, in addition to the previous infractions of withholding information from the police, impeding a murder investigation, breaking and entering, knowingly harboring a criminal, one who tried to strangle me. Let's not forget that. So what if I'm about to add grand theft auto to the list?

I take Mac's PIN pass from his desk and grab Calvin's leash. He's already waiting by the door. We head to a cash machine, and I take out as much as his daily limit will allow. I've memorized the PIN code I found with his list of passwords.

That's why you aren't supposed to keep them all in one place, Mac, but thanks for making it easy.

I rejected the option of transferring money directly from his account into mine. I don't want to establish any traceable links. If the entire house of cards comes crashing down, so be it. But my instinct tells me to stay off the grid.

We go to a small secondhand shop just across from the tram stop. It's called Karma, something I'm using up fast and furious, if I had any positive energy in my spiritual account to begin with. Calvin waits on the sidewalk as I sift through the meager collection of mismatched menswear and choose a couple of neutral short-sleeve shirts, a long-sleeved faded flannel work shirt, an extra-large sweatshirt, a pair of slightly frayed blue jeans, khaki carpenter pants with plenty of pockets, and a pair of baggy summer shorts. I also pick up a pair of comfortable-looking leather sandals and an inexpensive, but not too worn, black denim jacket. Socks and underwear from Mac's drawers will fit him well enough. It's not an extensive wardrobe but it'll have to do. The old British hippie behind the counter gives me a decent price on the lot without comment, even though everything appears a couple sizes too large for me.

Before heading back to the house, I stop in an all-purpose hardware store and buy a plastic laundry basket. Calvin wants to carry this home, however awkward it proves to be. He does admirably for a few blocks, but tires of the challenge by the time we reach the canal, dropping it abruptly for me to pick up. I pull the clothes I just bought out of the plastic bag and chuck them haphazardly into the basket.

He'd been asleep when I left, still slept a lot. But when we get back he's standing at the kitchen sink staring out the window into the garden.

- You forgot to pick up your laundry.

- What?

He turns around, startled, as I set the basket on the dining table.

- Your clothes? You must've put them in a dryer, come home, and never went back to pick them up. We were walking by the launderette and the old Indonesian man who runs it came out, yelling at me. He said he was about to get rid of them. Good thing he saw us, or you wouldn't have much to wear in France.

I don't know how I think up these ludicrous scenarios, but I'm getting used to them just popping into my head and running with them. He walks cautiously toward the basket, as if it might contain a nest of snakes, slowly lifts the items of clothing out, one by one, and examines them carefully. He holds a shirt against his chest, sets it down, and does the same with another. I almost hold my breath, wondering if he'll accept this fabrication, as he has all the others I've fed him.

He takes out the jeans, inspects them back and front, then slips off Willy's sweatpants and pulls them on. I guess there's no need to worry about underwear. The fit is a bit snug, but they look good that way. Damn good. He strips off his T-shirt and exchanges it for one of the lightweight short-sleeve models. He adds the sandals to his new ensemble and checks himself out in the full-length bedroom mirror.

Everything fits, and it dawns on me this is the first time I've seen him dressed in everyday street clothes. He reminds me of someone but I can't quite place who. Not Willy, it's not his style at all. Then it hits me. I've unconsciously chosen the calculatedly casual look of my college friends, not that I had much to choose from. He looks younger, cleaner cut, even with his mop of black curls. He turns toward me, lower lip quivering, eyes on the verge of tears.

- I forgot.

- Yeah. You forgot. It's no big deal. There's a lot more important stuff you don't remember than the laundry. Forget it.

- No. I mean, I forgot what I looked like, what I used to wear, what I like to wear. Is this me? It feels strange. Like I'm wearing someone else's clothes. Are these mine? Did I buy them?

- Of course they're yours. Who else's? You've just gotten a little too comfortable in those sweats.

I try to laugh it off, put him at ease, and then I realize that's not what he needs. He needs reassurance, acceptance. He needs his boyfriend to compliment him. Willy needs Dekker to tell him how great he looks, how sexy, how all eyes will be on him tonight, his opening night. Yes. In a sense, this is his opening night, his debut, his reawakening to the land of the living. Perhaps he feels this because his whole body begins to tremble, a tear runs down his face. I take him in my arms, hold him tight, and whisper into his ear.

- You look fabulous, kid. You do. This is exactly how you like to dress. This is what you were wearing the night we met. It's you, all you. Soon you'll remember. It'll all come flooding back like high tide on the beach. All the memories we've had. In the meantime, tomorrow we'll drive off and start making new ones. Trust me. Trust me. We're fine. We're gonna be just fine.

Of course, we're not fine. We are anything but fine. We're fucking light-years from fine. But for a moment, just a moment, holding him in my arms, cheek to tearstained cheek, I almost start to believe, believe it could be true.

II. Gadget/Willy

He can't sleep. Something is bothering him, something simple, something stupid, probably nothing but still something. The clothes. The clothes he forgot. Left in the launderette. Not the clothes exactly. Washing the clothes. His clothes. Only his clothes. He asked Dekker about it. Why did he only wash his own clothes? Why not Dekker's clothes, too? Dekker said he liked to wash his clothes separately because they were all black. He liked to use special detergent for only black clothes. It made sense but it didn't make sense. Did it?

There was something else about the clothes. What was that story about the king who always wanted new clothes, better clothes, the best clothes? A tailor promised to make him the most magnificent new clothes, but they were invisible. When the king put the invisible clothes on, everyone said how wonderful he looked in his new clothes. But secretly they all laughed at the king because there was no such thing as invisible clothes. The king was naked and everyone knew except the king. That was how he felt when Dekker looked at him in his new clothes, the clothes he forgot at the launderette. Dekker looked at him like he was naked, and that's how he felt. Naked.

Trust me. Trust me.

He wanted to trust Dekker, but Dekker was keeping secrets. He was certain. That's why he felt naked. Or maybe he was imagining it because he was naked now, naked in bed, naked with Dekker, naked together. Maybe there were no secrets between them after all. Nothing between them. Naked.

The white dog was lying in the doorway, head resting on the floor between his paws, not sleeping, watching. Watching him. Always watching him. The dog didn't trust him. He didn't trust Dekker. Something was going on, something he couldn't quite work out, but something, not nothing. If there was a secret, the dog knew. But the dog wasn't talking. The dog wasn't sleeping. He and the dog remained that way for a long time. Watching.

CHAPTER TWENTY-TWO

I. CALVIN

calvin sulking backseat riding / bastard talking soft&low
dekker driving badman laughing / windows open no&no
no wind blowing no smells scenting / new car
    smelling clean&bad
missing jax&willygone / bluebear waiting home&home
calvin sulking backseat riding evermore&evermore

II. DEKKER

Saint-Valentin turns out to be pretty much a one-horse town, barely worth the short detour we took to get here. I'd noticed it on the map before we left, almost missed it, wish I had. I got this strange notion the village might be useful for writing a new story, one where the setting could be a variation on Valentine's name instead of one of the characters. I'll be hard-pressed to come up with anything useful.

Next month there will be festivities based on a figure I'm sure they've invented called Saint Amour. February is, of course, when their biggest tourism event occurs, attracting couples from as far away as Japan who wish to marry on the special day dedicated to lovers. Straight couples only, no question about that, and all a total sham, really. The mayor came up with the idea about ten years ago, according the talkative petite French woman in the shop where we bought some delicious fresh-baked baguettes. St. Valentine never set foot in the village, nor did he die anywhere near it. There isn't even a church named for him. The whole faux celebration seems to be more Hallmark than Holy. Not that I'm a big fan of Holy, but disappointing nonetheless.

❖

We left Amsterdam early, as the light began to dawn and the streets were empty. I'd given Bastard's cage a good cleaning after determining it would fit neatly in the backseat and could be secured to one of the door handles for minimal jostling. It left plenty of space for Calvin but I knew he might not be too keen on being relegated to the rear of the bus, so to speak. I covered his side of the seat with his favorite sheepskin rug, but little good that did. Upon opening the rear door, he gave me a dubious look.

You're kidding, right?

Only after a firm command did he jump in. Without missing a beat, he squeezed himself between the front seats and took up his usual shotgun position.

Isn't there an easier way we could've done this?

It took considerable cajoling, with Bastard adding his obscene two cents' worth, to get Calvin to return to the backseat, where he stuck his head out the window, refusing to give me a second glance.

During this canine drama, The Kid stowed bags and supplies in the back. Calling him Willy still plagued me with guilt, so in my head I thought of him as The Kid, as in Sundance. I avoided calling him anything out loud. He loaded bags of dog food, bird food, water bottles. His clothes, my clothes, shared toiletries. A bag of basic foodstuffs so we wouldn't have to waste time or money in restaurants along the way.

I had moved Jax to what I hoped was a secure enough spot where parking was still free and grabbed my sunglasses from the glove compartment for The Kid. I'd claimed Mac's super-cool Ray-Bans for myself. The maps were in the leather case, routes charted, and we were ready to rock-and-roll. Calvin managed to whimper one last objection before I turned the key in the ignition and the engine roared to life.

The Kid was a surprisingly good navigator, kept close track of each city or village we passed and quickly estimated how long it would take to get to the next. It was almost as if he had traveled the route before, knew it by heart. Either that or he was a bit obsessive-compulsive. He seemed to enjoy the wind blowing in his face and hair almost as much as Calvin, who remained subdued and sulky. The farther we got from Amsterdam, the more I could feel myself relax, tension oozing out of my body in waves, anxiety shedding like Calvin's winter coat in spring.

We decided to stick with the main highway until we bypassed Paris, with only a rest stop or two as needed. I didn't think there would be any problem crossing into Belgium or France, since the European Union had opened the borders. I had brought my passport, just in case, but I didn't mention this to The Kid, didn't want him to be anxious about not having one of his own. It never occurred to him, the amnesia working to my advantage for a change. If it came up, I'd deal with it somehow. We could avoid hotels that ask for identification by sleeping in the car, off the beaten track, solving the dog and parrot dilemma as well. At least to begin with. Play it by ear after that.

One hour after we passed Paris, we arrived in Orléans, where I decided we would stop for lunch. It was early afternoon and the old bridges on the Loire River were bathed in sunshine. This was the city teenaged Joan of Arc helped liberate during the One Hundred Years' War in the fifteenth century, two years before she would be burned at the stake. It was once home to the French royal family whose symbol was the *fleur de Lys,* hence the motto: *It is by this heart that lilies flourish.*

The Kid had found an old guidebook on Mac's bookshelves and read out these historical details, pointed out noted landmarks with glee. It wasn't as difficult to park as I feared. We found a shady spot next to a park near the river, close to the city center, and chose to leave Bastard in the car, his cage covered so he would nap quietly.

Calvin's nose led him along the sidewalks in a near frenzy, with new and exciting scent messages to investigate from unknown canines. The French are particularly enamored of dogs, large or small. Elderly ladies with bejeweled miniature poodles in their laps sat at cafés, indoors or out. Young children laughed and played with scruffy mongrels in city squares. Some old hounds lounged lazily in doorways, and one cheeky bugger begged for treats in front of a butcher shop. I kept Calvin on his leash, although it didn't seem necessary. Many dogs roamed the streets without an owner in tow, or even in sight. They expressed little interest in the Dutch newcomer.

At the end of Rue Jeanne d'Arc stood the majestic Gothic Cathedral Sainte-Croix, where Saint Joan attended mass on her one-night stay in the city. The stained-glass windows depict her story and must be spectacular from inside but I wasn't about to push the limits of the dog-friendly city by attempting to enter with Calvin.

At the other end of the street was a small house, a reconstruction according to the guidebook, where Joan spent the night. The Kid seemed enthralled by everything about the martyred young woman, with a particularly morbid interest in her death. This worried me a little, but I hoped that once we moved on, his fascination would be directed elsewhere. We bought some chocolate croissants, walked back to the Loire, and found a bench along the tree-lined Quai du Châtelet, affording a panoramic view of the river's opposite shore.

- I wonder what it feels like to burn to death.

- Excuse me. It's not something I want to think about while I'm eating.

- It must be incredibly painful. Starting with your feet and gradually moving up your body. I'll bet her hair burst into flame and fried her brain like an egg.

Before I could reply, I caught his mischievous smirk, waiting for me to react. He was teasing me, reveling in my discomfort, actually enjoying himself. For the first time since the accident, he displayed a sense of humor, albeit one with a slightly sadistic bent.

- I'll fry your brain if you don't shut up about freaking Joan of Arc!

- Too late. My brain's already fried. Or have you got amnesia, too?

- Ha ha. Very funny. Let's hit the road, Jack.

- And we won't come back no more, no more, no more, no more.

He started to giggle. I couldn't help joining in, and then we were both laughing, laughing our asses off, laughing so hard our stomachs hurt, laughing all the tension out of our bodies, out of our fried-egg brains.

Calvin watched us with a curious expression, as if we were a couple of raving lunatics.

❖

We spend our first night in the car, on a wooded cul-de-sac just outside Saint-Valentin. We're both exhausted, me from driving most of the day and him from overstimulation. He adjusts his seat, leans back with a pillow against the window, and is lightly snoring almost immediately. In the morning we will continue south and drive along the coast to Arles. I'm looking forward to the famous light van Gogh talked about in his letters, the colors he saw. The cadmium yellow of the sun, dioxin purple of the earth. Will there still be peasants in the wheat fields, carafes of pale viridian absinthe in the cafés? Does the cobalt blue starry night still reflect in the aquamarine water?

I imagine Vincent on a late night like this, writing to his brother, describing his days, illustrating his work, waxing philosophical. Willy gave me a note before his last illness, a note still tucked into my wallet, paper worn ragged from too much handling, words memorized from too much reading. A short paragraph from a letter written to Theo from Arles:

> *Painters, being dead and buried, speak to following generations through their works. Is that all, or is there more, even? In the life of the painter, death may perhaps not be the most difficult thing.*

The sky is awash with countless stars, easier seen in the rich darkness of the countryside. It's something Vincent and I shared, our love of the stars. The stars I see now are the stars he saw a hundred years ago. The world may change but the stars remain the same. Calvin emits a soft growl, but he is only dreaming, like Vincent dreaming his paintings, dreaming his stars.

Chapter Twenty-three

I. Gadget/Willy

Orléans to Châteauroux to Limoges to Toulouse.

Willy liked being in charge of the maps, estimating the distance from one city to another, checking the mileage to see how accurate he was, predicting arrival times, and keeping track of everything in a notebook he found in the glove compartment. He wasn't sure if he had ever done this before, couldn't remember doing it before, but it came so naturally, felt so familiar, he must have done it before. Maybe not this exact route, but some other journey, to some other destination. Maybe with Dekker. He'd ask him later. Sometimes Dekker got flustered or annoyed when he started asking too many questions, but now they were having fun. Dekker liked driving and Willy liked navigating, and everyone was happy.

Everyone except Calvin.

He still couldn't figure out why the dog didn't like him, watched him like a hawk. Every time he turned toward the backseat, Calvin just stared at him. It really got on his nerves.

This morning he asked Dekker if Bastard and Calvin could switch sides. He'd rather look at that crazy parrot than that mean old dog. Willy liked Bastard. The bird was funny, hanging upside down, climbing up the sides of his cage, or swinging on his chain, the whole time swearing his damn fool head off. Bastard would take fruit or peanuts right out of his hand, real gentle. Calvin refused even his favorite bacon-flavor treats when offered. Wouldn't even sniff it if Willy left one on the floor. With the hairy mutt behind him now, he could sit back and enjoy the ride.

Toulouse to Carcassonne to Narbonne to Béziers to Montpellier.

Best of the Gipsy Kings blared from the speakers. He found the CD unopened in their house, and Dekker said to bring it along. The band was originally from Arles, according to the notes in the case. They were real gypsies and their music was upbeat and perfect for a road trip. He didn't know what they were singing about, but he had played it so many times that he was learning the words and could sing along. Dekker pretended to be sick of only listening to the Gipsy Kings, but his hands drummed the steering wheel to the lively tempo, so Willy knew Dekker liked the music, too.

Willy was going to have the best seat for a perfect view as they drove the less-traveled roads along the coast of the Mediterranean Sea. He was looking forward to that. In the guidebook pictures the water was a beautiful turquoise color. It was hard to believe it would be that blue but pictures didn't lie.

That was something else that bothered him. There were no photographs of Dekker and Willy at the house. Didn't most people frame pictures of themselves looking happy together? When they were in Orléans, a couple asked Dekker to take a picture of them with their camera. He asked Dekker if he had a camera, and Dekker said no, he didn't like taking pictures. Dekker liked to remember things in his head. Willy was worried he wouldn't be able to keep memories in his head. Maybe he needed pictures to help him remember everything he had forgotten. He didn't want to think about that now. He wanted to relax and enjoy the scenery. Maybe they could buy a camera when they got to Arles.

Montpellier to Nîmes to Arles.

They should get to their final destination at dinnertime. He hoped they would eat in a restaurant. He was getting tired of croissants and sausage rolls and baguettes with cheese. He was hungry for some real food, a big steak with fried potatoes, and one of those fancy pastries with brightly glazed berries and whipped cream on top for dessert. He was tired of Dekker deciding everything. Which way to go, where to stop, what to eat. He was a lot stronger now and wanted to make some of the decisions. They were a team, weren't they? He had observed other couples discuss what street to walk down, which café to have coffee. He wanted to start pulling his own weight on this trip.

Willy was getting sleepy again. He didn't realize how exhausting it could be sitting in a car and keeping track of the map. It should be easy. He wanted to close his eyes for a few minutes but he didn't want to miss anything. At that very moment, they rounded a bend in the road and the Mediterranean Sea spread out before them like an endless blue carpet, exactly like the pictures.

II. Calvin

scenting salty beachwater more&more&more / wanting
        out wanting out
now dekker now / lookit dekker lookit
        bastard / water&water evermore
stopping wagging happy barking dekker / jumping
        out jumping dekker
        - Hold on, Calvin. Hold on now.
calvin tugging pulling dekker water&water evermore&evermore

III. Dekker

If we hadn't stopped at the first available location with access to the sea, I don't think Calvin would've forgiven me. Ever. He's already pissed for making him switch places in the backseat. Why, I don't quite understand, unless he was still fuming about having The Kid usurp his position in front. He yanks at the leash as if he'd never used it before.

Lemme go, Dekker, lemme go.

True, at the beach in Zandvoort he's accustomed to jumping out of Jax and heading straight for the North Sea, unrestrained. I don't know if there are different rules for dogs here, so I'm not taking any chances.

Deal with it.

This isn't actually a beach anyway, just a roadside rest area to take in the view. It's easy enough to follow a path through the rocks to get to the pebbled shoreline and that's where Calvin leads me. The Kid hangs back by the car, staring out at the water, possibly aware that this stop is all about Calvin. When we're close enough and I don't see any signs with restrictions, don't see any other people around at all, for that matter, I let him off the leash so he can run the last distance alone.

I wave to The Kid to join us. He slowly makes his way down the path.

- Isn't it beautiful?

- Yes.

His voice is low, barely a whisper. He looks pensive, almost sad. It's impossible to know what he's thinking.

- Have I seen it before?

It's the new clothes all over again. What was it Yeats wrote?

I have laid my dreams at your feet. Tread softly, because you tread on my dreams.

- I don't think so. Not that you ever mentioned. Not since we've been together.

This is not a lie but I really have no idea. I take his hand in mine and we watch Calvin splash about in the sea.

- Thank you.

- Um. You're welcome. I think. I'm not sure for what.

- You know. For taking care of me. Being patient with me. Trying to help me. Bringing me here. Being here—seeing this—I'm not sure what I should feel.

- You don't have to feel anything. Just be here.

- With you.

- With me.

He squeezes my hand, tight, as if he were holding on for dear life. Perhaps he is. Maybe we both are.

An odd sensation tickles my stomach. Butterflies. Or not. I could be in bigger trouble than I thought. There's nothing wrong with my memory, I remember this feeling as if it was yesterday, and there is nothing, absolutely nothing I can do to make it stop.

We arrive at Arles in the early evening. The sun is low in the sky and the light is as I always imagined. Amber-tinted, soft, pure, magical. I want to walk in this light, bathe in this light. There will be plenty of time for that.

The Kid must be hungry although he has not mentioned it, has hardly said a word since we stopped by the coast. At lunchtime he said he was getting sick of eating bread for every meal since we left

Amsterdam. We both could use some serious protein. Then we need to find a good place to spend the night before it gets dark. I saw what looked like a campground just outside the city. Maybe someplace near there.

Several bistros with tables outside are open where we could sit with Calvin. I find a parking place on a narrow cobblestone side street. I put some dinner in Calvin's dish and set it down on the sidewalk for him, while The Kid gives Bastard a handful of peanuts and covers his cage. In only a couple of days, we've fallen into this simple routine as if we were a real couple, as if we had shared our lives for years.

- Dekker?

- Yeah?

- The place on the corner looks nice.

- It does. Good choice.

The Kid smiles and looks pleased with himself.

Calvin finishes his dinner, and the three of us walk down the street to the restaurant together.

IV. Gadget/Willy

The menu was in French but Willy discovered he could read French. He discovered he could speak French when the waiter came to take their order. It wasn't perfect, not especially fluent, but enough to be understood. He hadn't realized he could speak French yesterday when they stopped in Orléans. Dekker had been taking the lead, always asking the same question.

Do you speak English?

Willy hadn't been paying that much attention. Had Dekker known he could speak French? Was it another test? To see how much he would remember? When he would remember? Was this the reason for the trip to France? Why it might help his memory?

Questions didn't help. Questions gave him a headache. He didn't want anything to ruin his enjoyment of this delicious meal. The thick rich onion soup topped with a slice of garlic toast and plenty of crispy melted cheese was like nothing he had ever tasted before. He couldn't be sure but he had a feeling French food was a lot better than Dutch food. He wasn't even sure what Dutch food was.

Potatoes. The Dutch are potato eaters. It sounded funny.

- Am I a potato eater?

Dekker looked up from his plate.

- Are you what?

- A potato eater. I got this idea in my head that Dutch people are potato eaters.

- That's an odd way of putting it, but yes, the Dutch like potatoes. You like potatoes. You ordered them with your steak.

- *Pommes de terre frites*. I ordered *pommes de terre frites*.

- Yes. Potatoes. In French.

- Did you know I spoke French?

He hadn't meant to ask that question. It just slipped out and he immediately regretted it. Before Dekker could answer, the waiter returned with their main course.

La plat principal. Mais oui. Entrecôte avec haricot et pommes de terre frites.

He looked at Dekker, raised his glass of excellent chardonnay, and winked.

- *Bon appétit.*

Dekker laughed, raised his own glass, and clinked the two together.

- *Vive la France.*

They both laughed and dug into their delicious French food.

Chapter Twenty-four

I. Dekker

Our arrival in Arles could not have been timed better. The city buzzes with sights and sounds, the Saturday street market in full swing. Apparently it's one of the largest in Europe, nearly two kilometers of stalls that run through the town center's beautiful tree-lined boulevard, selling everything under the sun. Literally.

The Kid had charmed all we needed to know from the smitten waiter last evening, in what sounded to my untrained ear as quite fluent French. What time to arrive, where to park, the best bargains, the tastiest food. They got on so famously I half expected the man to invite us to move in with him. Maybe he would have if his wife had not been keeping a close eye on him from the kitchen. She was equally charmed by Calvin, brought him a bowl of water, scraps of meat, and a juicy marrowbone for the road.

❖

What I thought was a campground outside the city turned out to be a gathering of ramshackle gypsy caravans. Whether a long-term arrangement or just a temporary stopover, I couldn't be certain.

The Kid thought it would be fun to meet real-life Gipsy Kings. With no idea how they might react to strangers appearing in their midst, I told him gypsies could be dangerous. Besides, we were gypsy kings ourselves, packing up at the spur of the moment, looking for adventure on the open road, sleeping in the car. Their presence did seem to indicate that authorities might not bother us if we pulled off somewhere a little farther away.

I gazed up at the starry night, Vincent's starry night, as I smoked a cigarette. A few wispy clouds gently drifted overhead, one wholly contained within the Big Dipper, which slowly poured it back into the galaxy like celestial cream.

As I opened the car door, I saw a shooting star as it streaked across the sky, before the atmosphere extinguished the dying meteor's light. I would have made a wish if I still believed in them.

II. Gadget/Willy

Serrano, Fumée, Soubressade, Figue, Truffe, Noisettes, Royale, de Sanglier, Filet, Chevreuil.

Willy had never seen so many kinds of sausages. The different aromas emanating from all the stalls were intoxicating enough, but these in particular were making his mouth water. Dekker was having a difficult time keeping Calvin under control, even with the leash. Dekker's problem, not his.

Bastard perched calmly on Willy's shoulder, one end of the lightweight chain attached to the bird's leg, his finger slipped through a metal ring at the other end. Dekker said Bastard's wings were clipped, so he couldn't fly anyway. The chain was just an extra precaution. It was Willy who decided to bring Bastard along. The parrot was getting bored locked up in the car under the cover. He'd start plucking his feathers out if he didn't get some action. Willy didn't know how he knew this but he did. If Dekker could carry Bastard around on his shoulder, Willy could, too. They got along fine, unlike some stuck-up animals.

In Orléans, Dekker had gone on and on about how much the French adored dogs, pampered their dogs, gave Calvin so much attention because he was such a beautiful dog. Fuck Calvin. Today Bastard was getting all the attention.

Ah, magnifique! Il parle francais?

When it came to *parlez* Bastard was keeping his dirty beak firmly shut, but he enjoyed being outside having people gawk at him. Willy could tell.

Seafood stands, olive stands, spice stands, honey stands, wine stands, cheese stands, soap stands, lavender stands.

Willy was glad Dekker had decided to stay in Arles for a while. It was better than being cooped up in the house in Amsterdam. They were going to have a blast. There was so much to see here. He'd read the entire section on the city in the guidebook. Besides the market, the restaurants, cafés, and museums, there were ancient Roman ruins, including an arena where they still staged bullfights. There were the places where the artist van Gogh lived and painted and went nuts and killed himself. There was the Rhône River that ran right through the city, the Alpilles Mountains to the north, and the Camargue nature reserve to the south, where you could see pink flamingos. Willy wanted to see everything, do everything. Most of all, he wanted to remember everything.

Peppers, tomatoes, cucumbers, beans, carrots, aubergines, cougettes. Apples, pears, grapes, peaches, nectarines, melons. Strawberries, blueberries, raspberries, blackberries, currants.

The vegetables, fruits, and berries were perfectly laid out, making beautiful color patterns that drew the customers to the stands like flowers attracted bees and butterflies. He wanted to try each and every variety of each and every thing he saw, even the stuff he had never seen or tasted before. When Bastard began to nibble on his ear, Willy got the message. The bird was hungry, too. Bastard liked all kinds of fruits and vegetables, nuts and pasta, and pretty much anything except meat. Some grapes would keep him happy for a while.

Willy was about to ask Dekker for a few francs when he heard the sirens. That's when all hell broke loose.

III. DEKKER

As the police sirens get closer, louder, I force myself to relax my initial panic reaction. No Dutch authorities have tracked me down to the south of France. They don't have the slightest inkling I exist. I am the only one who knows about my opportunistic foray into a life of crime. But something unusual is definitely happening. The market crowd swarms with a chaotic excitement, heads turning, fingers pointing, laughter spreading, and above the growing din of voices and sirens, I hear a familiar voice cutting through the air like a bawdy boomerang.

- Fuck me. Fuck me. Fuck me.

I turn to see Bastard tangled in The Kid's mop of curly hair, furiously flapping his wings, spreading his tail feathers, and screeching frantically between curses. As The Kid tries desperately to disentangle himself from the frenzied bird, Calvin yanks the leash out of my hand and races forward, barking his fool head off.

- Calvin. Stop.

He acts as if he hasn't heard, snarling and nipping at The Kid's ankles. His own alarmed shouts add to the pandemonium as Bastard continues to pollute the sunny afternoon with screamed obscenities.

- Get him off me. Dekker, help.

- Motherfucker. Cocksucker.

- Calvin, stop. Sit.

- Suck it, asswipe.

I can't repress an inappropriate giggle, or maybe not so inappropriate in this case. The large crowd gathering to watch is also laughing. But a terrifying thought surfaces and stifles my amusement. If anything might trigger The Kid's memory of his ill-fated attack in the attic, it would be an incident like this.

I drop to the ground to get a good hold on Calvin's collar, at the same time trying to reach for the leash, when I sense someone beside me.

- I have his line. Help your friend.

A deep, heavily accented male voice. Young and eye-catching, I notice as I scramble to my feet.

The Kid has fallen to his hands and knees. Bastard balances precariously on the back of The Kid's neck, wings flapping and beak gripping hair. I see a trace of terror in his wild eyes as I bring my outstretched hands closer to his body. My aim needs to be precise if I want to avoid being bitten.

- Willy, hold on. Don't move. I've almost got him. Take it easy, Bastard, you crazy motherfucker.

- You're a motherfucker.

- No, you're a motherfucker.

- You're a motherfucker.

- No, you're a motherfucker.

And then I have him. He doesn't struggle, doesn't try to bite me. He looks me straight in the eye and has the last word.

- You're a motherfucker.

The crowd laughs and applauds as a middle-aged woman with a ruddy complexion, wearing a white apron, comes forward and helps extricate Bastard's talons from The Kid's black curls. She says something in French that I don't understand. I apologize with the only French phrase I know.

- *Pardon, je ne parle pas francais.*

- She said the police siren scared him.

The Kid has sheepishly gotten up off the pavement, and runs his hands through his disheveled hair.

- *Merci, Madame.*

He takes her hand in his, brings it to his lips, and kisses it with an air of chivalry. She giggles like a schoolgirl and the crowd gives yet another round of applause, showing their appreciation as if they've been treated to an impromptu street performance. Much to my relief, The Kid is smiling and taking a bow.

- My *Maman* is happy to help. Her *Maman* had such a bird when she was young.

Her son is the young man who took charge of Calvin. She hurries back to what I assume is their fruit and vegetable stall to wait on a customer.

- But I do not believe with such a way of talking.

The smiling Frenchman hands Calvin's leash over to The Kid. Calvin sits as far from him as the leash will allow, shooting me a disapproving look.

- I apologize for our feathered friend's foul language. I hope you and your mother weren't too offended.

- *Maman* likes to pretend she understands no English. I hear worse from the bullfighters at the arena.

He grins mischievously, a twinkle in his dark brown eyes. He has short-cropped hair and wears a black T-shirt that complements his well-defined biceps and dark Mediterranean complexion. He's the type that elicits the question *Gay or European?* The answer is nearly always *European.* Even when they appear to be flirting.

Stop staring, Dekker.

The Kid says something to him in French, and they both laugh.

I'm convinced they're having a joke at my expense, or maybe I'm just being paranoid.

- I must get back to work. I'm Sebastian, by the way.

- I'm Dekker. This is Willy. You met Calvin and Bastard.

He and Willy shake hands as I deposit the now-calm bird on my shoulder.

- The least we can do to thank you for your help is buy some of your mother's beautiful fruit.

- That will please her. She's very proud of our produce.

Again, The Kid makes a comment in French and Sebastian laughs before returning to the fruit and vegetable stand. There's definitely a flirtatious element to this exchange and I'm surprised by a slight stab of jealousy. To whom it might be directed I'm not sure. Our first morning and already this trip is not going the way I expected. What did I expect? I have no idea.

IV. GADGET/WILLY

- What did you say to him?

- I told him he was his mother's best product.

- That's pretty lame.

- Hmm. It sounded better in French.

Dekker shook his head and walked over to Sebastian's stand. Willy could tell Dekker didn't like it when he spoke French. He didn't like not being able to understand. He didn't like being left out. He didn't like feeling the way Willy felt since the accident, since he woke up with no memory.

He wasn't sure why but he liked speaking French so Dekker couldn't understand. He liked speaking French to Sebastian so Dekker couldn't understand. Even if it felt a little mean. Because it felt a little mean. Maybe he was just teasing Dekker. It was confusing. Better not to think about it. In fact, he continued talking to Sebastian in French while Dekker was busy choosing fruit with *Maman.*

Sebastian told Willy they lived on a farm about a fifteen-minute drive outside Arles. They grew almost all the food they sold on their stand here, and they had their own roadside stand at the farm. There were fields of vegetables, fruit orchards, and all kinds of berry patches.

He invited them to come out for a visit during their stay. Willy told him that would be great and Sebastian asked where they were staying so he could give them directions.

Willy wasn't sure what to say about that. Dekker was busy counting out francs with *Maman*. Willy didn't need to ask Dekker what to say anyway. He told Sebastian the truth, told him they'd been sleeping in the car, told him they didn't have a place to stay, told him they were worried about finding a hotel that would allow Calvin and Bastard in the room with them. Maybe they would just look around today and drive straight back to Amsterdam.

Willy knew the last part was not exactly the truth. As they were talking he'd been watching Sebastian's face carefully, and an idea began to sneak into his mind. Sebastian was already shaking his head.

- *Non. Non. Un moment.*

Maman was putting the money Dekker had given her into a box. Sebastian walked over to her and spoke in a soft voice so Willy couldn't hear. But he knew exactly what was being discussed.

Dekker came back with two bags full of fruit, Bastard on his shoulder.

- All set to go?

Willy smiled. They were more than all set to go. Sebastian was working his charm on his reluctant *Maman*. Dekker didn't know it yet, but Willy had arranged excellent accommodations for the rest of their stay in Arles.

CHAPTER TWENTY-FIVE

I. CALVIN

running chasing this&that way
twotails wagging circling back
chasing gigi chasing mimi / stopping barking running jumping
mimi gigi / sweet air scenting / more&more&evermore
gigi resting mimi joining / calvin watching joining resting
big tree shading / alldogs panting / evermore&evermore

II. DEKKER

Calvin gets a real workout with his new playmates, two black Labs. They lie together in the shade of a palm tree, Calvin nestling between the black beauties, one big breathing Oreo cookie. His usual ambivalence toward other dogs never surfaced when the young and enthusiastic French showgirls Gigi and Mimi greeted him. It was all sniffing and licking, pawing and necking, love at first sight from all sides, an indisputable canine ménage a trois.

Maybe it's something in the air. The rich earthiness of the vegetable fields and the fresh fruitiness of the orchards mix with the faintest sweet scent of lavender. An intoxicating combination, so unlike my grandparents' farm, or any other farm I can remember, for that matter. Calvin isn't the only one affected by it.

I sit in the front courtyard of the farmhouse with a cup of Madame

Clement's strong coffee and look up at the open window of the attic, or *la mansarde*. The Kid still slept soundly when I slipped out with Calvin early this morning. Not surprising, considering the night we had, another one of yesterday's unexpected turn of events.

Sebastian told us to bring the car around to the street behind the stand when the market was closing down at about one o'clock, and we could follow him to the farm. The Kid remained tight-lipped about what had been discussed between him and Sebastian, or between the French farmer and his *Maman*. He only said he had arranged a surprise for us. Something about his smug expression hinted that whatever he had up his sleeve, it was more than an afternoon ride through the countryside.

I waited with the Volkswagen while The Kid helped Sebastian load the unsold produce into his white van. Their logo was painted in green on both side panels, the name Clement above a bushy fruit tree, with the words *La Ferme Le Verger* underneath. When they'd finished, Sebastian maneuvered his vehicle easily out of the tight spot as The Kid jumped into the car.

- This will be great.

- What'll be great?

- You'll see.

Maddening as it was to be kept in the dark, I pulled behind the van and together we headed out of Arles.

The landscape as we drove north was somewhat more rugged than we'd seen arriving from the south. In the distance, the rocky Alpilles provided an entirely different backdrop than the coastal scenery we'd traveled through only the day before. Living in Amsterdam so many years, I'd forgotten how much the natural setting could change in such short distances. The Netherlands was as flat as its stodgy pancakes, the same from one end of the boring countryside to the other.

Willy and I had often talked about going to France, Italy, or Greece. But we'd never traveled anywhere together. Money was no object. His paintings went for thousands of guilders each and he sold a lot. Maybe not internationally, but he was unquestionably the most popular living Dutch artist. I hadn't thought much about it, but maybe he felt he didn't have time left to waste on something as frivolous as sightseeing. Maybe he felt ever-increasing pressure to produce a certain body of work, work that would leave a mark on the art world, a legacy worthy of the fame he had achieved. He once commented that van Gogh never sold a painting in his life but now a museum was devoted to his work and his paintings sold for millions, desired by every collector in the world. Would a Willy Hart hang any place other than a bank or a boardroom?

I had learned at those moments not to try to console him with banal flattery or praise. Commercial success had been just as devastating for him as financial failure had been for van Gogh.

I was about to banish such thoughts from my mind when one of the artist's paintings appeared before my eyes, in real life. I'd seen the original on a trip to Washington, even bought a poster of it for my room. Vincent van Gogh painted *Farmhouse in Provence* in 1888, not long after arriving in Arles, two years before his death. His sister-in-law sold the painting less than four months after he was gone.

❖

Up close the seventeenth-century stone farmhouse, or *mas*, looked no less like the artist's version. The stonework walls were lighter and cleaner; the green doors, shutters, and trim brighter, the contrast more distinct, and there was certainly no swimming pool in the *jardin* behind the house. This was a recent addition by Sebastian, over Madame Clement's strong but futile objections. She clearly loved her only son, and I imagine he often used that to his advantage. I should be grateful. It's surely how he charmed her into inviting two strangers to stay in their home. Although Bastard and Calvin may have given his argument some decided support.

The house had been added to over the years, centuries, giving the whole structure a unique if slightly slipshod appearance. The oldest part was a large two-story shoebox-shaped building, originally housing livestock on the ground level, with living accommodations above. After the animals had been removed to outbuildings and stables, a kitchen was added to the front half of one side, with a high lean-to roof. Later still, another extension from the rear of the main structure probably served as living quarters for servants and was now Madame Clement's bedroom. The newest section was an almost self-contained two-story annex built off the rear half of the original farmhouse, on the opposite side from the kitchen. Sebastian lived there in the ground floor's open-plan studio space. The second floor housed a well-equipped modern gym, and above that, under the steeply peaked roof, was the spacious unfinished attic. More than habitable enough for two men, a dog, and a parrot.

Upon our arrival, Madame Clement scurried to the kitchen to let the cook know there would be two more mouths to feed for lunch. The Kid helped Sebastian retrieve a couple of single mattresses from the former stables, which currently housed a handful of seasonal farm workers. I juggled Calvin, Bastard in his cage, and a suitcase of our things up the narrow stairway to the attic. As Calvin investigated the room with his nose, I opened the windows at either end of *la mansarde.* The view of the surrounding countryside was spectacular in both directions.

Lush green fields of well-irrigated crops, orchards of apples and cherries, peaches and nectarines, and scrubby olive trees. To the south, rolling hills leading to Arles, and to the north, the rocky peaks of the Alpilles. In the front courtyard covered with white pebbles, a wrought-iron table and chairs between the entrances to the main house and the annex. A palm tree surrounded by a collection of clay pots filled with a variety of leafy green plants, hardy succulents, and flowering petunias. The garden at the rear side of the *mas* was no less manicured but had been allowed a more overgrown, natural look. A gravel path lined with similar-sized rocks led to the modern in-ground swimming pool, protected by tall grasses, flowering shrubs, and an assortment of conifers and deciduous trees.

Sebastian appeared in the doorway, pulling one mattress into the room as The Kid pushed it up from behind.

- Do you need some help?

- We are good. The difficult job will be making the bed-stands *Maman* insists are necessary.

They both laughed, tossing the mattress on the floor along one of the walls and starting back for the other one.

- I told *Maman* that Bas didn't need to bother. Said we were used to sleeping on the floor in our own Amsterdam attic.

He gave me an exaggerated wink, turned, and followed his new friend down the stairs. I wasn't sure what bothered me more. His winking reference to the attic, his overly familiar use of *Maman* instead of *Madame*, or that he referred to Sebastian as Bas. I knew some Dutch men called Bas, but I'd never thought of it as short for Sebastian. Maybe it was. Something else The Kid just knew, like speaking French.

Calvin stood in the middle of the room, staring at me. This time his intention was clear.

What do I have to do to get a drink around here?

- Let's get your water dish from the car.

Before I finished the sentence, his wagging tail disappeared out the door and down the stairs.

Even during the long days of summer farm folk go to bed early, so it was not very dark when we retired to our *mansarde*. Madame Clement had brought clean linens, pillows, and lightweight duvets upstairs. The two single mattresses on either side of the room were fitted with military precision. Calvin helped choose the appropriate corner for his throw rug. The room was still warm from the day's constant sun beating on the roof, and the exposed wooden beams offered little in the way of insulation. Sebastian provided a couple of strategically placed revolving fans that at least kept the air moving. Although the room was supplied with electricity, there was no running water, but the gym on the floor below had a sink, toilet, and two showerheads in a large open wet room.

- It's hot up here.

The Kid peeled out of his sweat-drenched shirt as I pulled up a chair in front of a fan.

- I don't want to hear any complaints.

- I'm not complaining. I'm just saying. It's hot.

- You realize how lucky we are, don't you?

- Luck had nothing to do with it.

I recognized the cockiness he exhibited the day we met in the park. He might not have recovered his memory, but he was definitely recovering aspects of his personality. I had no idea if one might lead to the other, and that concerned me.

- Let's take a shower. That wet room downstairs looked really cool and plenty big enough for two. Let's try it out.

I had to admit, a cool shower before turning in sounded inviting. Folded clean towels were piled on a small table by the door. Madame Clement had thought of everything.

- Good idea.

- I'm full of them.

He slipped off his trainers, grabbed a towel, and headed downstairs. I slowly removed my shirt, socks, and sneakers, gave Calvin some head scratches.

Stay.

I grabbed a towel and followed The Kid's lead.

The shower was running as I walked through the gym. The polished wood floorboards were cool under my feet. Sebastian had spared little expense for this set-up. Free weights, cycling and running machines, gymnastics rings, high bars. No wonder he had such great biceps. The rest of his body must be equally toned.

One mirrored wall seemed to indicate a certain degree of exhibitionism or voyeurism.

The opposite wall was painted with a colorful mural clearly inspired by if not directly copied from Picasso's bullfighting series. It occurred to me Sebastian might be more than an avid spectator of the sport, despite its increased negative publicity in recent years. The Kid had read that the arena in Arles was one of the last places outside Spain where bulls were still killed in the ring.

I was surprised to find the wet room filling with steam. The water was running hot, not cold. The Kid's sleek, well-defined body had taken on a reddish hue. His prodigious appendage, though not erect, looked longer and more swollen than usual. I felt a stirring in my own loins.

- I thought the idea was to cool down?

- I did. Then I wanted it hot. Now I'm going to switch to cold again. It feels better that way.

I stepped out of my shorts, hung them from a hook screwed into the white tiled wall. Above each hook, a tile was decorated with a black bullfighting silhouette. Picasso again.

I stood under the second showerhead and turned on the water. The cold spray hit my body, and I involuntarily shuddered, more with pleasure than shock. It felt good to cool down, rinse the dust of traveling off my body, wipe away the sweat from sleeping in the car. I closed my eyes and let the water stream over my head, across my face. Suddenly, the water turned hot. I jumped back and saw The Kid had his hand on the silver knob, a wide grin on his face.

- Just try it. It'll feel great. I promise.

What the hell.

I stepped under what felt like boiling-hot water, but before my body could adjust to the temperature, he switched it to cold again. Then hot, then cold. Hot. Cold. I never experienced such a sensation, and he was right. It was fantastic. My whole body tingled, and every nerve ending quivered. As the spray and my body temperature became one, I felt him layer his body against mine from behind, put his arms around my chest, and hold me close.

We two boys together clinging.

I knew what was going to happen, what I wanted to happen, needed to happen. He butterfly kissed the back of my neck, and I let him. He turned my shoulders, my body followed, and his arms around my back held us close.

One the other never leaving.

- Let's go upstairs.

- Yes.

We didn't move.

- Now.

- Yes.

We didn't move.

- …

- …

He took my hand and led me out of the wet room, through the gym, up the stairs, through the door, and into the attic. We each pushed a mattress toward the center of the room until they became one mattress, one bed.

The dogs begin to stir from their short nap as I bite into the warm buttery croissant that Madame Clement forced on me, fresh from the oven. Although she knows I don't speak French, she could not resist telling me a story, which was not so difficult to understand. All I needed to hear were the words *Bastard* and *merde* and it was easy enough to fill in the rest. Her girlish giggle let me know that she took no offense, perhaps had taught him the word herself. It was she who insisted after lunch yesterday that we move his cage to a spot she cleared by a window in the kitchen.

It's not even mid-morning and the temperature is soaring. It's going to be a scorcher, and we have volunteered to help out in the fields or orchards, whatever Sebastian tells us needs to be done. It's the least we can do to earn our keep, since it was made clear last evening that no money would be accepted for their hospitality. I told them I'd grown up on a farm, and although it had been many years since I'd done a fair day's labor, I knew there was no such thing as enough help during the summer and looked forward to getting my hands dirty again. I haven't seen Sebastian yet today, am sure he's already working up a sweat somewhere on his vast estate. It's time to wake The Kid from his beauty sleep. I look up toward the attic window and there he is, shirtless, basking in the sunlight. He catches sight of me, waves, and throws a kiss before disappearing inside.

III. Gadget/Willy

The sun was shining, the air was fresh, and last night had been amazing. He wondered if sex had always been that good between them. Dekker had let him do anything he wanted, everything he wanted. Okay. There was that moment when Dekker had tried to do something he didn't want, and he felt a little bad about that. But it felt wrong, and Dekker hadn't seemed to mind, just turned himself over, raised his legs in the air, and let Willy do what he wanted again. And again. Until they were both too tired to do anything anymore.

Willy pulled on his sleeveless T-shirt and headed down the stairs, stopping at the gym to do a few pull-ups on the high bar. Sebastian took real good care of his body, the same as him. This was a sweet set-up, all the equipment to work the abs and keep the stomach tight, strengthen the arms and legs.

The place looked brilliant with that bullfighter mural. Bas said he'd take them to a bullfight next Sunday, could get the best seats for them, ringside. It was going to be awesome. Willy couldn't wait, would be counting the days.

He needed to do a few press-ups before he left the gym. He was out of shape. Strange. What had he just been thinking? About how he and Bas both liked to take care of themselves. How did he know that? Not about Bas working out, that was obvious. But that he did, too. He tried to imagine himself in another sports gym. Nothing came to mind. Strange.

He jumped up and raced down the stairs to meet Dekker. They had promised to help Bas with the farm work. He had no idea what that might entail, didn't remember ever being on a farm. This memory loss thing had some advantages after all. Every day was a new adventure. France, the farm, the sex. Everything.

Chapter Twenty-six

I. Dekker

I imagine this is where they stood, easels side by side, painting together for the first time, each with their singular vision of an identical scene. Not because it's what the plaque erected on the edge of the sun-parched pathway says, under a pedestrian reproduction of *Les Alyscamps*. But it's probably the reason this spot was chosen for one of the many signs that guide tourists to the places he painted. It feels right. The trees, the sarcophagi, the benches. Everything in the same position. The season is wrong, of course. Van Gogh and Gauguin stood here at the end of October. Their colors were autumnal. Cadmium oranges and yellows, pale greens and light grays, touches of Venetian red or Cerulean blue.

On this late afternoon, the hottest day of summer so far, a limited palette is enough. Titanium white for the limestone boulevard, mixed with ivory black for the granite graves, burnt umber tree trunks and viridian green foliage. Not dull, but not as vibrant. I see it now as they saw it, as Vincent saw it, as Willy might have seen it. Willy Then, not Willy Now.

I have no idea what he sees. Or maybe I do. The ruins of an ancient Roman necropolis, favorite burial ground in centuries past, bodies and bone disintegrated into ashes and dust. Although I had longed to visit this hallowed site, had hoped to experience it through Willy's synaesthetic soul, perhaps I made a serious error in judgment not to come alone. Now I see it through the eyes of another, whose vision is filled with shadows and darkness. The mind may forget, but what does the soul remember?

❖

The past few days I feel as though I'm reliving my childhood as an adult. Life begins early on a farm, especially during the hot weeks of midsummer when you need to get as much done as possible before the afternoon heat slows man and machinery to a near standstill. Every morning Sebastian assigns us to a different crew. We spent the first day in the vegetable fields picking sun-ripened tomatoes and cucumbers, haricot beans and snap peas, red, green, and yellow peppers. The next day we plucked cherries and peaches from the trees in the orchard. After an early lunch break, we filled baskets with strawberries, raspberries, or blueberries while the sun rose higher, as did the temperature. Though it's been many years since I've done such manual labor, it feels good to flex long-inactive muscles and work up a sweat.

I was concerned it might be too difficult for The Kid to manage, but I needn't have worried. He thrives, getting along easily with the other farm workers, sharing jokes with them. He prefers to work shirtless and seems immune to the sun's rays, eschewing sunscreen. His body has already acquired a dark tan. He tags along with Sebastian to do special chores, mending a fence or repairing an irrigation line, like an eager little brother or lovesick puppy.

Calvin accompanied me the first day, lounging in the sun or shade, rolling in the dirt. The following morning he made clear he would rather stay at the farmhouse with his two new friends Gigi and Mimi, not to mention Madame Clement, who spoils him shamelessly with treats and attention. Just as Bastard has found his special place in the kitchen, Calvin has been crowned King of the Courtyard by adoring consorts.

When Sebastian determines we've done enough for the day, we return home with him for a late-afternoon swim in the backyard pool, a privilege not afforded to the other farm workers, who continue their tasks into the early evening. We're being treated as members of the family. I'm not sure why but it probably has to do with the innocent, charismatic charm The Kid exudes. The air around him seems to buzz, drawing people closer and closer, like moths to a flame. The same thing was happening to me. Even though aware of it, I seem unable to break the spell.

Those damn butterflies. I remember the days and nights they fluttered in my gut at Willy's approach. The restless sensation of pleasure, unlike the trembling agitation they set off in me now. What was I thinking? I'm too old for a schoolboy crush. And whatever I call him, The Kid's not Willy, not in the same league, barely the same species. A gorgeous specimen, yes. No question.

So what? Have sex and move on. Don't confuse desire with—

I knew with what. The consequences of *what* were unfathomable, and exacting a toll on my messed-up psyche.

After dinner, Bas and The Kid worked out together in the gym while I sat in the courtyard with my notebook. As I tried to develop ideas for another Valentine story, I heard them through the open window, egging each other on and laughing. Part of me wanted to join them but something about their easy bond troubled me. I needed to step back so I could see it clearly, understand it, and discover where it was leading, if it was leading anywhere. Another part of me wished for an easy way out of my own dilemma.

Be careful what you wish for.

- Bas and I are going for another swim. Come on.

- No, thanks. I'm going to write some more.

- Suit yourself.

Then night would begin to fall and we would retire to our attic, push our mattresses together, undress each other slowly, kiss and be kissed, and lie naked in the warm breeze of the revolving fans, everything forgotten but rough caresses, skin against skin, and the tight embrace of long-lost lovers rediscovering a past that never existed.

He lies on a stone sarcophagus, eyes closed, ankles crossed, arms folded over his chest. As we approach, Calvin emits a soft, barely perceptible growl. I give a chastising tug on his leash and he stops, looks up into my eyes.

What? I wasn't doing anything.

The Kid doesn't move, doesn't even appear to be breathing.

- You ready to head back?

Nothing. I know he's just messing around, having fun playing dead. But I get this feeling unlike any other I've experienced. It's as if I'm having a *déjà vu* in reverse. No, that's not quite right. It's hard to explain. It's not the sensation of having been here before, it's more the impression I'll be here in the future. Not a premonition, but a memory. It makes no logical sense whatsoever.

A scream pierces the serene silence. I nearly leap out of my skin and Calvin starts barking aggressively, straining at the leash. The Kid laughs hysterically.

- Calvin, stop. Stop.

- You should see your face.

- Not funny. Not funny at all.

- Then why am I laughing my ass off?

- Because you're a twisted little shit.

I attempt to keep a straight face, but try as I might I can't hold back my own laughter. This is no *déjà vu*. This has happened before, more than once. We're laughing, laughing hard, uncontrollable, like we laughed together the day we met. The day he tried to kill me.

II. WILLY/GADGET

- You know what would be great? To go back there after dark. With all those thousands of tombs, the place must be full of spooks at night.

Dekker didn't answer, but Willy knew he wasn't asleep. It was too hot to sleep, even with the fans on, even after sex. Besides, Willy was still wound up after their visit to *Les Alyscamps*. Dekker only wanted to see where the two artists painted. Willy wanted to see it all. He'd read everything in the guidebook about the place. The name was some corrupt version of the Elysian Fields. He didn't know what the fuck that was, but Dekker said it was a part of Hades where the gods sent heroes after they died, where they could keep doing all the shit they loved to do when alive. Willy knew what he'd be doing. Sex, sex, and more sex. Forever. No wonder everybody in Europe used to want to get buried there. Even what they called it was cool. Necropolis. Sounded like a comic book city. A comic book city of the dead. That was funny.

There was other interesting stuff. Jesus Christ himself attended a funeral there and left his knee print on the lid of a sarcophagus. No shit. The wildest thing related to this saint he'd never heard of named Genesius. He was some ancient Roman civil servant who refused to persecute the Christians. His punishment was to get his head chopped off, and a bizarre thing happened after Willy read this. He could see it happening, as if he was there himself. He heard religious chanting music and saw the poor guy stretched out naked on a slab. Did they really strip all his clothes off, for humiliation or something? He saw a black-robed figure in a black mask raise a wicked sharp sword over his head with both hands, and watched it swoosh down, severing the saint's skinny neck. He saw the blood gush out and the head thud to the ground. The freakiest thing of all was that Genesius looked almost exactly like Dekker. If he'd been sleeping, that was the kind of dream a shrink would spend a lot of time blathering on about. But he'd been wide-awake. It must have been some kind of a hallucination, like when you drop really good acid. Wicked.

He decided not to tell Dekker. He'd get bent out of shape, want to talk about it and shit. Maybe he could tell Bas. Or maybe keep it to himself. He didn't want to take a chance Bas might tell Dekker. He didn't want to take a chance anything would fuck up their plans for the weekend. Tomorrow they were going to help Bas at the Saturday farmer's market, and on Sunday Bas was taking them to see a real bullfight at the old Roman arena in the middle of Arles.

Bas knew everything about bullfighting. His father had sent him to a bullfighting school when he was ten years old. *Maman* had never approved of the idea and put her foot down after the old man died. Still, Bas had a whole repertoire of classic matador moves and taught Willy some in the gym. Dekker wasn't so excited, probably felt too much sympathy for the bulls. Stupid animals. They were born to die, that's what Bas said.

Willy was psyched. Big-time. Sunday was going to be a day he would never forget.

III. Calvin

always watching never sleeping / watching
    badman sleeping dreaming
watching dekker ever guarding / listening
    badman sleeping talking

Chapter Twenty-seven

I. Valentine

Everyone thought they were brothers, some even thought they were twins. In fact, they were not related in any way, were not even from the same country. They looked as similar as their names but Valyu was Hungarian and Vali was Romanian.

They had traveled together since they were teenagers, from season to season, farm to farm, following the migrant path where work appeared and paid enough to put some aside for leaner times. It made no difference to them whether they planted or harvested vegetables in fields, picked grapes in a vineyard or olives in an orchard, scythed sweet-scented lavender or pulled rows of rhubarb stalks.

They spoke a unique blend of their native languages, barely intelligible even to their countrymen. They ate together, bunked together, and kept their distance from the other workers. They never joined in the drinking or card games after dinnertime.

Valyu was slightly heavier and Vali was slightly taller, but still it was difficult to tell them apart, with their equally swarthy complexions, thick mops of unruly hair, and the same worn clothes, which they appeared to share. On the rare occasions they removed their shirts, their tightly muscled arms, broad chests, and packed torsos looked identical, except for a scar on Valyu's lower back that may or may not have been made by a knife. It was never spoken about, and no one knew for sure.

The scar was the secret that bound the two men together, the secret that they would carry to their graves. Valyu and Vali were lovers, passionate and steadfast as any pair that ever lived or would live again. Their story is complicated but what happens between them under cover of night, when they are sure they are alone, is the stuff that homoerotic dreams are made of.

There's a space between the curtains on the window at the back of their caravan. I'll hoist you up on my shoulders so you can peek into the bedroom. But only if you promise to keep the dark secret they hold so close to their hearts.

(To be continued…)

II. DEKKER

It's easier to write about sex when you're not having it. I thought spending time alone would help, so I offered to stay behind and look after the dogs while The Kid accompanied the Clements to the market. I wouldn't be much help anyway, not speaking French. I look back over what I've written and am tempted to toss it away. Where did that odd *Dear Reader* voice suddenly come from? I can hear the editor's response.

I pay for dick, not Dickens.

I close my notebook and watch Calvin play canine tag with Gigi and Mimi. They chase each other around the courtyard trees, roll in the parched grass between the *mas* and the fields. It has not rained since we arrived, perfect weather for a holiday. If only. This beautiful place, this dream of a life, this sense of time standing still. If only I could hold on to these things and forget the real reason we're here. Then what?

Tomorrow we're off to the bullfights. As a kid I used to play in the field with a red kitchen towel and a rubber-headed spear, taunting our placid bull with shouts of *Ole, Ole!* I ran for the fence if the bull so much as turned his impressive set of horns in my direction. Perhaps I'd seen it in a movie or read about it in a book. I don't remember. It was a summer afternoon of child's play. Tomorrow will be the real deal, something I never imagined I'd witness live.

I didn't know bullfighting took place anywhere other than Spain or Mexico, but apparently it's still popular in this region. Sebastian says the tradition dates back to the early eighteenth century, and there are regular calls for *la corrida* to be granted national heritage status. I asked him if that decision wouldn't be too controversial for the government to take now. He shrugged and said bullfighting has always had its detractors. Victor Hugo wrote that torturing a bull for sport was not merely the torture of an animal, but the torture of conscience.

Sebastian preferred Hemingway's view on the subject, that bullfighting was not a sport but a tragedy, a great tragedy played out over three acts, and ending with the death of the bull.

Death in the afternoon.

Was Mac's death a tragedy? Certainly. A great tragedy? I think not. Were there tragedies still undiscovered? I fear so. Was there a great tragedy yet to come? Could it be averted?

Someone once said *Comedy is tragedy plus time.* Is that what I hoped would happen by coming here? Buy the time necessary to change the ending of an ill-fated story? Was it possible to uncross the stars of two unlikely lovers? Or had I inadvertently taken steps that did nothing more than accelerate the arrival of the inevitable conclusion?

Calvin sits in the middle of the driveway flanked by his black paramours. All three gaze in the same direction, toward the road from Arles, silent and motionless, ears alert. Far in the distance a faint white speck of a vehicle appears over the crest of a hill. How did they anticipate its appearance before it could be seen or heard?

Teach me that trick, Mister Calvinator. It could really come in handy right about now.

III. Calvin

badman coming gigi&mimi / waiting watching sitting still
dekker looking never knowing never seeing /
    only calvin gigi&mimi
gigi&mimi listening calvin / calvin teaching gigi&mimi
gigi&mimi holding maman&bastian close /
    only calvin gigi&mimi
badman smiling gigi&mimi / smiling laughing hiding true
calvin guarding everknowing everseeing / only calvin gigi&mimi

IV. Willy/Gadget

After they unloaded the truck, Willy went straight up to the attic and changed into the swimsuit Bas lent him.

Those damn dogs.

It was enough to deal with Calvin always watching him, but now those two French bitches had joined in the game. He just didn't get why people thought dogs were so great, so smart, so lovey-dovey. Even Bas. It pissed him off. It made him think of different ways to torture them, make them suffer.

Those damn dogs gave Willy a splitting headache.

❖

He had the pool to himself. Bas was busy with *Maman* sorting out the bookkeeping from the morning market, and Dekker was helping prepare lunch. That was fine by him. He liked swimming alone, cutting through the water like a great white shark. One night he slipped out of bed, tiptoed down the stairs stark naked, and swam silent laps while everyone was sleeping. Watched the stars as he floated on his back.

Willy jumped into the water cannonball style and generated a huge splash that drenched the deck chairs. He sank to the bottom and stayed there as long as he could, cooling his body and slowing his heartbeat. He opened his eyes, and the blue underwater world wriggled around him. He pushed himself up from the bottom and started the strict routine of laps he had developed in the past week.

Freestyle, breaststroke, backstroke, butterfly, and repeat. Freestyle, breaststroke, backstroke, butterfly, and repeat.

With each cycle the tension eased from his body, the headache subsided. The muscles in his arms and legs worked in perfect harmony, matched the rhythm of his deep breaths.

Freestyle, breaststroke, backstroke, butterfly, and repeat. Freestyle, breaststroke, backstroke, butterfly, and dive.

He liked sitting at the bottom of the pool. He slowly let air out of his mouth, watched as blue bubbles rose and burst on the surface. A flicker of movement caught his eye. The sun was shining on the water so he couldn't tell what or who it was. It might've been a branch swaying in the breeze. Or it might've been Bas trying to sneak up on him, ready to jump in and scare him when he ran out of breath and came up for air.

He pivoted his body and scanned all four sides of the rectangular pool. He thought he could make out a crouched figure, just above him at the deep end.

Ha. Bas.

If he managed the right angle, he could pop up at lightning speed, and he'd be the one scaring the shit out of Bas. He got himself into the perfect position.

Three, two, one, and push.

He broke through the surface with a barbaric roar, leaning forward as his hands groped the edge, and found himself nose to nose with a pack of rabid, snarling, barking beasts from hell.

The fucking dogs.

He instinctively thrust his whole body backward and plunged into the pool again, inhaling a huge gulp of the chlorinated water. His anger turned to panic, his throat and chest burned as if he'd swallowed white-hot coals. His arms flailed as he tried to come up for air.

He felt more than heard a powerful splash right beside him, then another, and another. His head broke the surface, and he opened his eyes long enough to see he was surrounded by the fucking dogs, barking their fucking heads off. One of the monsters bumped into his back, and he went under again, taking in another mouthful of water. Why weren't his arms working?

He let himself sink to the bottom, pushed off with his feet, and when he emerged, tried to scream for help, but only managed a strangled gurgle before sinking again. He was going to die in this pool.

The fucking dogs were drowning him.

Suddenly he felt himself being lifted up, up and out of the water. Strong arms held him across his chest, hauling him to the side of the pool. He wanted to help himself, but his body had no strength. He was as limp as a sodden rag doll. He let himself be pulled up onto the stone deck and felt hands press against his chest. Water spewed from his mouth. He gagged, sucked in fresh air, and began to cough.

Bas was kneeling beside him, massaging his shoulders, his chest, his back, easing the pain from his tightened muscles. Bas was talking to him, saying he would be fine, everything was good now.

Take it slow, catch your breath.

Soft, whispered comfort. Then he heard Dekker's voice.

- What's going on?

- Willy had some little problem in the pool. Maybe cramp. I heard the dogs barking like mad. When I came out he was struggling in the water.

- Are you okay?

Dekker knelt down on the other side of him.

- The dogs.

His barely audible voice was hoarse. It hurt to speak.

- Yes. The dogs. They saved you, *ce va?*

- Not saving.

Another fit of coughing interrupted him.

- Not saving. Drowning.

Dekker began to laugh first. Then Bas joined in. Did they think the idea that the dogs tried to drown him was funny? Clearly they did. They thought it was the most ludicrous thing they'd ever heard.

It wasn't funny. Not the least bit funny. It was true. The fucking dogs deliberately intended to keep him under the water long enough to kill him. Dogs drown their puppies if they can't take care of them, don't they? That's what heartless shits they are. Why didn't everybody see it?

The fucking dogs.

A flash of recognition seared his synapses. Not a dream, not a premonition, and certainly not a graveyard hallucination. It was a memory. He was certain. A memory that came and went in the wink of an eye. He didn't know what it was he remembered, or why he remembered it, or even if he really remembered anything at all. But one thing he would always remember was how those evil mutts humiliated him in front of Bas and Dekker.

Sooner or later it would be payback time, and he knew exactly which fucking dog he was going to take on first. The sooner, the better.

CHAPTER TWENTY-EIGHT

I. DEKKER & WILLY/GADGET

In a letter to his sister, a letter in which he mentions reading Dostoevsky, van Gogh wrote that when you suffer as he had, you see everyone you know at a great distance, as from the far end of an immense arena. He was, of course, referring to the Roman amphitheater in Arles. However, in his one painting of the ancient arena, the bullfight is merely sketched in the upper corner. The focus of the work, like a camera zooming in for a close-up, is on the upper tier of spectators, including friends who appear in other paintings. Many of the *Arlesiennes* are turned away from the ring. Two well-dressed women gossip under a red parasol that protects them from the sun. The crowd, closest to the action below, is painted with dark jagged strokes and splotches of color, a roiling sea of anonymous humanity.

The fashion may have changed, parasols replaced by sunhats, but the locals and tourists that fill the steep bank of seating above a red-painted fence surrounding the oval of white sand have not changed in one hundred years, or two thousand years. Most remain as blissfully ignorant of Hemingway's tragedy as they are of Hugo's torture of conscience. They are here for the spectacle of *la corrida*. They are here for the blood.

Sebastian used his connections to get us seats in the first row above the fence, directly across from where the bulls will enter. I didn't realize there would be more than one, and I'm not sure I'll enjoy being so close to the action. But he insists it's the only way to experience our first bullfight. It would be rude to protest, especially since he refuses to accept payment for the tickets. Maybe he got them for free. I don't ask.

In stark contrast to my reservations, The Kid can barely contain his excitement. I'm glad to see his moodiness of last night, after the incident in the pool, has been replaced with boundless enthusiasm. He asks Sebastian countless questions, which the Frenchman answers with good-natured patience. As the musicians herald a loud brass fanfare and two columns of men in white uniforms march into the arena, I'm infected with as much eager anticipation as any of us.

❖

Bas told Willy the fighting of each bull was made up of three acts. The first featured the picadors on horseback with lances, and the matadors who tried to protect them from the bull. Sometimes the bull killed a horse. Act Two belonged to the *banderillos*, which Bas said would be easier to explain when they were brought into the ring. The last act was the best, just the matador and the bull, man versus beast, a fight to the death. Blood in the sand.

He couldn't wait for the boring procession to be over so the real show could begin. He watched the wooden gate across the arena from where they sat. Willy knew that was where the bull would be waiting, snorting, pounding his heavy hooves into the sand, preparing to charge into the ring as soon as the gate was opened. Maybe if the music wasn't a stupid opera march, the action could really get going. The Gipsy Kings would be perfect.

The crowd yelled and chanted as men in brightly colored outfits walked around the ring and saluted with their hats. The picadors on horseback entered the ring and paraded in circles. Three immaculately dressed matadors stood in the center, soaking up the adulation of the spectators. Willy could tell each one thought he was better than the others. They looked proud and aloof, almost as if they were bored by the opening ceremony, too.

Most of the participants began to leave the ring, all except one young matador and three picadors. They rode their horses directly in front of Willy, backing hindquarters toward the fence, and faced the gate across the sand.

Something flew over Willy's head and was caught by one of the picadors. The key to the bullpen. Two of the picadors galloped their horses around the edge of the arena, and the one with the key tossed it to the man who would open the gate. The players in this act were in place, and a hushed silence fell over the crowd. The man unlocked the sliding bar on the red door, which had a white circle painted in the center, a bull's eye. That made Willy laugh. The guy lifted the bar up and, in one smooth practiced movement, pulled the gate open and stood hidden behind it. Everyone seemed to hold their breath, waiting.

Suddenly a massive darkness emerged from the shadows, burst into the bright sunlight, a colossal black behemoth with lethal curved horns and eyes full of murderous intent.

I thought I knew what to expect, having grown up on a farm with a herd of cows and a succession of stud bulls. A domestic bull bears as little resemblance to a fighting bull as a dog does to a wolf. I'd tangled with mean bulls, faced down their bravado, gotten a rope around their neck, and led them obediently to the barn. But this exceptional specimen, like the lone timber wolf, was clearly a wild animal. It was purposely bred for size and speed, strength and viciousness. Born with a killer instinct, he was about to fulfill his destiny.

It takes no time at all to zero in on his target. Head lowered, he charges forward with an almost graceful gallop that picks up speed at an unbelievable rate. The horse must make a hasty retreat, but is slow to react to the spurs. The picador's pole is useless against the raging assault, as the bull twists its neck with precision and plunges a horn into the horse's side.

I gasp with the crowd as horse and rider rise into the air and fall to the ground with a sickening thud. I expect the bull to attack them again, but another horse and rider gallop past to attract the beast's attention away from their fallen comrades. The maneuver works, and the fierce creature sets his sight on the fresh prey, turning, snorting, and charging again. Everything is happening much faster than I had imagined.

The matador comes forward fearlessly, flashing his red cape before the bull's charging horns, deftly directing its charge as he dances out of harm's way.

Ole! The Kid screams with the crowd.

For the first time since the bull appeared I am aware of his presence beside me. He and Sebastian high-five each other, and the matador continues his cape work.

Ole! Thunderous roars accompany each pass as the bull narrowly misses the agile matador. He finishes with a flourish and turns his back on the now-confused bull, walks to the fence, and leans casually against it. His face glistens with sweat. The crowd cheers their appreciation. The injured horse has been dragged from the ring.

The bull stands alone, breathing heavily, waiting for his next challenge.

❖

- The swings of the cape are called *veronicas*.

Bas had to shout into his ear to be heard over the crowd, but Willy liked learning the names of the moves. He wondered if he was too old to become a bullfighter. Bas explained the *veronicas* were a kind of foreplay to gauge the bull's ability and temperament. That made sense. Fighting the bull must be like having hot, rough sex, the final plunge of the sword into the animal's neck the ultimate climax. Willy got hard just thinking about it.

Of course, he'd have to change his name. No bullfighter could be called Willy. He'd be laughed out of the arena. Maybe something like Gachet, that artist's doctor. It had a familiar ring to it, and a hint of danger, of mystery. Gachet. That's what he'd call himself. *El Gachet.*

He didn't have time to think about that. A man entered the ring with an armful of colorfully decorated spears, each one about a meter in length. Bas told him these were the *banderillos*, and the man was the *banderillero.* His role was to prepare the bull for the final act by sticking the harpoon-like points of the *banderillos* into the hump on the bull's back. Bas said it was one of the most difficult techniques to learn in bullfighting.

The *banderillero* lifted the spears dramatically and pointed them toward the bull.

Toro! Toro!

Willy watched, mesmerized, as the bull turned and charged.

The *banderillero* rose on his toes like a ballet dancer, curving his body as the bull raged toward him. Just as it appeared the bull was going to barrel him down, the man almost gently dropped two spears into the hump, one on each side. The bull stopped, startled, then recovered his composure and charged again. And again. Each time the bull got two more *banderillos* in his hump.

When the unusual *pas de deux* was completed, the man took his applause and the bull was once more left alone. The beast had lost his initial raging thunder, unable to shake off the festive dangling *banderillos* embedded securely in his body.

That's when something strange happened.

The air in the arena shimmered in the sunlight like a scene in a science fiction movie.

Willy shook his head, and everything shifted back into focus. But now the spectators were all wearing white robes or togas as in ancient Roman times. Their enthusiastic cheers turned to disdainful jeers. Dark cloud formations spread across the sky, blocking the sun.

The bull had disappeared from the center of the ring. In its place, a nearly naked male figure was tied to a pole, his wrists bound together behind his back. His body was pierced with arrows that hung at odd angles. Blood from his wounds dripped onto the sand. Willy recognized the image from an old engraving he had seen somewhere. *The Martyrdom of St. Sebastian.*

He was no longer standing in the crowd with Bas and Dekker. He was also in the ring, staring from a considerable distance at the victim tied to the pole. He was holding a bow. He was the archer who shot Sebastian full of arrows. He looked at the martyr's suffering face. Sebastian was Bas. He felt no sense of remorse for his actions, no trace of regret for the death of his friend.

Bas wasn't really a friend. He deserved to be punished, deserved to die for his sins. Had Sebastian sinned? Or was he confusing Bas with someone else? Another sinner who deserved to die. What was his name?

His head started to ache. He closed his eyes. What was his name? What was *his* name? Not Willy. His name was not Willy. Something else. Gachet. Like the doctor.

No, not Gachet. Not the doctor. He never saw the doctor. His head hurt. Hurt bad. Gachet. Something like Gachet. Not the artist's doctor. Nothing to do with the artist.

Dekker? Gachet? Something like Gachet.

The darkness returned, wrapped its softness around him, protected him, enveloped him, and everything changed once more.

❖

Sebastian and I ease The Kid down into his seat. The combination of the sun, the heat, and the excitement must have gotten to him. At least I hope that's all it is. I can't be sure this isn't related to his concussion, even though it's been weeks since the accident. The last thing I need is to take him to a doctor. I wipe the sweat from his forehead and Sebastian fans him with the souvenir program. Before I get too panicky, The Kid opens his eyes, looks at each of us, and smiles.

- What's up, Docs?

An odd thing for him to say, but I suppose Bugs Bunny is universal. I'm too relieved to care.

- You fainted. Probably a little sunstroke.

- No way. I'm fine. I just closed my eyes for a second.

- It is not a big deal, my friend. You are not the first person to pass out in the heat of a bullfight.

Sebastian punches him lightly on the arm and suggests we leave to find some shade and a cold drink. The Kid doesn't want to miss the end, but Sebastian tells him there will be two more fights this afternoon.

- They always save the toughest bull and the best matador for last. We'll be back in plenty of time.

I don't think I could've convinced him, but Sebastian has an irresistible *je ne sais quoi* that works every time. He speaks to the men sitting nearby, I assume to tell them we'll be back. As we stand and make our way to the exit, the matador returns to the ring for the final act, the killing of the bull. Seeing that only once will be enough for me.

II. DEKKER

We stand on the quay as the streetlights of Arles turn on, reflecting across the mirror-calm surface of the Rhône. The Big Dipper rises in the night sky, van Gogh's Great Bear, the same stars he saw, the same starry night he painted. Not the famous one. Not the one reproduced on everything from calendars to coffee mugs, not the one of madness that attracts viewers in the museum like a human magnet. The other one, the first one. The one he painted from this very spot. Aquamarine, royal blue and mauve, russet gold and bronze, stars of green and pink, above two lovers walking along the river. Willy's favorite.

Willy. The other one, the first one.

❖

Sebastian was right. The last bullfight of the day was far more spectacular than what we saw of the first. The bull was larger, smarter, and more vicious. He gored two of the three horses, one critically enough to be put down as soon as it was removed from the ring. He threw the *banderillero* over his horns, would have trampled him had there not been men ready to intervene. Even the matador seemed to treat the animal with greater respect and caution before delivering the final sword into his neck.

I was right, as well. One bloody fight to the death was one more than I wished to witness. However, I cheered with the rest of the spectators, honoring the matador and his worthy opponent, as did Sebastian and The Kid. He remained a bit subdued after his fainting spell, but not so as anyone else would notice. As we left the arena, he complained about missing most of the first two rounds. But the break outside had been a good idea, and he must have known that.

We had dinner at the Van Gogh Café on the Place du Forum, near the amphitheater. Of course, it's been renamed for the Terrace painting, repainted bright yellow for the tourists. Tables outside, as the artist painted them, made it a pleasant enough place to eat less-than-average French food and drink pedestrian French wine. People who spoke any language but French strolled by or stopped to take a photograph so they would never forget their evening in Arles.

As we drive back to the farm, I sense our time here is drawing to an end. It's probably not safe to return to Amsterdam so soon, but is it safe to remain here? Anywhere?

The Kid has barely spoken a word since he blacked out at the bullfight. He flashes his charismatic smile when addressed, nods or shakes his head in answer to a question. But he is withdrawn, guarded, and I cannot read what he might be thinking. Would he show any signs if he's begun to remember his gruesome past? How might his memory return? In momentary fits and starts, in the glint of a glance, or the twinkle of a star? Or would it all come rushing back in one treacherous tsunami, like the near-silent charge of a bull? That didn't seem likely, but a shiver of fear runs through me at the thought. Was there a message to be read in his uncanny silence?

And what about the last few days? His creepy behavior at the necropolis, the near-drowning incident at the pool, the bloody battle to the death in the arena.

Hey, I've got an idea. Let's take a road trip to Arles. It's a beautiful place. Maybe it'll help you remember.

Could I have chosen a more auspicious spot to spur the lost memories of a murdering psychopath? Could I have chosen a place with more romantic associations to my own past with Willy? What was I thinking?

That's the point, really. I wasn't thinking, I haven't been thinking for a long time. I've simply been reacting, living in the moment, in Calvin's *Now*. That should be the difference between us. I need to return, not just to Amsterdam, but to the real world, to thinking, to planning and seeing a future. No matter what it might hold.

It's dark when we arrive at the farmhouse, but Calvin and the girls are waiting in the courtyard to greet us. They don't move from their sprawled positions under the palm tree, but their tails wag happily. Sebastian suggests a swim to wash away the dust of the arena. The Kid shakes his head, mumbles something about being tired, and goes inside alone. I offer Sebastian an apologetic shrug.

- He's had a big day, as my grandma used to say.

Sebastian laughs, throws a friendly arm over my shoulders, and we head for the pool.

III. WILLY/GADGET

They wouldn't see him watching from the high attic window, with the room in darkness behind him. He had returned from the darkness and he knew about watching. He liked to watch.

He didn't remember everything but he remembered enough.

Dekker lied to him. Dekker lied to him about everything. Dekker was never his boyfriend. He never had a boyfriend. The idea of a boyfriend disgusted him. The word alone repulsed him.

Boyfriend.

Dekker had never been anything to him but an obstacle to overcome, a loose end to be dealt with. He wasn't sure what had gone wrong, but he knew he had to make it right. He needed time to think. He needed time to make a plan.

He watched Bas and Dekker racing laps, back and forth in the pool, naked. Bas should have been way ahead but he wasn't really trying. He didn't want to show off. He didn't want to beat Dekker. Bas wanted to have sex with Dekker. Like he had sex with Dekker. Bas pretended to be friends with him so he could get to Dekker. That's the way the faggot world worked. He knew it well. Knew how to play the games. Knew how to make them work in his favor.

He didn't remember everything but he remembered what he was. He would make no move tonight. Tonight he needed to sleep. He needed to prepare for battle, as meticulously as the matador prepared for the bull. It wouldn't take long. He had been preparing his whole life.

IV. Dekker

I lie next to him and stare at the peaked ceiling. He lies on his side, one arm tucked under his pillow. He was already asleep when I stole quietly into the room.

My psychopathic Sleeping Beauty. And I, his Prince Not-So-Charming-After-All.

From his deep slumber he murmurs words that rip the wry smile from my face.

- *Fucking dog...kill me...kill the fucking dog.*

My body freezes, then starts to tremble.

Subconsciously or not, he is beginning to remember. Once the floodgates of his memory open, there will be no turning back the tide. *Finis.* End of story.

I know what I have to do. I've known from the beginning. No driving off into the sunset, no happily-ever-after.

Death may perhaps not be the most difficult thing.

I cannot stop shivering. I'm afraid I might wake him. I listen to his breathing for a moment and slip silently out of the bed.

Calvin raises his head, I gesture him to come, and we steal out of the attic together.

PART FOUR: THE BEACH

"I have found myself—I am that dog."

—Vincent van Gogh

Chapter Twenty-nine

I. Dekker

The three of us sit together on the sand. He and I, arms around shoulders, and Calvin a short distance away, muddy tennis ball between his paws. A vermilion sun sinks slowly into a Prussian blue sea. It's more beautiful than I remember, when Willy and I sat in almost the same spot so long ago, some year BC. *Before Calvin.* I asked him how it might look if he painted it, synaesthetically. He wouldn't tell me. Instead, he asked me how Vincent would have painted it. I laughed, said I couldn't say. He told me to close my eyes, imagine a blank canvas, and let the colors appear. Then he whispered into my ear.

- *Zandvoort aan Zee. Zandvoort aan Zee. Zandvoort aan Zee. Do you see it?*

- *Yes.*

- *All the colors?*

- *Yes.*

- *That's how I would paint it.*

I don't consider broaching the subject with The Kid. Whatever his past, our time in Arles convinced me that art appreciation is not one of his special interests. Yet again, he surprises me.

- It looks like something your artist would have painted.

My mind does a little back flip because I was thinking about Willy, although I know he's referring to van Gogh.

- It does. I didn't think you paid all that much attention to his work in France.

- I paid attention. Will there be a test?

- Very funny. Did you have a favorite?

- Nothing we saw there. Another one. In the museum. Something with blackbirds. Crows. A murder of crows.

He must mean *Wheatfield with Crows*. It's considered by some to be van Gogh's last, painted just before the artist killed himself. More than a little unsettling, and not only because this seems to be something he remembers from his past. I don't think he realizes this, and I have no intention of pointing it out to him. It's impossible to tell. The words were spoken in a remote monotone, the same tone of voice he's used for what little he's said since we left Arles.

I expected an argument when I told him we were leaving, on the morning after the bullfight. I said I was worried about his head injury after his fainting spell, thought it best that we see his doctor for a check-up, to be on the safe side. He offered no resistance, simply nodded and began to pack his things into a bag.

Sebastian was the one who vigorously expressed his objections, how much he needed our help, how much he enjoyed our company. He pleaded and cajoled, begged and bullied, even got Madame Clement involved in the one-sided discussion. I didn't need to be fluent in French to know that most of her excited tearful argument centered on Bastard. She had become extremely fond of our profanity-prone parrot. The bird often perched happily on her shoulder as she busied herself in the kitchen.

In the end I made a promise, a promise I knew I'd be unable to keep. I said we'd return once the doctor assured us nothing was seriously wrong. To add strength to my feeble falsehood, I suggested that Bastard stay with Madame Clement until then, embellishing the lie by saying the long car journey had not particularly agreed with him. Sebastian still looked dubious, but Madame Clement seemed mollified. The matter was settled.

We loaded our meager belongings into the car, including bags of bread, fruit, and vegetables, which Madame Clement insisted we accept. I bid a brief good-bye to Bastard, whose reply was equally succinct.

- Fuck off.

Gigi and Mimi fussed over Calvin, but when I opened the door, he jumped into the backseat without hesitation. The Kid mumbled a sullen *au revoir* and lurched into the front seat with no further ado. Sebastian gave me a warmhearted hug that felt somewhat more than brotherly. I watched him waving in the rearview mirror with a twinge of regret as we headed for the road toward Arles and the highway back to Amsterdam.

❖

I fake a swig from the half-finished bottle of wine and pass it to The Kid. He takes a long drink and clumsily hands it back to me. His eyelids are beginning to droop. The sun has set, and although it is still quite light out and will remain so for at least another hour, it's time to make a move. Timing is everything now.

- You look tired. Let's get back to the jeep?

I pack up our stuff, offer him a hand, which he refuses.

- Calvin. Come on.

He must be tired, as well, because he offers no resistance. He picks up his ball and trots toward the wooden stairs that lead to a parking lot behind one of the beach cafés. I forgot it would still be open at this hour, which means a change of plan. A better plan, I think.

We arrived back at the canal-house late last night and The Kid went straight to bed without a word. When I was sure he was sleeping, I quietly went upstairs and found what I had hoped was included in Mac's attic stash of recreational drugs. There were two packets, ten of the little blue pills in each. It had to be enough. I needed him out cold long enough for the second part of my plan. If I could pull this off it would be a miracle.

Downstairs in the kitchen I crushed them into a fine powder with Mac's stone mortar and pestle. I rolled the glossy page from a magazine into a funnel and tipped the drugs into a bottle of white wine from Mac's fridge.

Have I thought of everything, Mac?

I hoped so, because if this had a prayer of working, there was little room for a stupid mistake. I went over every detail I could think of in my head a few more times before falling asleep on the sofa.

I woke early and while taking Cal out for his morning walk, I moved the jeep to a space in front of the house. I gave it as thorough a going-over as possible, removing everything from the back and the glove compartment. I vacuumed the inside and washed the outside. It would be impossible to get rid of every trace of the years Calvin and I drove in it, but I was counting on the fact that no one would use a fine-toothed comb. My fingerprints had never been taken, so I didn't worry about trying to wipe them away.

The Kid didn't wake until noon and still seemed lethargic after a cup of coffee. I suggested he go back to bed. If he felt up to it later, we could spend the evening out at the beach. He shrugged noncommittally and disappeared back into the bedroom. While he dozed, I finished cleaning the jeep and packed a bag that would be easy to carry.

At the top of the stairs leading to the parking lot, he stops and looks back at the ocean for a moment. I wait for him as Calvin trots ahead to Jax. When he turns back toward me, he sports a wide grin.

- I know what you're doing.

- What are you talking about?

- You're trying to get me drunk.

- Why would I want to get you drunk?

- Because I'm your boyfriend.

He laughs, takes my face in his hands, and kisses me hard, forcing his wine-soaked tongue into my mouth. He's caught me off guard. I want to resist but it's more important not to upset him at this point. I kiss him back, with the same intensity, if not passion. When he breaks away, somewhat unsteadily, he gives me a romantic wink.

- Let's take a walk in the dunes before we go.

His voice is a little slurred and I fear I'll have to carry him back if we walk too far. But I need him to stay calm.

- Are you sure you're up for it?

- I'm very up for it, if you know what I mean.

His grin gets wider as he grabs and adjusts his crotch.

- Let me just put this crap in the jeep first.

I hurry, hoping he will interpret it as my urgent desire for sex.

Shit. I didn't count on him getting horny. Sex? Now? When I open the tailgate to stow our stuff in the back, Calvin is ready to jump in as well.

- Hold on, Mister. We're gonna walk before we go. Give the ball.

He places the ball in my hand and looks at me, confused.

You're not the only one, buddy.

I fake a throw toward the dunes. He gets the message and takes off at a run. Then I really throw the ball, as hard and as far as I possibly can.

II. Gadget

What a fucking idiot.

Gadget had him hook, line, and sinker with the old boyfriend routine. This was working out even better than he'd planned.

As soon as Dekker mentioned an evening at the beach, Gadget's mental wheels had started to turn. He'd learned that opportunities were best taken when suggested by the target. It lulled them into a false sense of security and increased the element of surprise. He'd never executed one of his performances in the dunes. New locations were exciting. This was going to be better than the attic.

Gadget took Dekker's arm and leaned into his body as they walked in the direction where the fucking dog searched for his ball. Arm in arm, just like a married couple.

Yeah, right. Not in this lifetime, asshole.

He stopped suddenly, and as he slipped his hand into the pocket of Dekker's shorts to retrieve the jeep keys, Gadget gave him a quick peck on the cheek.

- We forgot the wine. You head over there where it's nice and private. I'll catch you up.

Before Dekker could object, he set off back to the parking lot. He turned once, continuing to jog backward, and saw Dekker heading through the wispy grass deeper into the dunes, just as he'd been told.

Good boy.

No one else was in sight on this summer evening.

No one else but the fucking dog. Perfect.

He knelt on the passenger seat to get the bottle from the satchel in the back. He set it on the ground and, shielded by the open door, pulled out the cache he had secreted away under the seat while Dekker was in the shower. He tucked the handkerchief into his pocket. He secured the coil of rope under the elastic band of the swimsuit under his sweats. He slid the roll of duct tape around his wrist.

Last but not least, Gadget tenderly pulled his most prized procession from its hiding place, the treasure he had briefly lost but happily found. Like his memory. The sheathed weapon tickled his skin as he slid it along his leg beneath the sweatpants. He tightened the drawstring to hold it in place. It was a bit loose, but it would hold long enough. The most excellent sabre would not be hidden from view for long.

Chapter Thirty

I. Calvin

seeking sniffing searching finding / old&old ball dried&warm
pawing digging nudging / snorting sand&dirt /
    tickling calvins nose
shaking stopping sensing danger / badman rising bad&bad
seeking finding / lookit dekker / badman danger more&more
evermore&evermore

II. Dekker

Calvin barks me to come see what he's investigating. Officially dogs are not allowed in the dunes, much less digging in them. I give him a shout. He stops, looks around, barks twice, picks up what appears to be two balls, and races back, dropping them directly in front of me. He barks me to throw them both at the same time, and I do.

Who's your daddy?

He barks again and takes off after them.

What the hell are we doing out here anyway? A sexy tumble in the dunes won't change anything. So why does The Kid's sudden romantic behavior tonight have me thinking maybe I've gotten it all wrong? Maybe he was just having a bad dream in Arles. Maybe I overreacted, let my imagination run a little wild. Maybe he'll never remember what he truly was.

Is. What he is, Dekker.

That's the point. What he is will never change, will always be the same, will always lie in wait, under the surface, ready to reemerge and begin again.

Remember what he did to Mac. And God-knows-what to that Canadian guy. And to you, for fuck's sake.

No bump on the head is going to change that, no more than prison ever cured a psychopath. He's Jeffrey Dahmer and Ted Bundy rolled into one.

I turn and see him heading toward me, bottle in hand. I look for Calvin and see him in the distance, still tracking down his tennis balls. Maybe there's another way to deal with this before he gets his memory back. My resolve is slipping away into the dusky dunes as the light steadily fades.

He comes up behind me, nuzzles his face into my shoulder and covers my neck with his butterfly kisses. He pushes against me, and I can feel he is fully aroused. The corked bottle drops in the sand with a soft thud.

Oh, shit.

I'm getting hard as well.

What the hell, go with it. One last time.

- Willy, wait.

His body disengages from mine.

- My name's not Willy.

I sense more than see both his arms come smashing down onto my shoulders, intense pain forces my knees to buckle, and I fall forward. Before I can recover, he pushes my face into the sand. He lands a vicious kick to my side. I roll onto my back, gasping for breath. He kicks me directly in the balls.

Fade to blessed black.

III. GADGET

He knew from experience that a couple of kicks didn't keep anyone out cold for long, so he wasted no time. He pulled the sabre from inside his sweatpants and laid it carefully on the ground. The coil of rope he'd remembered from the attic was silky smooth, and he had plenty of practice tying tight knots. He bound Dekker's wrists and ankles together behind his back.

- Your turn, ass-wipe. How does it feel?

He took the red handkerchief from his pocket and wiped the sand from around Dekker's lips, then stripped off a piece of duct tape and sealed his mouth closed. Gadget was breathing hard, adrenaline pumping through his veins. He grabbed the wine bottle, popped off the cork, and took a healthy swig. His quarry was beginning to come out of his temporary stupor.

- Willy? What kinda queer-boy-faggot name is that? I'd kill myself before I let anyone call me Willy. Sorry. I got that backward. Anyone who called me Willy I'd have to kill. I told you my name the day we met. In the park? Remember? You got a problem with your memory? It's Gadget. Got it? Gadget. Next time, Gadget, got it?

He threw his head back and laughed like a deranged mental patient. That usually freaked them out but good.

It's all in the game.

That was one of those English expressions the Dutch said more often than the English themselves. He laughed again. He was totally back, thinking Dutch and English at the same time. He could think in French, too. Even Spanish. He was a smarter motherfucker than anyone ever gave him credit for. That was the key to his success.

- Oh yeah, I'm back. Thanks for the trip. Have a nice fall?

This totally cracked him up. Gadget thought he was gonna bust a gut, he laughed so hard. For some reason, his future ex-*boyfriend* didn't seem to be amused.

- Really. It's funny. Your fucking dog was the reason I lost my memory and your fucking dog helped me get it back. That's an amazing fucking dog you got. Where is he, by the way? I'd like to thank your amazing fucking dog for totally fucking with my life.

Gadget picked up the old sabre, knocked the sand off it with his foot, and drew it slowly from its sheath.

Dekker had a real panic attack, jerking and bucking like a roped-up calf. Too bad there was nothing he could do about it. He was completely helpless. Gadget lived for that, to see pure terror widen their eyes like glow-in-the-dark flying saucers.

- Caaaaaaaaaalvin. Calvin. Caaaaaaaaaalvin.

He turned and saw the dog atop a nearby dune, sitting there, staring at him.

- There you are, my white werewolf. No heroic gestures to save your boss this time? We'll see about that.

Gadget retrieved the handkerchief from where it lay on the ground and shook the sand out straight into Dekker's face.

- You want to play games with my name? You don't like Gadget? I got another name you might like better, inspired by our little road trip. You remember your artist's *doctoro*? Get it? Doc-*toro*. Behold, El Gachet!

He raised the sabre and threw the red handkerchief into the air with a flourish. It floated toward the ground, but just before it touched the sand, he lifted it back up with the point of the sabre's blade. Perfectly executed.

- Bravo, El Gachet! Bravo!

He heard the deafening cheers and enthusiastic applause of the spectators, took an exaggerated bow, and caught sight of the wine resting on the sand. He seized it and made a flamboyant show of draining what remained in one long swallow.

- Act Three. A fight to the death between man and beast. Watch and learn.

Gadget threw the bottle in a high arc, clear over Dekker's head. Slowly, dramatically, he rotated his body until he was face-to-face with the fucking dog.

CHAPTER THIRTY-ONE

I. DEKKER

- Toro! Toro! Toro!

Gadget pitches his voice high, a lilting, friendly taunt that sounds eerily like Dorothy calling for Toto.

Stay, Calvin, stay.

I want to scream, but the tape stuck across my mouth prevents anything more than a barely audible grunt. Calvin cocks his head, keeping a quizzical eye on the man he justifiably never trusted. He shows no sign of moving from his higher and, for the time being, safer vantage point.

Although I knew this nutcase was a psychopathic killer, I'd not seen the full scope of his helter-skelter personality. If his attic attack had been successful, clearly it would've been the last thing I ever saw. It's unfathomable to think I'd taken care of this maniac, kissed him, had sex with him, fallen in love with him. What the fuck was wrong with me? If stupidity was a capital offense, I deserved whatever Gachet, or Gadget, or whatever his name was, had in store for me.

I watch with increasing terror as he struts in a circle, kicking up sand, shoulders thrown back, head erect. He performs a series of graceful passes with the sword and red handkerchief, a nightmarish but accurate imitation of what we witnessed in the arena.

Sebastian told us the bullfighter never admits the possibility of his own death. Arrogance is etched on his face, his supercilious sneer brims with confidence. He gyrates his body, deftly shifting his weight from one side to the other, never losing sight of his prey for more than a few seconds. He acts as if I'm not here, just as the matador ignores the roar of the crowd and remains focused on the bull.

Sebastian said something else that resonates with new meaning.

Bullfighting depends on the bravery of the bull.

Calvin is brave, of that I have no doubt, but he is up against a dangerous opponent who knows no fear, an adversary who will show no mercy. His enemy is a bloodthirsty psychotic with one objective, to bring the beast to its knees and deliver the *estocada*, the final thrust of the sword into its heart. And in doing so, cause the greatest suffering imaginable, far worse than what will follow when he turns the blade on me.

Finished with his improvised choreography, he slides the handkerchief gently along the razor-sharp blade and points the sword toward Calvin. A low, rumbling laugh issues from his throat. I remember one last point Sebastian noted.

It is the true enjoyment of killing that makes a great matador.

I've had the unfortunate privilege of encountering the perfect candidate.

II. Calvin & Gadget

growling grumbling soft&soft / badman moving strange&slow
waiting watching lookit dekker / badman stopping downbelow

❖

El Gachet awaited the charge of the bull, scarlet *muleta* in his left hand, sabre in his right. They stared each other in the eye but the bull did not move. He must be provoked.

El Gachet took a step onto his right foot, allowing his left knee to bend and touch the ground. His body leaned forward, both arms stretched back behind him, never breaking the stare as he willed the bull to charge.

El Gachet bellowed at the bull. The bull brayed back.

❖

barking snarling standing barking / badman staring calvin more
jumping barking badman waiting / calvin gnashing more&more

❖

The bull was agitated but refused to charge. El Gachet waved the *muleta* forward and back to entice the beast. The matador must remain patient, use his guile to outsmart the bull, draw him close.

At last, the animal charged toward the inviting *muleta.* El Gachet was ready for him. The bull jumped for the scarlet cloth, all horns and fangs.

The matador rose and pivoted his body, performing a perfect *pase natural*. The bull twisted around and came from behind El Gachet, just as the matador had planned. He prepared for the *pase de pecho*, forced the beast to pass directly in front of him. He raised the sword and jabbed at the bull's hindquarters, felt contact, and pulled the weapon away.

❖

something stinging hurting yelping / scurrying fast away&away
stopping sitting licking tasting / badman moving slower closer
calvin standing backing snarling / badman stopping standing still

❖

Blood on the sand.

The crowd roared its disapproval of the strike from behind, a cowardly maneuver. El Gachet didn't care. He was playing his own game with the bull. Besides, he had barely pierced the hide of the beast. The wound was superficial at best, but enough to achieve his true goal. Out of the corner of his eye he caught Dekker's wince, as if he had taken the hit himself.

This fueled the ecstatic fire that burned through El Gachet's body, filled him with godlike pride. He was the one and only immortal conqueror. The brilliance of his star surpassed all others. The matador was ready for his *pase del la muerte*, pass of the dead one. A classic move, but El Gachet, supreme artist that he was, had a deadly new twist. He would combine it with the *estocada*, the kill thrust.

Instead of staring the bull in the face, he stood in profile, holding the blood-red cloth at his waist, stretching it out with the tip of the blade. All he needed now was to incite the bull to a final charge and let his perfect reflexes do the rest.

❖

badman calling taunting calvin / anger growing more&more
calvin tensing hackles rising / badman waiting more&more
ready steady holding tensing leaping higher evermore

❖

Gadget screamed as the fucking dog leapt toward him and gnashed its teeth onto the wrist nearest his waist, holding him in the vise-like grip of its jaws. He dropped the sabre and tried to pull free.

Excruciating pain shot up his arm. The fucking dog would not let go, even when he batted at its head and neck with his free fist.

Gadget had never been so infuriated in his life. No one attacked Gadget. No one. Ever. He stumbled, managed to keep his balance. But the fucking dog kept yanking his arm, yanking it hard. He felt as if it was going to pop out of his shoulder socket.

This is not happening. Absolutely. Not. Happening.

The world turned red with rage.

Gadget became oblivious to the pain. He channeled his fury, and with a ferocious roar, he planted a vicious kick into the side of the fucking dog's body.

❖

falling falling falling fast / hitting sand
gaping gasping / sucking air blowing hard
rolling turning twisting / breathing / holding hurting more&more
badman falling / holding hurting / looking calvin eye&eye
crawling reaching / badman standing / breathing loud&loud

❖

Gadget felt dizzy when he stood up again, sabre in hand. The fucking dog had brought him to his knees, made him crawl in the sand.

Enough is enough.

He glanced at Dekker, who still grunted unintelligible protests under the duct tape. Gadget took a step toward the pathetic panting animal stretched out on the ground. It didn't move. Just kept staring at him. Another step. Nothing. Good.

Klaar is Kees. Or, as the clever rabbit used to say, *That's all, folks.*

- Maybe some fucking dog will pull Calvin's head out of the fucking water.

Something was wrong with his voice. He had trouble getting his mouth around the words. Almost like he was high. Right? He was high, all right. He was the high priest about to slaughter the sacrificial lamb.

Gadget laughed and raised the sabre high above his head, gripped it with both hands. He tried to shake off another bout of wooziness when, without warning, the dunes, the beach, the sky, the whole wide world began to spin.

III. DEKKER

Just as I'm about to close my eyes I detect a change in the murderer's stance. The weight of the sword seems to unbalance him. He totters, lurches a step forward, reels back, and stops. For a few seconds the maniac is perfectly still, framed against the darkening sky like the statue of a warrior from a distant time. Then he simply keels over, face first into the sand.

Tears of relief cloud my vision. I was afraid the drugs had had no effect on him at all, that Calvin and I were destined for the same fate as Mac.

We weren't out of the woods yet, far from it, but we had a chance.

Calvin has not moved since the brutal kick that nearly defeated him. I'm in awe of the raw animal instinct that emerged for him to attack Gadget as he did, a kind of wolf-courage, written deep in his DNA. He's panting heavily but doesn't appear in great pain.

I'm bound in such a way that any movement is difficult. How would Houdini have escaped? He could dislocate his thumbs in order to squeeze out of handcuffs. I know I couldn't bear the pain, even if I had a clue how to accomplish that feat. Tight knots hold the rope around my wrists and ankles, which seem connected to each other. At least the rope isn't wrapped around my neck so that if I move I'll strangle myself. I saw that once in a movie.

I try rubbing the tape over one side my mouth in the sand. It accomplishes nothing, but I catch sight of a large rock not too far from my head. It has a rough edge that might do the trick if I can wriggle closer. It's not as easy as I thought it would be, but I maneuver myself an inch or two at a time until I can lift my head up to the rock. I slide my face along the edge, hoping to loosen the tape.

At first it doesn't seem to be doing any good, but after a couple more tries, I begin to feel the tape tugging off my skin. I keep at it until I can suck some air into the side of my mouth. I taste my own blood and notice the rock is smeared with it as well. I couldn't care less about scratching my face. I've done what I needed to do. There's just enough space to speak from the corner of my mouth, like a ventriloquist.

- Calvin. Calvin, come.

Though my voice is muffled and nasal, Cal's ears prick up at the sound of his name. He slowly pushes his front paws in the sand, rising to a seated position. He looks around and barks once in my direction.

It's about time.

He stands with some difficulty, attempts a halfhearted shake, and shows signs of a limp as he moves around Gadget. He is hurt, but true to his stoic nature he refuses to acknowledge the pain. He makes his way to where I lie and licks my face.

- Good boy, Calvin. Yes. Yes. Good boy.

I'm not sure he's up to my next request, but it could get us out of here faster if he is. A trial run will check out his mobility and maybe get him in the right frame of mind.

- Where's the ball? Find the ball.

He looks at me with his cocked-head expression of doubt.

The ball? Really?

But he trots away, already looking steadier on his feet. I see blood smeared on his hindquarters. The wound doesn't seem too serious. Giving his prone opponent a wide berth, he climbs the side of the dune where he'd dropped the two balls before the battle began. Leaving a ball behind is not an option, and it takes him a moment to secure both of them in his mouth at the same time. He saunters back and drops them in front of me.

Now for the more challenging task.

- Good boy. Where's the stick? Calvin's present. Find the present-stick. Go find.

He looks completely confused. He understands stick. He understands present. Putting the two words together might be a leap too far for him to grasp. It's been weeks since he dug the present from its hiding place in the shrubs. And I didn't let him carry it home, so it may hold no proprietary interest for him. Add to that its use as a weapon against him, and I fear I'll be inching myself through the sand, losing precious time.

And then I remember. Not a present. *Garbage.*

- Calvin. Find garbage-stick. Go find. Bring to me.

Calvin goes, nose to the ground, probably unsure what he's scenting, but determined to satisfy my command. Again he avoids getting too close to Gadget, circling around him.

The sword has lodged its blade into the sand a few feet from his head. Calvin stops, looks at the weapon, looks back to me. Before I can confirm it's what I want, he sniffs it, backs away, and barks in my direction.

- Yes. Bring. Bring to me.

He gingerly grips the handle with his teeth and pulls it out of the ground. Without letting go, he half drags, half carries the unwieldy prize straight to me. He drops it by my side, tail wagging with pride.

- Good boy. Good boy.

He executes a nonchalant shake and sits, waiting for the next game.

It's my turn to perform a trick. I get my body in position so the sword lies parallel to my back and gently roll myself on top of it. I feel the blade cut into my left arm, reminding me that both edges are razor sharp.

Forget the pain. It's just a scratch.

I arch my back to put some space between the sword and my wrists. It's awkward but less difficult than I imagined. I position the blade and begin to push the knotted rope against one edge. With short back-and-forth sawing motions, careful to keep the sword in place, I feel it begin to sever the silky rope, strand by strand.

Sweat pours from my brow, runs down my face, and stings my eyes, but I keep at it until the blade slices completely through. The knots loosen, start to unravel, and finally one wrist is free. The other is still held by the short length of rope attached to my bound ankles. I roll onto my side, grab the handle of the sword, turn over onto my back again, lift my feet, and slice through the rope.

As I stand, the parts of my body not in pain are numb. I give myself a quick Calvin-shake to get my limbs in working order again. Calvin stands, shakes as well, and looks at me.

Let's get out of here!

- We're not home free yet, buddy.

It's almost dark and the streetlights have turned on in the distant parking lot. Part of me wants to run like hell to the jeep, hightail it back to the canal-house, pack up our stuff, and keep driving, put as much distance between me and this psychopath as possible.

But where would I go? Back to France? That's probably the first place he'd come looking for us. And I have no doubt that he will come looking. Even if I didn't return to the farm, I've put Sebastian, his mother, and everyone else there at risk. How many more victims will die before he's caught? If he's caught. No. I see no logical choice but to stick to my plan, insane as it may be. It's time to put an end to this madness, once and for all. His and mine.

- Calvin. Where's Jax? Get your balls. Go find Jax.

He picks up the balls without hesitation and looks at me.

Are you coming?

I'm not sure how he might react to what I'm about to do, and I don't want to take a chance he'll make a scene. I point toward the jeep insistently.

- Go. Now.

He obeys my command, suppressing his reluctance to leave me behind, and heads into the darkness, a white ghost-dog disappearing into the dunes.

I pick up the sword and walk toward the unconscious body lying in the sand.

Chapter Thirty-two

I. Dekker

I resist the temptation to race back to Amsterdam. The last thing I need is to get pulled over for speeding and be forced to explain to some Dutch cop why my passed-out passenger is bound and gagged.

You see, Officer, my boyfriend is a vicious serial killer who twice tried to kill me, so this is the only way we can travel together, unless I bash his head against a wall and hope for another round of amnesia.

I intended to carry out the last part of my plan in the deserted parking lot. It was dumb to forget the beach café stayed open late, but it was no use beating myself up about it. Night Watch Lane was perfect, dark and quiet, hidden by the trees at the edge of the park, no foot traffic at night. Plan B should've been Plan A in the first place.

I could even keep an eye on the jeep from a safe distance within the park, if the mosquitoes don't eat us alive. Calvin seems immune to them, but they love the taste of me. Small price to pay, considering the alternative.

I'm not a religious person, and if I were this would be pretty sacrilegious anyway, but I take a deep breath, look up at the starry night through the windshield, and whisper a short prayer.

If anybody is listening, could you please give a guy a break?

After burying the sword as deep in the sand as I could with my hands, I retrieved the duct tape and secured his wrists together behind his back. I didn't bother with his ankles, hoped it wouldn't be necessary. I didn't want to waste any more precious time. I did take the precaution of taping his mouth shut. Next came the task of getting him back to the jeep.

In the movies it always looks so easy. The hero hoists his fallen friend or partner or even a complete stranger across his shoulders in a fireman's lift and carries him to safety. In reality it's a little more difficult, maybe because I never tried it before. I pulled him into a sitting position but couldn't work out how to get him onto my shoulders. I realized he needed to be upright.

I laid him back down, rolled him onto his stomach, and tucking my hands under his armpits, managed to pull him to his feet, facing me. That's when I figured out it was still not possible because I'd bound his wrists together behind his back. I thought of trying to cradle him in my arms, the way I used to carry Willy, but his dead weight was simply too much for me at that point. There was only one thing left I could think of to do.

I wrapped tape around his ankles, increasingly worried he might come to at any moment. I ran back to the parking lot where Calvin waited patiently by the jeep, opened the tailgate, and told him to jump in. Fortunately, the Dutch are not big on fences or railings, even along the canals. There was nothing to keep me from driving the jeep straight into the dunes. But even in four-wheel drive, this was going to be tricky.

I started the engine and looked around to make sure no one was in the vicinity. I didn't want to risk turning on the headlights and attracting attention. But there was just enough light left, and we weren't going far. A well-trodden path made the short drive easier than I anticipated.

Appealing as the thought was of just running him over a few times, I dismissed it for all the same reasons I'd quashed my momentary desire to use the sword on him in the same way he had planned for me. We spent enough time at the beach for someone to have noticed the jeep, or the two of us, or even Calvin, and later remember when a dead body was discovered. I stopped, dragged his dead-weight ass into the passenger seat, and took the time to turn the jeep around so the reverse taillights wouldn't come on. I drove slowly back through the dunes to the parking lot and onto the open road toward Amsterdam.

❖

I flick off the headlights as we turn onto Night Watch Lane. It doesn't make much difference under the soft illumination provided by the streetlamps, but it might help conceal the black jeep from anyone looking out a window from the nearby high-rise apartment buildings. I pull into a spot under the trees alongside Rembrandtpark, midway between streetlamps where the light is dimmest.

I'd already disconnected the interior lamp so it won't turn on when I open the door. I leave it open while I let Calvin out from the back. He gives himself a shake and immediately heads toward the bushes for a sniff and a piss. I feel around for Calvin's two tennis balls, find them, and put them into the knapsack. I pull out the screwdriver I brought from the house. Not a soul in sight as I remove the license plates and tuck them into the bag as well.

My passenger has not stirred the entire trip back. My fear that perhaps I had used too many of the little blue pills proved unfounded. He's still breathing. I consider moving him to the driver's seat later but decide to risk it now. It's tricky getting him past the gearshift but I manage. I lean him forward to remove the duct tape from his wrists and re-tape them individually to each side of the steering wheel. I wrap tape three times around the back of the seat and across his chest to hold him in place. If he doesn't regain consciousness, it won't have been necessary. At this point I'm taking no chances. I pause for a moment before completing the final part of my plan.

Like the fireman's lift, thinking about it was easy. Faced with actually carrying it out, I'm paralyzed with doubt. I know I'm dealing with a psychopath. But in Greek that literally means a suffering soul. Doesn't that make me a psychopath as well? We don't put suffering souls out of their misery. And in a way, aren't we all psychopaths?

- Seriously, Dekker? This freak has been killing people. You're no murderer.

- I'm about to become one. What if I go home and call the police? Let them deal with him.

- Sure. Be the good citizen. How do you think that'll play out with your own list of crimes?

- Okay. Fine. So I get into some trouble. Maybe this guy just needs therapy.

- Evil doesn't get therapy. It gets locked up for as long as possible, preferably in a cage on some desert island.

I read somewhere that Eskimos have a special name for a man who repeatedly lies, steals, and rapes women. I don't remember the word, but when asked what the tribe would do with such a person, one Eskimo explained that somebody would push him off the ice when nobody was looking. That's what I need to do. Push him off the ice.

I pull the rubber hose from beneath the driver's seat, take it to the rear of the jeep, and attach one end to the exhaust pipe, sealing it in place with the tape. I carefully check the length of hose to ensure there are no obstructive kinks. I leave it lying on the ground as I crack open the window and reach inside to turn on the ignition. I need to hold the key in my right hand and at the same time use my left to push down on the gas pedal. It's a tight fit with his wrists taped to the steering wheel. I force myself under his arms so that my chest half leans against his lap. I breathe in a not unpleasant combination of sea, sand, and his all-too-familiar body.

At the moment I hit the gas, turn the key, and the engine starts, I hear a loud grunt. His bound feet slam on top of my arm, pressing it hard against the brake and clutch pedals. I shriek, more from shock than the sharp pain, and Calvin starts barking. I clumsily attempt to extricate myself, at the same time telling Calvin to shut the fuck up. I lose my balance, fall from the jeep, and land butt-first on the lane's stony shoulder. My arm feels like it's broken, my palms and elbows are scraped from trying to break the fall, and my ass hurts like a hell. I am well and truly pissed off. The psycho's eyes, wide with fury, stare down at me.

II. GADGET

Goddamnmotherfuckershitpisscuntscrew.

Gadget wanted to scream. He had regained consciousness too late, as Dekker wrapped tape around his body, securing him to the seat. He had no idea what the asshole had done while hidden from view behind the jeep, but whatever it was couldn't be good. He had a very bad feeling and was powerless to do anything about it.

He watched as Dekker stood, brushed the gravel from his bloody hands, and bent down to pick something up off the ground. A rubber hose.

What the fuck?

As soon as his intended victim put the end of the hose through the narrow opening at the top of the window, Gadget smelled the exhaust fumes and knew what the cocksucker had planned for him. As the driver's door slammed shut, he struggled fiercely, but could not budge the tight bands of tape that bound him. If he could lift his legs, he might be able to sound the car horn. Impossible.

No. No. No. No. No.

This was not happening. He had to calm down, slow his breathing, give himself time to think, or it would all be over very quickly.

The window was beginning to turn opaque with condensation as the fumes clouded inside the jeep. He could just make out Dekker standing in the bushes at the edge of the park, ghostly white dog sitting at his feet, both of them staring at him.

Why were they doing this to him? Dekker was his boyfriend, took care of him when he was hurt. That fucking dog had come between them, turned Dekker against him.

Dekker was an idiot. What kind of stupid shithead chooses a fucking dog over a gorgeous hot young stud like Gadget? Gadget was every faggot's dream. One night with Gadget was worth a thousand and one nights with anybody else.

Isn't that true, Dekker?

Gadget was good. Gadget was God.

Nobody fucks with Gadget and gets away with it.

His head hurt. He had trouble keeping his eyes open. Somebody must've put something in Gadget's drink. That was it.

Somebody wanted Gadget all soft and cuddly. Somebody was shy, too scared to ask Gadget for what they really wanted. Somebody wanted to suck on Gadget's willy. Gadget had a beautiful willy. Everybody wanted Gadget's willy.

Wait. Willy. Dekker called Gadget Willy. Bad Dekker. Don't call Gadget Willy. Gadget is nobody's Willy.

Fuck you, Dekker. Fuck you and your fucking dog.

Gadget was tired.

No. No. No. Not tired.

Don't sleep, Gadget. Stay awake.

Don't fall asleep like the little kittens Mama put in the box. Put in the box and gassed with the car.

Mama, don't put the kittens in the gas box. Don't put Gadget in the gas box.

Gadget doesn't like it in the box. The priest put Gadget in the box.

Let Gadget out of the box. Now. Gadget wants out of this fucking box.

Fuckers. Put the fucking dog in the box.

Next time, Gadget. Next time.

Gadget wanted to sleep, his whole body vibrated with the need to sleep. The warm sun on his face, the soft breeze on his skin, the gentle rhythm of the waves. He wanted to lie here on the vibrating beach forever and ever and evermore.

Next time, Gadget.

Something with blackbirds.

Next time...

III. Calvin

waiting watching badman sleeping
watching waiting badman gone
tail wagging soft&soft

IV. Dekker

In the dead of night. Here we are in the dead of night.

Jax runs out of gas, sputters his last gasp, and dies. Not a living soul has come anywhere near while we waited, watching on Night Watch Lane.

The jeep is full of cloudy fumes. The longer they remain there, the better. It's time to go. But like it or not, I have to approach the jeep one last time.

I pull the folded flyer I nabbed from the window of the snack bar out of my back pocket.

I softly command Calvin to stay. He doesn't move. I look up and down the street, hurry toward Jax, and slip the paper under the windshield wiper.

I can barely make out his motionless figure in the driver's seat. I carefully remove the hose from the window and quietly open the door. The acrid fumes unfurl around me. His eyes are closed, his skin the palest shade of blue. I gently unwind the tape from his ankles, from his wrists, from his body, from his mouth. I close the door silently and replace the end of the hose in the narrow opening at the top of the window.

I return to the shadows. Calvin needs no further instruction. He trots ahead of me, leading the way home.

CHAPTER THIRTY-THREE

I. CALVIN

salty water spraying splashing / bigwave coming fast&fast
calvin jumping soaking dunking searching finding ball&ball
two balls finding yes&yes
dekker laughing shouting waving / calvin splashing
    water dripping
lookit dekker two&two / dripping water shaking flying
two balls dropping yes&yes
calvin&dekker always playing running happy running fast
throwing balls finding balls giving dekker more&more

II. DEKKER

Summer is over and this is our last visit to the beach. I stare across the water and try to envision the future there, beyond the western horizon. That's the direction we'll head soon. With the help of a less-than-scrupulous lawyer, who asks no unnecessary questions as long as his fees are paid, arrangements have been made to clear and sell the little canal-house for a surprisingly high price. It will be torn down and replaced with a new multistory building of luxury apartments. The neighborhood is in the early stages of gentrification.

Someone is coming by tomorrow to look at the Volkswagen, a done deal as far as I'm concerned. It's amazing what the appropriate documents and a brisk air of confidence can achieve.

As for Valentine Mackenzie, he will simply disappear from the relentlessly flat landscape of the Lowlands, as will Jason Dekker. Our time here didn't have much of an impact.

Mac did make one rather extravagant purchase before he left for parts unknown, a purchase that he promptly signed over to me. Call it a parting gift. Mr. Scrupulous handled the sale from one of the more expensive galleries in the *Spiegelquartier* for a handsome fee.

The large canvas depicts what most would call an abstract figure, head turned over one shoulder toward the viewer. It's painted with brash bold strokes of thalo green, burnt sienna, pale cadmium yellow, and Tyrian purple, with a faint fading trail of Venetian red. Tiny black markings in the lower left corner read JD#33 above the artist's signature. It is not dated.

Mac will live on, in a sense. I emailed the webzine editor to tell him Valentine was taking a break. He was pretty upset. Apparently the popularity of the sexy stories is growing. I wrote back that I'd be in touch, so to speak. His curt reply: *No jokes. Just sex.*

The name people would've remembered during our time in Amsterdam was that of our nameless mutual friend and psychopath. His body was discovered in the jeep, funnily enough by a dog walker. His death was thought to be a suicide. He was linked to the murder of the Canadian tourist, whose decomposing corpse was found on a building site where construction had been suspended. He was never identified. For some reason that's difficult to comprehend, I'm sorry I never knew his real name.

All's for the best in this best of all possible worlds.

Voltaire was being ironic, of course, but I don't believe van Gogh was. He referenced that quote in numerous letters he wrote from Arles. He had every reason to be depressed. His paintings aren't selling, his best friend runs out on him, he gets committed to a mental hospital, and through it all he keeps working. Despite all his misfortune, financial difficulty, and bouts of profound loneliness, his letters are fueled with this determined unflappable optimism.

I wonder what happened in the field on that cloudy summer day. Nobody knows. Not really. But sometimes I think I do.

He once wrote he loved nothing more than a blue sky. His favorite color was cobalt blue and his starry nights were full of it. I'll never forget the starry nights in the south of France. I was tempted to return to Sebastian's farm, but know it's not the place for me. Not now. Maybe someday. I need to find my own starry nights.

Calvin, of course, has no clue we're about to leave his birthplace. It won't matter to him as long as there's the promise of a ball to throw, a stick to fetch, or a pond to swim in. It's not particularly bright of me to bring him to the beach the day before I plan to sell the car. It's going to totally stink of wet dog.

He answers my unspoken complaint with a big body shake, drenching me in a cold shower of seawater as the cadmium yellow sun sets in the cobalt blue sky.

III. CALVIN

lookit dekker wagging calvin
lookit calvin wagging dekker
evermore&evermore

AUTHOR'S NOTE

In the interest of full disclosure, I should mention that during the summer of 1995 I was homeless in Amsterdam, living in a jeep with my dog Calvin. One morning in Vondelpark, we did come across a crime scene similar to what is described in this book. A dog had pulled a garbage bag from a pond with the same grisly contents. My only thought at the time: Thank God it wasn't Calvin. I never heard any more about it. Three years later I began to develop the story by asking: What if...?

Flash-forward thirteen years. At ThrillerFest in New York, with an early draft tucked under my arm, I related these details to a journalist. She asked what had actually happened in the case. I said I didn't know. She suggested that answer was not good enough. So I returned to Amsterdam and did some research. According to a Dutch database of murders in the Netherlands, the Vondelpark victim was never identified, the murder never solved.

To be perfectly clear: *Calvin's Head* is a work of fiction. I have no knowledge of the crime upon which it is based. Apparently the killer got away with it. Unless...

—DS

About the Author

David Swatling grew up in upstate New York and studied drama at Syracuse University. He has done experimental theater in Poland, performed mime on the streets of NYC, and made his Off-Broadway debut in *The Passion of Dracula*. He also worked for twenty-five years at Radio Netherlands Worldwide as a newsreader, reporter, and producer. His culture program, *Aural Tapestry*, was chosen as one of the Ten Best Shows on World Radio. His documentaries have won international prizes, and he is a three-time winner of the NLGJA Excellence in Journalism Award. He hosted a live LGBTQ radio show, wrote for Amsterdam's first gay weekly, *Trash in the Streets*, and reported for *The Daily Friendship* newspaper during Gay Games '98. He currently edits material for Pride Photo Award and regularly blogs about LGBTQ issues—from Amsterdam and elsewhere. *Calvin's Head* is his first novel.

Books Available From Bold Strokes Books

Calvin's Head by David Swatling. Jason Dekker and his dog, Calvin, are homeless in Amsterdam when they stumble on the victim of a grisly murder—and become targets for the calculating killer, Gadget. (978-1-62639-193-2)

The Return of Jake Slater by Zavo. Jake Slater mistakenly believes his lover, Ben Masters, is dead. Now a wanted man in Abilene, Jake rides to Mexico to begin a new life and heal his broken heart. (978-1-62639-194-9)

Searching for Grace by Juliann Rich. First it's a rumor. Then it's a fact. And then it's on. (978-1-6263-9196-3)

Dark Tide by Greg Herren. A summer working as a lifeguard at a hotel on the Gulf Coast seems like a dream job…until Ricky Hackworth realizes the town is shielding some very dark—and deadly—secrets. (978-1-62639-197-0)

First Exposure by Alan Chin. Navy Petty Officer Skyler Thompson battles homophobia from his shipmates, the military, and his wife when he takes a second job at a gay-owned florist. Rather than yield to pressure to quit, he battles homophobia in order to nurture his artistic talents. (978-1-62639-082-9)

Fifty Yards and Holding by David Matthew-Barnes. The discovery of a secret relationship between Riley Brewer, the star of the high school baseball team, and Victor Alvarez, the leader of a violent street gang, escalates into a preventable tragedy. (978-1-62639-081-2)

The Fall of the Gay King by Simon Hawk. Investigative journalist Logan Walker receives a mysterious erotic journal that details the sexual relations of a corporate giant known in the business world as the "Gay King of Kings." (978-1-62639-076-8)

Tristant and Elijah by Jennifer Lavoie. After Elijah finds a scandalous letter belonging to Tristant's great uncle, the boys set out to discover the secret Uncle Glenn kept hidden his entire life and end up discovering who they are in the process. (978-1-62639-075-1)

Backstrokes by Dylan Madrid. When pianist Crawford Paul meets lifeguard Armando Leon, he accepts Armando's offer to help him overcome his fear of water by way of private lessons. As friendship turns into a summer affair, their lust for one another turns to love. (978-1-62639-069-0)

The Raptures of Time by David Holly. Mack Frost and his friends journey across an alien realm, through homoerotic adventures, suffering humiliation and rapture, making friends and enemies, always seeking a gateway back home to Oregon. (978-1-62639-068-3)

The Thief Taker by William Holden. Unreliable lovers, twisted family secrets, and too many dead bodies wait for Thomas Newton in London—where he soon enough discovers that all the plotting is aimed directly at him. (978-1-62639-054-6)

Waiting for the Violins by Justine Saracen. After surviving Dunkirk, a scarred and embittered British nurse returns to Nazi-occupied Brussels to join the Resistance, and finds that nothing is fair in love and war. (978-1-62639-046-1)

Turnbull House by Jess Faraday. London 1891: Reformed criminal Ira Adler has a new, respectable life—but will an old flame and the promise of riches tempt him back to London's dark side…and his own? (978-1-60282-987-9)

Stronger Than This by David-Matthew Barnes. A gay man and a lesbian form a beautiful friendship out of grief when their soul mates are tragically killed. (978-1-60282-988-6)

Death Came Calling by Donald Webb. When private investigator Katsuro Tanaka is hired to look into the death of a high profile lawyer, he becomes embroiled in a case of murder and mayhem. (978-1-60282-979-4)

Love in the Shadows by Dylan Madrid. While teaming up to bring a killer to justice, a lustful spark is ignited between an American man living in London and an Italian spy named Luca. (978-1-60282-981-7)

In Between by Jane Hoppen. At the age of fourteen, Sophie Schmidt discovers that she was born an intersexual baby and sets off on a journey to find her place in a world that denies her true existence. (978-1-60282-968-8)

The Odd Fellows by Guillermo Luna. Joaquin Moreno and Mark Crowden open a bed-and-breakfast in Mexico but soon must confront an evil force with only friendship, love, and truth as their weapons. (978-1-60282-969-5)

Cutie Pie Must Die by R.W. Clinger. Sexy detectives, a muscled quarterback, and the queerest murders…when murder is most cute. (978-1-60282-961-9)

Going Down for the Count by Cage Thunder. Desperately needing money, Gary Harper answers an ad that leads him into the underground world of gay professional wrestling—which leads him on a journey of self-discovery and romance. (978-1-60282-962-6)

Light by 'Nathan Burgoine. Openly gay (and secretly psychokinetic) Kieran Quinn is forced into action when self-styled prophet Wyatt Jackson arrives during Pride Week and things take a violent turn. (978-1-60282-953-4)

Baton Rouge Bingo by Greg Herren. The murder of an animal rights activist involves Scotty and the boys in a decades-old mystery revolving around Huey Long's murder and a missing fortune. (978-1-60282-954-1)

Anything for a Dollar, edited by Todd Gregory. Bodies for hire, bodies for sale—enter the steaming hot world of men who make a living from their bodies—whether they star in porn, model, strip, or hustle—or all of the above. (978-1-60282-955-8)

Mind Fields by Dylan Madrid. When college student Adam Parsh accepts a tutoring position, he finds himself the object of the dangerous desires of one of the most powerful men in the world—his married employer. (978-1-60282-945-9)

Greg Honey by Russ Gregory. Detective Greg Honey is steering his way through new love, business failure, and bruises when all his cases indicate trouble brewing for his wealthy family. (978-1-60282-946-6

Lake Thirteen by Greg Herren. A visit to an old cemetery seems like fun to a group of five teenagers, who soon learn that sometimes it's best to leave old ghosts alone. (978-1-60282-894-0)

Deadly Cult by Joel Gomez-Dossi. One nation under MY God, or you die. (978-1-60282-895-7)

The Case of the Rising Star: A Derrick Steele Mystery by Zavo. Derrick Steele's next case involves blackmail, revenge, and a new romance as Derrick races to save a young movie star from a dangerous killer. Meanwhile, will a new threat from within destroy him, along with the entire Steele family? (978-1-60282-888-9)

Big Bad Wolf by Logan Zachary. After a wolf attack, Paavo Wolfe begins to suspect one of the victims is turning into a werewolf. Things become hairy as his ex-partner helps him find the killer. Can Paavo solve the mystery before he runs into the Big Bad Wolf? (978-1-60282-890-2)

The Moon's Deep Circle by David Holly. Tip Trencher wants to find out what happened to his long-lost brothers, but what he finds is a sizzling circle of gay sex and pagan ritual. (978-1-60282-870-4)

The Plain of Bitter Honey by Alan Chin. Trapped within the bleak prospect of a society in chaos, twin brothers Aaron and Hayden Swann discover inner strength in the face of tragedy and search for atonement after betraying the one you most love. (978-1-60282-883-4)

Tricks of the Trade: Magical Gay Erotica, edited by Jerry L. Wheeler. Today's hottest erotica writers take you inside the sultry, seductive world of magicians and their tricks—professional and otherwise. (978-1-60282-781-3)

Straight Boy Roommate by Kevin Troughton. Tom isn't expecting much from his first term at University, but a chance encounter with straight boy Dan catapults him into an extraordinary, wild weekend of sex and self-discovery, which turns his life upside down, and leads him into his first love affair. (978-1-60282-782-0)

In His Secret Life by Mel Bossa. The only man Allan wants is the one he can't have. (978-1-60282-875-9)

Promises in Every Star, edited by Todd Gregory. Acclaimed gay erotica author Todd Gregory's definitive collection of short stories, including both classic and new works. (978-1-60282-787-5)

Raising Hell: Demonic Gay Erotica, edited by Todd Gregory. Hot stories of gay erotica featuring demons. (978-1-60282-768-4)

Pursued by Joel Gomez-Dossi. Openly gay college student Jamie Bradford becomes romantically involved with two men at the same time, and his hell begins when one of his boyfriends becomes intent on killing him. (978-1-60282-769-1)

Timothy by Greg Herren. *Timothy* is a romantic suspense thriller from award-winning mystery writer Greg Herren set in the fabulous Hamptons. (978-1-60282-760-8)

Lightning Source UK Ltd.
Milton Keynes UK
UKHW04f0626260918
329553UK00001B/175/P